Sword of Vengeance

KIT MCQUEEN—Reckless, bold, quick-tempered, a man like his father, burning with love for his country. Having once faced death, he must prepare to do so again . . . for a nation's survival.

IRON HAND O'KEEFE—Maimed by the British, taken in by the Choctaws to become a powerful chief, he saved McQueen's life. But the Americans call him traitor, and Kit McQueen has sworn to capture him or see him die.

BILL TIBBS—He fought by Kit's side in wilder, younger days, but the power of gold seduced him until honor and friendship were destroyed. Now they will meet again, to settle an old score.

RAVEN O'KEEFE—Like her father before her, she saved the life of Kit McQueen. Will the twice-owed debt of a life—and his love for the proud, beautiful Choctaw— keep Kit from discharging his patriotic duty?

WOLF JACKET—The fiercest Creek warrior chief, leader of the Red Sticks, who fight in league with the British. He burns with hatred for the Choctaw, the white men, and especially Kit McQueen.

★ THE MEDAL ★
Book 2

SWORD
OF
VENGEANCE

Kerry Newcomb

DOMAIN ™

BANTAM BOOKS
NEW YORK • TORONTO • LONDON • SYDNEY • AUCKLAND

SWORD OF VENGEANCE (THE MEDAL #2)

A Bantam Domain Book / June 1991

ISBN 0-553-29029-0

Published simultaneously in the United States and Canada

PRINTED IN THE UNITED STATES OF AMERICA

OPM   0 9 8 7 6 5 4 3 2 1

For Patty, Amy Rose, and P.J.

SWORD
OF
VENGEANCE

PART ONE

The Sword

Chapter One

July 4, 1811

Kit McQueen laughed as thirty-six inches of watered steel blade missed decapitating him by inches. He ducked, lowered his shoulder, and rolled against his attacker's legs. The Turkish guard's momentum carried him up and over the balcony railing. The guard cried out in astonishment and tossed his broad-bladed tulwar aside as he fought to catch a handhold on the railing. But luck had abandoned him, and the captain of Bashara al-Jezzar's janissaries dropped out of sight and crashed into the spring-fed pool below. Kit heard a splash of water followed by a sickening crunch as the captain's head slapped against the marble fountain built along one side of the spring.

Kit heard footsteps behind him. He swung around and leveled his pistol at Bill Tibbs, his fellow privateer.

"Please don't kill me, Christopher." Tibbs held out his hands in mock supplication.

Kit grinned and shook his head. "It's tempting,"

he said. "But I still might need your help before this night is through."

There came a hammering on the harem's bolted doors, and from the hall passageway sounded the savage outcries of the pasha's guards, who at any moment might break into the room and tear the two infidels limb from limb. Elsewhere in the city port of Derna, the rumble of distant cannon and rifle fire signaled the revolution against the pasha's rule was still in progress. Fortunately, the insurrection had drawn most of al-Jezzar's janissaries into the streets.

"Where are the jewels?" Tibbs asked, realizing for the first time his companion was empty-handed.

"I thought you had them." Alarm washed across Kit's sun-darkened features.

Tibbs looked horrified. "I took the lead to ensure our escape route while you pilfered the treasure house. Good God, have you lost what we climbed the cliff for?" Tibbs blurted. Then he knew he'd been set up as Kit roared with laughter and pointed toward the wall behind his fellow thief.

A large leather pouch dangled from a wall bracket that supported a heavy silk tapestry depicting the pasha in all his finery sitting a white charger and trampling his foes beneath the animal's flashing hooves. Kit did not feel the least bit guilty stealing from Bashara al-Jezzar, for the old brigand was one of the Corsican brotherhood who had been preying on American ships for several years. It was high time the thief got a taste of his own medicine.

Tibbs hurried over to retrieve the bag of stolen booty. With a sharp tug he worked the pouch loose and saw it drop to the floor. The pouch fell open and the ruby-encrusted hilt of a scimitar along with a necklace of gold clattered out onto the sandstone floor.

"The Eye of Alexander!" a man gasped from a nearby doorway. Kit looked around and noticed a bald, robe-clad eunuch staring at the scimitar from the entrance to the private quarters of the pasha's many wives. Several young women, dark-haired and doe-eyed, in various stages of undress, tittered among themselves and gestured toward the intruders. Such women were kept in seclusion and allowed only the company of eunuchs until they were summoned to al-Jezzar's bedchambers to await his pleasure—though there was seldom pleasure to be found in the nobleman's often cruel embrace. The women crowded the entrance despite the eunuch's efforts to force them back.

The aroma of incense, burning spices for which Kit had no name, wafted into the corridor and clouded the senses of the intruders, luring them to enter and lose themselves to desire. For here were two young men fit to fan the fires in any woman's heart, be she Turkish princess or slave.

Bill Tibbs, at twenty-eight, was a tall, strapping fellow, whose stark white skin was in sharp contrast to his pitch-black, shoulder-length hair. His eyes were deep-hued, his gaze often guarded and yet ever scrutinizing, as if he were always trying to gain the upper hand.

Kit McQueen stood several inches shorter than his towering friend. And yet it was to him that many of the women offered their inviting glances, for they had seen him move with catlike grace and quickness and they sensed an aura of power about him. His mane of scarlet curls was partly hidden by a bandanna of yellow silk, and his eyes were as bronze as his well-muscled torso. A gold ring glimmered in his right ear. He was younger than Bill Tibbs by a couple of years, but that didn't keep the larger man from deferring to his partner's judgment. It was an influence Kit tended to exude in moments of crisis.

He caught Tibbs by the arm as the man started toward the women, drawn by lust and a hunger for the forbidden and exotic fruits of the pasha's nubile garden.

"Bill, we don't have much time."

"I don't intend to be very long," Tibbs replied, a lascivious smile on his face.

"You must not take the Eye of Alexander," the eunuch interjected in his high-pitched voice. He placed his flabby body between the privateer and the harem women. "I don't know who you are or how you gained access to my honorable lord's domain, may he live a thousand thousand years and be blessed with the strength of a thousand thousand stallions—"

"Oh, shut up," Tibbs said, and shoved the pasha's servant aside.

"But you must hear me. The sword is the Eye of Alexander the Great, given to that most illustrious one by the priests of Persia after he conquered all the world. Cursed be the infidel who disturbs its rest among my lord and master's treasures. So it is written."

"Cursed be the fool who doesn't take it when he has the chance, old one," Kit said. "I do not blame you for trying to protect the pasha's belongings. But we are only stealing it from one who stole it himself. So the curse, if any, rests with Bashara al-Jezzar." Kit managed to catch the leather pouch of necklaces and gold anklets and the jeweled sword as Tibbs casually tossed it back over his shoulder. Tibbs caught up the nearest woman, a mere girl of sixteen, and lifted her into his arms. The silks and bangles she wore rubbed against him, and she pressed her small, pointed breasts against his lips as he held her in the air and then lowered her, running his tongue along her neck and up to her ear.

Kit shouldered the leather pouch. He could hear the wooden bolt begin to splinter in the courtyard below.

"You don't understand," the eunuch entreated, but no one was paying him any mind.

Kit hurried over to the balcony just as the courtyard door caved in and the pasha's guards who had been alerted to the intruders' presence crowded through the doorway. A wheel-lock pistol roared and blasted a fist-sized hole in the balcony.

Kit returned the favor and fired his heavy-caliber flintlock into the center of the janissaries, who were packed together by the door and struggling to untangle themselves and head for the stairway. Kit aimed low. He didn't want to kill anyone unless he had to. The heavy lead ball from his pistol took down three men with a variety of crippling wounds before its energy was spent. The fallen men only served to block the entrance. A pistol shot rang out from behind Kit, and the privateer spun around in time to see Tibbs standing over the eunuch. Blood streamed from Tibbs's ear. The eunuch was propped against the barren sandstone wall. He had dragged the pasha's tapestry down around him like a burial shroud as he slid to the ground, blood oozing from a nasty wound in his round belly.

"The bastard bit me," Tibbs said.

"You didn't have to kill him," Kit snapped angrily.

He had shipped with Bill Tibbs for the better part of two years. They had been friends and trusted shipmates aboard the sleek little Baltimore clipper the two men had pooled their resources to purchase. In all that time Kit had found only one thing to complain about with his friend, and that was Bill Tibbs's temper. The man had a short fuse, and he seemed forever primed and waiting for the right spark to set him off.

"C'mon," Tibbs said sheepishly, and clapped Kit on the shoulder. He blew a kiss to the harem women, who had recoiled in horror at the sight of the dying eunuch. Tibbs broke into a run.

Kit took a step toward the pasha's eunuch. The man's eyes were already glazed over. But he was still breathing.

"I'm sorry," Kit whispered. Then the clatter of swords and rifles below spurred him into motion. He charged the top of the stairway curving up from below.

The stairs were crowded with a dozen of the pasha's heavily armed harem guards. Their naked swords were thirsty for the blood of infidels. To the lead janissary, Kit seemed to come out of nowhere, a blur of motion like a pouncing tiger. The soldiers in the court-yard struggled to bring their guns to bear on the daring young thief. Kit never gave them the chance. He stiff-armed the balcony rail, and pivoting on his strong right shoulder, he leaped up and drove both booted heels into the lead janissary, a swarthy Turk in a black burnoose and flowing robes. The guard was hurled backward and began a chain reaction that toppled the entire column of men on the stairway. Weapons discharged into the air as the soldiers tumbled over one another all the way to the courtyard below.

Kit hit the floor running. Something slapped the pouch on his back and clanked against the metal inside. He nearly lost his balance but managed to reach the door hidden behind another tapestry at the end of the corridor.

Tibbs was waiting at the top of the winding stair-way. The quick-tempered thief held a crudely drawn map that he had purchased from an old beggar in

Constantinople, a withered relic of a man who claimed to have been in the pasha's service. The beggar had been a harem guard who had been discovered with one of al-Jezzar's wives. The poor soldier had been summarily castrated and driven out into the desert to die. However, he had survived and, remembering the location of al-Jezzar's own private escape passage, had furnished a map for the two Americans.

It was in Constantinople, too, that the privateers had heard the rumors of an impending assault on Derna by al-Jezzar's enemies. They had timed their own intrusion to coincide with the attack on the city.

"We promised we would leave the map with Salim's name upon it for Bashara al-Jezzar to find," Kit reminded his friend. Tibbs placed the parchment outside the corridor, where the guards and the pasha would be certain to discover it. The beggar of Constantinople would have the last laugh, after all. Kit removed the pouch and fingered the bullet hole in the center of the bulging surface. A gold anklet had turned the rifle ball and saved Kit's life.

Kit led the way down the stairs. He risked life and limb on the narrow tread as he descended at a run. Rough stone walls sped past as Kit circled around and around, as if burrowing like a corkscrew into the very earth. Only there was light, not darkness, at the end of his journey: yes, light and the smell of the salt sea air!

A few minutes later Kit emerged from the base of the villa onto a wide ledge carved into the face of a cliff overlooking the sparkling blue expanse of the Mediterranean, some three hundred feet below. What looked like an impossible sheer cliff face had, on closer examination, a narrow footpath chiseled into the stark surface. The narrow switchback was just wide enough for one man to edge along the wall, angling back and across all the way to the water's edge. Though a precipitous journey, it promised to be a far easier task in daylight than it had been in the predawn hours.

Anchored thirty yards offshore, the *Trenton* rode easy on the wind-rippled surface of the bay. The *Trenton* was a Baltimore clipper, only seventy feet from bow to stern and armed with a swivel cannon amidships. Half of the clipper's crew, six heavily armed men, waited by the johnboat on order of the clipper's captain. The landing party was ready to fight or run at a moment's notice, whatever the *Trenton's* joint owners required.

"The janissaries will probably start shooting at us from the walls once they discover what we've done," Kit said, dabbing the perspiration from his face on the sleeve of his loose-fitting linen shirt.

"But they are poor marksmen, these Turks," Tibbs said. His features were sweat-streaked and smudged with black powder.

"And they might even pry loose a few rocks to drop on our heads," Kit said in a sage voice.

"No problem, my good friend. The pasha's curse will be our good fortune." Tibbs lovingly stroked the bejeweled hilt of the scimitar jutting from the leather pouch. Then he reached inside his leather belt and removed a silver flask embossed with the family crest, a mailed fist holding a cross. He passed the brandy to Kit, who grinned and lifted the flask in a toast.

"To Alexander's luck," he said.

"To Alexander's luck," Tibbs echoed.

Nothing could stop them now.

Chapter Two

Thirty-five days later, "Alexander's luck" played out. After a particularly violent and stormy night, the morning tides washed the wreckage of the *Trenton* onto the seaweed-littered sandy shores of northeast Spanish Florida, two miles north of the thriving mission of St. Augustine. Fragments of a shattered jib, several barrels, a freshly carved coffin, and patches of a sail littered the shore, along with planks of wood ripped from a reef-shattered hull and a section of mizzenmast as long as a man was tall. A johnboat had also been left by the storm-swept waves that had lashed the coast in the hours just after midnight. The rowboat now rested on its side and was rocked to and fro by the surf.

Two men lay as if dead in the bottom of the boat, and a third was sprawled in the froth where the waves played out upon the beach. A leather pouch lay at his side, tethered to his right arm by a single strap. His matted red hair was patched with mud and dried blood.

Little Maria, an eight-year-old, brown-skinned, hazel-eyed bundle of curiosity and courage, gingerly approached the wreckage the winds of fate had wrested from the sea.

"Go on, Maria," said the boy behind her. Esteban, her brother, was older by five years. He was already grown, as tall as many of the men in his village, but what he had gained in size he had lost in courage, and he held back. These Yankees had been touched by the sea, or worse, by the Angel of Death that the padre told of in his stories. Either way, it was best, Esteban decided, that he not touch such men. Far better to send his nosy sister to tempt fate, and if she withered and died on the spot . . . well . . . where was the loss? No doubt his mother would make more sisters. Maybe she even carried another sister for Esteban right now in her swollen belly as she baked the bread for the padre's noonday meal.

"Go on, Maria. What is there?" Esteban called out. "Are you afraid?" he chided.

"I am not!" the little girl retorted, taking affront at even the mere suggestion of fear, though to be sure her insides were about to turn to jelly and her bare legs trembled as she crept up to the johnboat and peered over the battered bow. She saw the two men up close, and yes, they were indeed Yankees, but as to whether they were alive or dead she could not tell.

One of the men was very big, with large hands whose backs were matted with black hair, and his black-bearded features were red and peeling from sunburn on his forehead and cheeks.

The other man was average in height, as best as she could tell; he lay curled up like a baby in his mother's arms, only his mother this time was the bottom of the boat. He was bearded too, with a thick brown beard, and his mouth was open and she could glimpse a line of broken yellow teeth. And his thinning brown hair was plastered to his skull. There was a knot on his forehead, a swollen, purplish mound that was flecked with blood. Both men wore torn shirts and breeches tucked into high-topped boots.

The larger of the two men had a brace of pistols jutting from the broad leather belt circling his waist.

"Señor?" the girl found her voice and spoke to the men in a soft whisper. After all, she did not wish to wake the dead. Neither of the men stirred, for which she was profoundly grateful. Esteban might like the Yankee's pistols, but then let him come and take them.

The girl backed away from the boat and crossed over to the red-haired man lying facedown in the sand. He was smaller than the others, only a little taller than Esteban, but she could see he was powerfully built, for his shirt was in shreds and his shoulders and back, even in repose, were corded with muscles. She knelt by his side, her eyes on the pouch whose strap was looped around his sun-bronzed right arm.

Esteban took a few tentative steps closer and repositioned himself, the better to see what Maria had found. He craned his neck, and his bare feet trampled a pattern of nervous circles in the moist sand.

"The pouch, Maria, the pouch. Open it."

"I will," Maria hissed back, angry at her brother's incessant instructions. She had her own way of doing things and was not about to be rushed. The pouch appeared to be waterlogged. She reached for the corner flap, attempted to untie the fastenings, and eventually succeeded.

Overhead, a flock of gulls began to gather in lofty spirals. These scavengers of the coastline were willing to wait their turn because their turn always came.

Their high-pitched squawking cries filled the air like the banter of shrewish spirits caught between heaven and earth and complaining about the quality of both.

Maria reached down and picked up a six-inch-long, fanlike shell from the sand underfoot. Using the shell, she lifted the pouch flap and gasped as the golden sword hilt fell into view. Sunlight played upon the finely worked grip, and the rubies seemed to pulse as if with a life of their own, like embers waiting to burst into flame. They drew her like a moth. Esteban, too, once he caught sight of the sword, moved closer, youthful greed overcoming his cowardice. Here was something special, and he couldn't allow his younger sister to claim what ought to be rightfully his.

"Take it out, Maria. Let me see." The boy inched toward his sister and the red-haired Yankee who must surely be dead. "Bring the whole pouch to me."

"Perhaps we ought to bring the padre."

"Foolish girl," Esteban snapped, and he trotted the rest of the distance and drew up alongside his sister. "The padre will take what we have found and give it to God, or worse, hand it over to Sergeant Morales and his men. Is that what you want?"

Maria was impressed by her older brother's argument. She had to admit he made a lot of sense. She did not like Sergeant Morales. Every time he paid a visit to the mission he always caused trouble. Once he had taken her mother inside the jacal and would not allow the children to enter, and when her mother appeared later she was crying and Maria knew the sergeant had hurt her. Father Ramon had been furious, too. No, she was not about to hand over anything that was hers to the sergeant. And as for God, well, she had seen the golden cup that the padre drank from during

Mass, so it seemed to her God had enough pretty things.

"I want the pretty red stone," she said.

Esteban grinned. He envisioned buying his sister's silence with a single stone and keeping the rest of this treasure from the sea for himself.

"Yes—yes, a pretty red stone," he agreed, and shoving the eight-year-old aside, he caught up the pouch and attempted to drag it free of the dead man's arm.

The arm suddenly tensed, and the "dead" man partly rose from the sand and turned a bruised and swollen visage toward the startled children as he violently pulled the pouch from their grasp and snarled, "No!"

Esteban screamed and released the pouch, his blood turning to ice water. Maria screamed alongside her brother. She didn't remain there long. A second later, and she was scampering down the beach and calling out, "Father Ramon! Father Ramon!"

Esteban whirled around and lost his footing in the sand.

"Wait," the voice behind him ordered.

But the boy was not about to obey the entreaties of a corpse sprung to life. The red-haired man reached for him, and the boy screamed again, leaped away, and ran for his life. He could sense the other dead men leaping out of the boat and pursuing him down the beach, their dead arms flapping, and leering at him with their hideous pointed teeth. The image gave wings to his feet, and the boy soon caught up to and passed his sister.

Maria cried out to him to wait up for her, but alas, she had become expendable once again. So she plowed the moist sand with her chubby little brown legs and ran for her life. Ghost crabs scurried out of harm's way. The two children headed inland, spooking a flock of sanderlings and sending them winging into the sky.

Kit McQueen watched the brother and sister disappear beyond a rise topped with beach grass and seaside goldenrod.

"Oh, hell," he muttered, and sank to his knees. He had to brace himself on all fours as he tried to make sense of his surroundings. His head ached terribly. He remembered the storm. Like a fool, Captain Clay had tried to outrun the elements to shore and got caught in treacherous waters. He had fought to turn into the wind and lost when the Trenton had ripped its hull open on a submerged reef. Buffeted by the gale, the clipper had capsized. Kit had managed to survive the catastrophe and through sheer luck and determination had found one of the johnboats, climbed aboard, and managed to retrieve two of his shipmates from the black waters.

Kit doubled over and retched, leaving a puddle of muddy water on the sand along with the contents of his stomach. His head throbbed. He staggered back from the water's edge, noticed the johnboat, and managed to stumble over to the battered craft. He rounded the bow and saw that Bill Tibbs and Augustus LaFarge, the Trenton's first mate, were sprawled in the boat. He reached down, probed LaFarge's neck, and felt no pulse. The sailor was stone cold dead. But Tibbs moaned, and his eyelids flickered as Kit shook him.

Kit tossed the treasure pouch onto shore, then caught Tibbs underneath the arms, dragged him out of the boat, and stretched the big man out upon the sand well away from the lapping waves. Kit stumbled, then braced himself on his friend's shoulder and gasped for breath.

"Christ almighty," he muttered, and gingerly felt his scalp, probing the lump at the base of his skull. He winced and brought his hand away; the fingertips were moist and red. Blood trickled down the back of his neck. It felt like sweat. Kit's stomach flip-flopped, and he almost heaved. But he fought it and won, though the victory left him gasping for breath.

He staggered toward the broad leather pouch that had almost cost him his life by dragging him under the wind-churned waves of the night before. He bent over, grasped the leather strap, and the world tilted on its axis and he fell over. Shards of broken seashells dug into his knees. His skull felt as if it were coming apart. A groan of agony escaped his lips as he rolled onto his side.

"Damn," he cursed softly. He needed help. So did Tibbs. Where did the children go?

He began to crawl on his hands and knees toward the fringe of beach grass that the children had vanished behind, while the gulls overhead kept up a merry chorus of jeers. Kit pulled himself along; he didn't know how far he had come because he never looked back. He concentrated on moving one leg after another, one arm after another. At last he gained enough confidence to try to stand again. He balanced on his wobbly legs like a year-old taking his first steps, and he lasted about as long. He pitched forward and never remembered hitting the ground.

Chapter Three

Men can always find ways to get themselves killed.
The crew of the *Trenton* did. The Baltimore clipper
had battled the gale-force winds to within two miles of
shore when Captain Horatio Clay tried to "thread the
needle" between two reefs and brought his ship and
crew to ruin. Kit McQueen, having fought his way to
the wildly pitching deck, had tried to lend a hand as
best he could under the worst of circumstances. In his
dream, he watched once more the waves crashing over
the deck and the valiant efforts of the crew to trim the
sails in direct disobedience of the captain's orders.

Clay had been a man so sure of his skill that he
could not imagine failure, not even when the bow
reared up with a great grinding and splintering of
wood and the whole ship shuddered like a mortally
wounded beast. The mizzenmast came down in a
tangle of canvas and timber and rope that buried the
captain and several of the crew. The rest were pitched
into the storm-tossed sea as the *Trenton* capsized.

Kit could feel the cold embrace of the water.

Something cracked him across the back of the skull. He choked as the turbulent waters carried him under, borne down by the weight of the treasure pouch. To his horror, the pouch flap had torn loose and gold bracelets, rings, and necklaces spilled into the depths.

Clutching the bag, he fought the ocean's grip, refusing to release his hold on the treasure pouch as he clawed at the black water. He managed by sheer chance to catch hold of a rope lashed around a section of mast. Hand over hand, he pulled himself to the surface, thrusting his head out of the ashen sea to gulp air and cling to life.

Where was the *Trenton*? Surely not that shapeless mass of timber coming to pieces on the submerged reef.

Seawater stung his eyes. Waves lifted him and carried him toward the distant shore. God, how much of al-Jezzar's gold had the sea reclaimed? There was no time to look. Despite his pain-blurred vision, he glimpsed a johnboat riding the crests of the storm-swept surface. The boat leaped like a dolphin and crashed with a thud against the section of mast Kit had found. He reached for the side of the boat, stretched his trembling fingers. In another couple of seconds it would be too late.

Reach. Reach, damn you, or drown.

Kit opened his eyes and found himself groping toward a wall of mud and coquina shells. He rolled on his back and stared up at a cedar-plank ceiling. Sunlight spilled into the room through an open doorway and the unshuttered windows permitted a gentle cross breeze through to freshen the hut's interior. A crucifix hung above the doorsill. Kit was lying on a hard but not uncomfortable cot set in one corner of the coquinawalled hut. Kit noted at a glance he was not alone in the room. Long-legged Bill Tibbs was stretched out on a second cot, his bootheels dangling just inches above the floor.

A comely Creek Indian woman in the late months of her pregnancy sat on a stool alongside Tibbs, who was not only conscious but propped up to receive the broth she was spooning into his mouth. His upper torso was naked, and his shoulder was bandaged. If Tibbs was in pain it didn't show. He obviously enjoyed the attention he was receiving from the woman. The rope and wood frame of the cot creaked as Kit shifted his weight. The woman turned at the sound, and on seeing the second Yankee was awake she set the bowl of broth on the floor within Tibbs's reach and hurried from the room.

"Well, you sure spoiled that." Tibbs scowled at his friend.

"From the look of her, she was spoken for," Kit replied. He sat back against the wall and felt a sharp, stabbing pain lance through his skull. He brought a hand to his head and touched a cloth bandage.

Across the room, within view of both men, the large leather pouch had been securely fastened and left on a narrow but solid-looking table crafted from the dark wood of a young loblolly pine. An oil lantern, a worn leatherbound Bible, and a quill and ink had been left on the table, no doubt by the room's owner, but shoved to one side to make room for the treasure pack.

"Spoken for, indeed...but talking was the farthest thing from my mind." Tibbs sighed, a wicked grin on his face.

"Half drowned and still as horny as a goat." Kit chuckled and then sucked in his breath as his wound sent a sharp protest from his head to his shoulder blades.

"Goats? Yes, we have goats," a brown-robed priest said from the doorway. He had brought another bowl of soup.

Father Ramon Saucedo at sixty moved with the grace and energy of a man twenty years younger. His skin was as dark as that of the Creek Indians he served, the color of old bark. Indeed, the lines and wrinkles that creased his features gave his skin not only a barklike color but the texture of some aged forest monarch that had survived wind and rain and fire. His hair was stringy, silver and unkempt, but his mustache and goatee, also silver, were neatly trimmed. And if he had lost the beauty of his youth (once women had called him handsome and contested with one another to catch his eye), he had replaced such a transitory appeal with an air of wisdom and dignity that shone from his features as brightly as the Florida sunlight.

"Good morning, my friends," the priest said. His sandals shuffled softly over the packed earth floor of the single-roomed cabin. "It has been a while since I have spoken English. I am Padre Ramon Saucedo. You understand me, yes?"

He handed the bowl of soup to Kit, who nodded his thanks and chanced a sip. It was salty, and chunks of fish and scallops floated in this broth. He found the sample to his liking.

Father Ramon pulled over a three-legged stool and sat down. "You washed ashore on the island. Barely a strip of sand and beach grass. I go there to cast my nets. Maria and Esteban found you and brought me to you. Which was fortunate for you both." The padre toyed with the wooden cross dangling from a leather string around his neck. "My humble house is a palace compared to the prison Sergeant Morales would offer you at the garrison in St. Augustine."

"Prison?" Kit said. He set the wooden bowl aside and introduced himself and Bill Tibbs and then continued with his initial question. "Why prison?"

"There has been much trouble of late. Yankees from the north have come across the border and declared all of Florida a republic, free of Spanish rule. But the mission Indians have been well treated. Our colonists are of Spanish descent. We do not wish to break ties with our mother country, so we fight. The soldiers have hunted these Yankees down and killed or imprisoned most of them."

"Be we are . . . uh, traders," Tibbs blurted out. "We've nothing to do with any of this. A storm wrecked our ship, or we would never have troubled you."

"I believe you," the padre said, leaning forward. "But then my heart is filled with peace toward all men." Father Ramon kissed the cross he wore. "Sergeant Morales is a soldier, a man of war. If he discovers you, then . . ." The padre shook his head. The implication was quite clear: Their fates would be sealed.

"Do not worry," the padre spoke reassuringly. "I am no friend of Sergeant Morales. You are safe here. He seldom comes to visit. I have promised him the wrath of God if he touches one of my flock again." The priest seemed momentarily lost in thought, and he looked back to the barefoot Indian woman standing in the doorway. In a matter of weeks Sara would be having Morales's child. The woman disappeared into the sunlight; she was none of his guests' concern. He returned his attention to the matter at hand. "I will not reveal your presence here. But you cannot remain long. You will be in danger until you cross the border."

"How far away are we from Georgia?" Tibbs asked.

"Two days by horse."

"Good," Tibbs exclaimed. "We can make it. We'll rest up and then tomorrow or the next day borrow a couple of your horses and ride out. This Sergeant Morales will never know a thing."

"No," Father Ramon said.

"We will pay you for the animals, of course. Probably more than what they are worth," Kit said, thinking of the gold trinkets that had almost drowned him, the treasure of Bashara al-Jezzar.

"Of that I have little doubt," the padre conceded drolly. He glanced knowingly over his shoulder at the leather pouch behind him on the table. "Maria and Esteban spoke of the treasure. And I must admit I, too, examined the beautiful things you rescued from the sea."

"Our treasure," Tibbs emphasized. Just because a man donned a brown robe, sandals, and a cross didn't mean Tibbs felt obliged to trust him. He began to eat while scrutinizing the priest.

"Yes. Of course." The padre ignored the man's suspicious gaze. "It is yours alone."

"So you see we can offer you much more than what a couple of your horses are worth." Kit was worried that Tibbs would antagonize the old padre. They owed the priest their lives. Father Ramon could easily have turned them over to the authorities. Kit didn't want the old one to regret his decision. "Surely a portion of our wealth might prove useful for a church or a school outside St. Augustine."

Tibbs all but choked on a mouthful of fish. They hadn't even divided the spoils taken during the Derna raid, and already Kit was giving some away.

"It is impossible," Father Ramon replied.

"Why?" Kit asked.

"Because I have no horses," the priest replied. "I sent Esteban for help. Four Creek men carried you here upon the very pallets on which you rest."

"Damn!" Tibbs muttered.

Father Ramon gave him a pained look.

"But across the St. John's River, back in the woods, is the cabin of Alsino Escovar, the trapper. He has boats, horses, and a thirst for the shiny metal. He will sell you anything."

"How far past the river is his cabin?" Kit asked. Even with the pain hammering in his head he had begun to plan, to set his options and gather all the information necessary should the situation become desperate and the Yankees need to escape with this Sergeant Morales in hot pursuit.

"An hour, if a man is running," said the priest. "But much longer for these old bones." The Franciscan shook his head. "Enjoy your youth, my friends. Savor your days like rare wine. For the glass is soon drained. Ah, too soon." He clapped his knees and stood. "How I prattle on when you need your rest. We will talk later. Sleep, compadres. You are safe for now. Heal yourselves. I shall pray for the return of your strength. And my prayers are always answered." The padre winked and vanished through the front door into the yellow glare.

Kit sat upright and watched the brown-robed figure through the window. Father Ramon had barely stepped past the corner of the cabin when he was immediately surrounded by a gaggle of excited children and a half dozen Creek braves. The men were dressed in breeches and worn, patched linsey-woolsey shirts. They might have been Spanish settlers save for the reddish-brown luster of their skin and their shiny, shoulder-length black hair that hung straight and framed their flat, dark faces.

The cluster of mud-walled cabins appeared to be set well back from the shore and nestled in a clearing of live oaks and black willows draped with spanish moss.

"What do you think?" Tibbs said. He managed to stand and shuffled across the floor to the table, where he began to painstakingly unfasten the torn flap of the large leather pouch. The jewel-hilted scimitar that contained the Eye of Alexander fell into his hand. He sighed with relief. But his humor quickly faded on further inspection of the bag. All that remained of the stolen wealth was a handful of trinkets—a few solid gold bracelets, a couple of necklaces of pounded gold set with emeralds, and a golden goblet inlaid with pearls and lapis lazuli.

This was wealth, to be sure, but only a fraction of what they had taken from al-Jezzar's treasure room.

Tibbs's face became livid as he slowly turned to show Kit how they had been robbed.

"Damn their souls, they've taken it all. Robbed us blind, by my oath. Blood will flow for this!" Tibbs pounded the tabletop with his fist.

"They took nothing," Kit spoke up from the cot. He propped himself against the wall. "The pouch ripped open when the *Trenton* dumped me into the sea. I saved what I could."

Tibbs glared at his companion. Somehow he managed to calm himself. There was nothing to be said. He stared at the pouch as if willing the return of what had been lost. But he was no conjurer. At least something had been salvaged. A man could make a good life for himself on what remained. Tibbs returned the Eye of Alexander and lowered the flap.

"You did well, my friend," he said in a gentler, calmer tone of voice. "Best we heal up and quit this place as quickly as we can." He gingerly stretched out upon the cot.

"At least we're among friends," Kit added, trying to make the best of the situation.

"Sure. Friends," Tibbs echoed, unconvinced. "Only where are our guns?"

Kit swept the room at a glance. A knot of fear re-formed in the pit of his stomach. Tibbs was right about one thing. Their weapons were gone. *If Sergeant Morales and his soldiers came,* Kit thought, *we would be completely defenseless.*

"You think we can trust the priest?" Tibbs muttered, eyeing the open doorway and the empty sunlight that had suddenly lost its warmth.

Kit looked from his friend to the window and the brown-skinned men and women of the village who had grouped together to keep the Yankees' cabin under observation.

"I don't think we have a choice," he said.

Chapter Four

The next day dawned with a rumble of distant thunder. Kit had rested fitfully, dozing for a while, then lying awake. For the past hour he'd lain motionless, staring at the ceiling and listening to the patter of the summer shower. One by one he counted the beads of sweat that rolled off his neck and soaked into the cot beneath his head. As dawn's gray light seeped into the hut Kit rose from his bed and managed to stand, swaying in the center of the room. After a few moments he gained his sea legs.

A dull ache lingered in his skull, but the pain had lessened enough overnight to convince him he had suffered no permanent damage. He'd been willing to debate the matter earlier. But for now, as long as he could see and walk and he hadn't been clapped in irons by the Spanish, Kit was satisfied.

A loud snore erupted from the opposite side of the room. Bill Tibbs mumbled something in his sleep and then curled over on his side. Kit padded across the room, leaned over his partner, and caught a whiff of Jamaican rum about the same time his bare toe nudged the cool, brown glass bottle Tibbs had left by his bed. The bottle toppled over, rolled beneath the cot, and clattered off the wall.

"Helped yourself, did you?" Kit accused. "And not so much as a drop for your friend. Ah, Bill Tibbs, you can be a selfish son of a bitch sometimes. Still, we've pulled each other out of tight scrapes and saved one another's neck, so I guess I can pardon your oversight."

Tibbs snored, then smacked his lips, and his long fingers fluttered as if he were clawing at the earth. Kit never considered attempting to rouse his friend. Tibbs had drunk himself into this stupor, and time, not man, would·have to drag him out of it. Kit left his besotted companion and walked across the room to the table. He started to reach for the treasure pouch, then changed his mind and turned back to his cot, where he retrieved his belt from the foot of his humble bed. He was happy to note his knife was still in its sheath. He slid the six-inch blade from its scabbard.

Back at the table Kit discovered half a dozen hollow reeds of varying thickness that Father Ramon had intended to convert into writing pens. Kit selected one, and with knife in hand, he settled himself in the doorway and watched the overcast sky lighten in hue as somewhere beyond the clouds the sun rose above the horizon. Kit worked the blade point into the reed and dug out a series of four evenly spaced holes. From time to time he paused to stare out at the rain-spattered earth, the gray clouds reflected in the puddles, the dull green sheen of the willows and loblolly pines that screened the village from the coast.

A pair of Creek warriors hurried toward a partly

completed coquina brick structure in the center of the village. Kit guessed it was the mission church.

The Creek men were about Kit's height, and like the seafarer, they were well muscled and moved with quiet, quick steps. Between them, the two braves carried a load of timber into the church structure with only a glance in Kit's direction. They kept their heads bowed to the rain.

Kit resumed carving on the reed, adding the appropriate air holes and shaving and tapering the mouthpiece. He put the crudely honed instrument to his lips and played a couple of trilling notes. One of the holes needed enlarging, and he went to work on it. He finished, blew away the debris, and tried the flute again. This time the sound came clear and piping and sweet upon the rain-washed air. Kit smiled with satisfaction, then looked up and was surprised to find he was no longer alone.

Maria, the little girl from the beach, and two of her friends, both boys, peered around the corner at the red-haired stranger in the doorway. One of the boys, a chubby, sweet-faced child with rust-colored eyes, held a makeshift cage in which a seaside sparrow hopped from perch to perch and eyed the world through a cage made of twigs and bound together with strips of cloth. The sparrow's brown plumage was streaked with ashen gray feathers. The feathers on its breast were tinged yellow, and nature had placed a spot like a sunburst between its eyes and gray beak. It sang high-pitched notes to match the flute.

"I am called Kit," McQueen managed to say in his fractured Spanish.

"I am Maria," said the little girl. "I found you," she added proudly, as if the Yankee were her very own prize.

"I'm glad you did," Kit told her.

"And this is Mateo and Juan."

Kit noted that Mateo held the bird cage while Juan, who seemed a trifle more reticent, stared longingly at the flute. Mateo held up the bird cage for Kit to examine. He proudly described how he had rigged the snare and captured the bird all by himself. Kit understood only snatches of the lad's account, but he nodded approvingly and gave the appearance of being most impressed. All the while Juan continued to scrutinize the man from the sea.

"He does not speak," Maria said, indicating the long-faced boy to her right. "Even after Father Ramon baptized him, he still did not speak," she added, incredulous that no miracle had occurred to give the mute child his voice. She shrugged and took a step toward him. "I am not afraid of you."

"*Bueno.*" Kit smiled and placed the flute to his lips. He blew softly and his fingers danced over the holes to produce a merry tune of his own composing. The music danced upon the rain. The children smiled with delight, and Maria began to dance in little circles. Mateo held his bird cage out so its occupant might sing along with the carefree melody. Only Juan seemed unaffected. However, appearances were deceiving. His appreciation was far more subtle in its display. He remained perfectly still, as one transfixed by the redheaded piper and the tune he played while sitting in the doorway.

Kit finished his song, much to Maria's chagrin.

"Play it again," Mateo said.

"Not me," Kit replied. He pointed the flute at Juan. "Him."

He held the flute out to the silent boy. Time seemed to hang still as the child summoned his courage. Then, slowly, he stretched out his arm and opened his fingers. Kit placed the flute in the boy's palm.

"Now you have a voice," Kit said.

The boy closed his hand and dashed off into the rain, with Maria and Mateo at his heels. The silent boy was halfway to his parent's jacal when he skidded to a halt in the mud and turned back toward the man in the doorway. He raised the reed flute to his lips and piped a chorus of notes with such wild abandon that his whole body shuddered with the joyous sound. Then he turned and scampered off into the rain.

"You're welcome," Kit said.

His head started to throb. The dizziness had returned, though less severe now. Kit decided to weather his discomfort lying down. A thundercrack startled him as he stood in the doorway and braced himself against the wall of the house. Overhead, the storm tracked to the north and loosed a torrential downpour that all but obscured most of the village behind its watery gray sheets. Kit glanced over at Tibbs's still slumbering form. A hurricane could spring up and blow them all away and Tibbs wouldn't stir. Kit had to admire the potency of the padre's rum.

The cot creaked and groaned as Kit stretched out, folded his hands behind his head, and closed his eyes. With nothing but the droning downpour to relax him, Kit's thoughts turned to home, the Hound and Hare Inn on the Trenton Road.

His father, Daniel McQueen, a veteran of the War for Independence, had cared little for the bickering between political factions that oftentimes divided the populace. He had retired to the life of a blacksmith— honest labor, he called it. Kate McQueen, Kit's mother, managed the inn. She had a daughter to help her while Kit labored alongside his father at the forge, working iron and learning to shape steel to his will. Kit heard once more his father's strong, truthful voice speak in his soul, touching young Kit with words of caution and encouragement.

Captured like some living portrait in his mind, Kit watched the embers of a forge glow with life. He saw himself, a twelve-year-old boy, working the bellows. He cried out with glee as he sent a column of sparks like a whirlwind of miniature suns coruscating up into the black iron chimney.

These were good memories, the kind that anchored a man when he might be feeling hurt or lost and alone. They carried Kit into a place of rest and healing. The sound of the rain faded. Asleep, he did not even hear the storm slacken, the downpour lessen, until it became no more than a fine settling mist. Asleep, he did not hear the patter of footsteps across the puddled ground, nor could he be aware yet of the giggles and whispered asides of the children, all ten of them who had followed Juan and Mateo and Maria back to the hut. There the children crowded around the door to wait in respectful silence for the red-haired flutemaker to awaken—thirteen children with hollow reeds in their hands and hearts full of expectation.

Chapter Five

"Why do the young die?" Father Ramon Saucedo muttered softly. "Why does anyone die?" He stared down at the two-week-old grave of a young man who had been bitten by a cottonmouth and succumbed to the poison before reaching the village. "Joseph was my first altar boy. I myself taught him to read and write. He wanted very much to be a priest." Father Ramon glanced at the Yankee standing at his side.

It was late afternoon and Kit had been looking for the Franciscan for the better part of an hour. He'd misinterpreted little Maria's directions and been forced to retrace his steps after becoming lost on the edge of the very same swamps that had claimed Joseph's life. It was only by sheer chance Kit had stumbled onto the Creek Christian burial ground where the priest was wont to visit and read from the worn, leatherbound Bible he carried.

"Answering that question is your job, Padre. Not mine," Kit replied.

"Perhaps you are right, my young friend," the

priest conceded. "Then again, I have often suspected there is no answer. Only the search for it, as we seek the truth of our lives." Father Ramon placed his hand over the crucifix he wore. A gentle breeze tousled his thin, silvery hair and ruffled the voluminous sleeves and hem of his coarse brown robe. "The cross is the only truth I know." He snapped his Bible shut. He folded his arms across his bony chest and studied the Yankee he had rescued from the rising tide. "What truth do you know?"

Kit shrugged. Like most young men he intended to live forever. Thoughts of the hereafter were far from his mind. He believed in his quickness, in his strength and daring. He believed in the power of dreams and what a man might accomplish if he remained watchful and resolute.

"I believe, my friend, that I will leave tomorrow," Kit said. "We have been hiding for three days. We dare not stay longer."

Kit noted the padre did not try to hide his relief. He couldn't blame the priest. Having the Yankees in the village threatened the very survival of the mission settlement. For three days, Kit and Tibbs had remained in hiding, allowing their wounds to heal until both men felt well enough to travel.

Oh, the two adventurers were still sore and hardly up to their full strength, but Tibbs had declared he was confident of their ability to make the journey home. And Kit agreed. Anyway, they were bound to find a settlement along the Georgia coast in which to heal the last of their hurts. What mattered now was getting under way. Every day they remained in the village heightened the risk of discovery.

"I will have my people prepare food for your journey," Father Ramon told him.

"My thanks. And while you are at it, why don't you have them return our guns?" Kit carefully watched the padre's expression, searching his features for any sign of duplicity.

Father Ramon did glance up rather sharply, and he started to protest. But lies had no place on his lips. "Guns . . . yes. I suppose I must." He sighed and hooked a thumb in the rope belt circling his waist. "I thought it best to keep them until you were ready to leave. My Creeks have learned the ways of peace, unlike most white men. I took your guns in hopes of protecting them."

Father Ramon glanced up at the black willows and oak trees that even in this place of death were alive with the antics of the gray squirrels, chattering and scolding one another while dark-winged birds darted among the branches and multicolored butterflies fluttered lazy spirals in the warm summer air.

"Do you know," the priest continued, "Saint Francis of Assisi could call the birds from the treetops and the animals from the depths of the forest. He would sing to them, talk to them, and tell them of the love of their creator. I have walked this clearing day after day in prayer and have yet to summon so much as a bee from a flower." The old man in the brown robe made a soft, sibilant sound as he exhaled. Father Ramon spoke like a man questioning his belief, Kit thought to himself, yet Kit doubted the padre had even begun to tap the depths of his faith.

"You've made your mark, Padre. I wouldn't worry about whether or not you can charm the birds from the treetops."

"My mark . . ." Father Ramon muttered ruefully. "Is that what a man should live for? Is that what you think?"

"That or for gold. And the power it can bring."

"I do not think you know yourself as well as you think you do. I have seen you, carving flutes for the children as they gathered at your door. The heart speaks that which lips often deny. I trust a man's heart." With a gesture of his hand he led the way back to the path that wound through the woods to the village.

Kit started to follow, then paused, noticing the grave marker of Augustus LaFarge. Memories of the coarse, good-humored sailor returned. Poor LaFarge, he deserved better than to drown so close to home. But there were worse places to await the unfolding of eternity than here amid the willows and oaks and pines, here where the play of the distant tide lingered on the wind, where flowers bloomed and an old priest came to pray and consider the meaning of life. At least LaFarge had a marker, which was more than could be said for the rest of the *Trenton's* crew.

"Augustus, sleep well. You know the truth of it now, I warrant." Kit turned and started after the padre. Father Ramon waited for him near a fallen log that had rotted away from the inside. A swarm of bees had chosen to build a hive within that brittle cover of bark.

"He lies in sanctified ground," the priest said, nodding toward LaFarge's grave.

Kit had to laugh. "Padre...old Augustus had a lot of attributes. But sanctified wasn't one of them."

"It is now." The priest stroked his silver goatee and smiled. "I am glad I did not hand you over to Sergeant Morales." He had begun to like this young man. Where Bill Tibbs was guarded and suspicious of every overture, Kit McQueen had ventured among the people of the village and treated the Creek with respect.

"But you won't be sorry to see me leave, either," Kit mentioned.

"No, but one day, perhaps you will return and—"

"Father Ramon!"

The priest straightened, a look of concern on his face. The voice that called him with such urgency belonged to little Maria.

The girl appeared, breathless, out of the green gloom at the east end of the path where the tall grass grew in patches and sunlight struggled through the moss-draped trees to illuminate the shadowy interior of the woods.

Father Ramon hurried as best he could toward the girl. Maria spied the familiar figure in the brown robe and ran to him as fast as her little brown legs could carry her.

"What is it now, my child?" the priest said as the girl ran to his open arms. Kit felt the goose bumps rise on the back of his neck. An image of the village beset by a detachment of Spanish troops from St. Augustine flashed through his mind. But the danger this afternoon came from a different source, one Kit knew only too well. The girl blurted out her message in a mixture of Spanish and Creek. Kit was unable to follow her. He waited patiently for Father Ramon to translate for him.

"It is her brother, Esteban. She fears for his safety." The priest reported worriedly. He glared up at the patch of blue sky. "*Madre de Dios*," he muttered. "Esteban has been watching and waiting for you and Señor Tibbs to leave your hut. He told Maria he intended to help himself to one of your yellow metal bracelets."

"He better hope Bill Tibbs doesn't discover him," Kit said. His friend hadn't been the same since Derna. And the disastrous shipwreck, with the loss of so much of their treasure, certainly hadn't helped. Perhaps when they were safely out of Florida and strolling the streets of Charleston, Tibbs would see things in a more favorable light. Part of a treasure was better than none at all.

"Come, my young friend," Father Ramon said. "Perhaps we will be in time to stop trouble before it begins."

By the time the priest and Kit reached the clearing and the circle of huts that made up the Creek village, things had already gone from bad to worse. The men of the village, those who were not down by the beach tending their nets, were gathered outside the hut where Kit and Tibbs had recuperated. The men and several of the women clustered by the door of the hut were visibly angry. The men were armed with wicked-looking war clubs inlaid with jagged pieces of shell.

Word spread among the villagers that Father Ramon had returned. The priest and Kit quickly became the center of attention. Father Ramon stopped to talk to the first men he met in order to find out for himself what had happened. Kit continued through the crowd, which grudgingly parted before him, until he was almost to the hut.

Then a broad-shouldered Creek warrior blocked the white man's path. The man looked to be several years older than Kit. He wore a headdress of shells and plumage woven together. His war club sported not only a ragged line of razor-sharp shells but a wicked row of shark's teeth inlaid in the wood where it curved to form a wicked crook.

Kit was unarmed save for the knife in his boot sheath, but he wasn't about to back away. Any sign of weakness on his part might bring him a crushed skull. He met the warrior's stare and waited for the man to make his move. To his surprise and relief the warrior stepped aside. Kit moved past the man and halted a couple of yards from the door.

"Come ahead, Kit," Tibbs shouted from within. "I found our guns in the padre's hut. I've got them loaded and primed."

The shadows had begun to steal across the land as the sun sank beyond the trees and disappeared into a pool of incandescent orange and vermilion clouds.

"Bill, come out here!"

"Like hell."

"Come out and tell me what happened."

Movement in the doorway, a shift of shadows, then Tibbs materialized in the doorway, guns dangling at the ends of his long arms. Another brace of pistols was tucked in his belt. His dark eyes surveyed the crowd. His nostrils flared as he readied himself to fight. "You satisfied? I searched the priest's quarters and found our guns. When I arrived back here I caught one of these little heathens trying to rob us. I gave him the back of my hand and chased him out. The next thing I know, the whole damn village is standing outside the door shouting for my head. I showed them my guns, though, and none of them wanted to be the first to taste lead."

Kit closed his eyes a moment and shook his lowered head. Tibbs was going to get them both killed. Somehow he had to defuse the situation.

"The man who blocked your path is Esteban's father," Father Ramon said, moving up on Kit's left. The Franciscan priest folded his arms across his chest. "It is an unheard-of thing for an adult to strike a child among these people." The padre began to stroke his whiskers. "Unheard of," he repeated absently. "Now Esteban has run off, and I don't—"

But Kit had already headed straight for the hut

and forced Tibbs to retreat as he entered. Tibbs mis-read his intentions, thinking his friend had come to help in the defense of the hut.

"Good," Tibbs said. "If we charge them together they'll probably give way." He tried to pass a pair of the flintlocks to Kit.

"Don't be ridiculous." Kit untied the leather pouch on the table and dug into its contents. Gold bracelets and jeweled necklaces clinked and rattled off one another.

"What are you doing?" Tibbs asked, a scowl on his face. His features began to pale. "Oh, no...."

"Saving our lives," Kit replied. He selected a broad band of pounded gold and retraced his steps outside before Tibbs could even sputter a protest. Kit headed straight for the man with whom he had almost come to blows. The warrior kept a tight grip on his war club. He suspected the white man of treachery despite the fact that Father Ramon spoke soothingly in the man's ear, keeping his voice soft as he asked the warrior to give Kit a chance to prove himself.

Kit stopped directly in front of the warrior. He glanced at the padre. "What is his name?"

"He is called Isaiah. That is his Christian name."

"Tell Isaiah that my friend is not well. That his hurt inside caused him to harm the boy. Say that we wish to offer Isaiah a gift to honor him and his family." Kit waited for the priest to translate, then held out the gold bracelet. It gleamed in the light of the setting sun. The band of precious metal was etched with winged serpentlike creatures of myth.

The warrior accepted the golden band and reverently slipped it onto his wrist. Then he held up his right arm so that all the men and women around him might see. Everyone was suitably impressed. The warrior turned back to Kit. He nodded and placed the war club at Kit's feet. Kit, relying on instinct, picked the war club off the ground and returned the weapon to the warrior. Isaiah grunted his approval, then swung around and started back through the crowd, which had already begun to disperse.

Father Ramon remained behind. "You did well, my son." He looked past Kit to Tibbs, who remained in the doorway, glowering. "I will find Esteban. Then I will see to food and water for your journey. Rest now. You will need your strength tomorrow." The old priest turned and joined those he called his "savage children" as cook fires were lit and life in the village returned to normal.

Kit started back toward the hut, where Tibbs waited, speechless and flushed with anger. Before Tibbs could vent his rage, Kit went after him.

"Let it be, Bill. Just let it be. This gold means as much to me as it does to you. But one trinket isn't worth our lives." Kit crossed to the table and poured himself a drink from the water jug that had been left for them along with a platter of smoked bluefish and fry bread. "You've changed, my friend. For the worse. It will bring you ruin."

Kit sat on the edge of his cot and waited for the inevitable outburst. To his surprise, it never came. Instead, Tibbs slumped on the cot across from him and leaned forward on his elbows.

"Hell, you're right, Kit." Tibbs wiped a hand across his face, breathed in deep, and exhaled slow and easy. "I'm sorry." His handsome face suddenly split with a grin. "Maybe it's because I had so many dreams, and now we're back where we started, after almost two years, with nothing to show for it."

"Nothing?" Kit stood, walked over to the table,

and held up the jeweled scimitar that had once belonged to Alexander the Great. A golden shaft of sunlight poured into the hut as the setting sun seemed to hang suspended between a gap in the trees. A beam of light washed over Tibbs and made it seem as if he were afire, as if he had become one with the precious wealth he had hungered for and would kill to protect.

"Like I said, Kit. You're right." Tibbs held out his hand. "Friends?"

McQueen clasped the offered hand. "We've never been anything else, you hardheaded, quick-tempered bastard," he said with a grin. The sunlight had faded. Darkness crept into the room.

Chapter Six

Sergeant Pablo Morales had spent the entire night scouring the forests below St. Augustine for some sign of the Yankee stragglers attempting to make their way home after trying to foment a revolution in this Spanish colony. For weeks now, rumors had run rampant throughout the settlement concerning the remnants of such an expedition, one that had marched out of the north to free Florida from Spanish control. First, word came of a sizable Yankee army loose in the interior and marching on St. Augustine. But what gossip and hearsay had called an army became a desperate, hungry band of ragtag militia whose only interest now was scurrying to the safety of the country that had sent them . . . and left them unsupported to do or die in the swamps and forests of Florida.

However, even this rumored collection of fugitives proved as intangible as a will-o'-the-wisp. Sergeant Morales had spent most of the night laying traps for *Inglés* stragglers who apparently never even existed.

Morales eased his wide girth out of the saddle

before a darkened tavern in the center of the settlement. The twelve bone-weary dragoons under his command arranged their horses to his left, dismounted, and tethered their horses. Morales was a large man with a belly that hung over his belt like a bay window. His shoulders were sloping and heavyset; his torso was thickly padded with watery rolls of fat. His jowls were dark with a three-day-old stubble of beard. Sweat glistened in the gritty folds of his bull neck. His fists were huge and covered with coarse, black hair as he hammered on the door.

"Open up, you son of a worm," Morales shouted. "Valdez! You trickle down your father's leg, open this door. My men and I are tired and thirsty and have little patience. Open the door, or we will kick it in!"

A lamplight glimmered in the room above the cantina. A muffled voice could be heard through the shuttered window muttering curses to whatever deity might listen. Morales continued to hammer on the door. It didn't matter to him in the slightest that it was an hour before sunrise, when all decent souls were catching the last few precious minutes of sleep, living the last of their dreams before waking to the harsh realities of survival. Morales did not care who heard him or whose sleep he disturbed. After all, he had exhausted himself supposedly protecting these very same people whose peace he shattered.

The door creaked open on its iron hinges, and a slight-built, balding man, middle-aged and wearing a mask of long suffering, moved aside as the sergeant swept past him and into the cool confines of the cantina.

The cantina held no more than six tables that the owner had built from driftwood. The building itself, like most of the others in St. Augustine, was built of a mixture of mud and coquina shells, which when dried turned hard as stone and able to withstand the forces of nature.

However, it seemed that no home, business, or place of worship was safe from the likes of Sergeant Morales. He went where he pleased and did as he pleased. The inhabitants of the settlement tolerated him; they had no choice in the matter. To give him his due, the sergeant was a fighter to be reckoned with, ruthless and cruel and giving no quarter. He had fought Indians and the French and now the *Inglés* invaders from the north. And if he acted like a bastard once in a while, at least he was their bastard. Aside from his occasional outbursts of bad temper and drunken forays, he was the settlement's protector, and St. Augustine's inhabitants for the most part felt better for his presence.

Tomas Valdez, the owner of the cantina, waved in the dozen soldiers who followed the sergeant out of the warm, muggy air. They were a weary, mud-spattered lot and wanted nothing more than to slump into the closest chair and wash the swampwater taste from their mouths with the cantina's sangria.

"Welcome, my good friend," Valdez said with false cheer. "All my good friends." He closed the door and hurried to light a few more lanterns. Soon the net-strewn walls were bathed in an amber glow.

Morales strode across to one of the interior walls. He unfastened his sword belt, coat, and shirt and pressed his naked, round belly and hairy chest against the earthen wall. His face, too, switching from cheek to cheek, he cooled against the hard-packed surface.

"Too damn hot," the sergeant muttered. "And the mosquitoes, the size of black-backed gulls, I tell you. And they came in swarms and damn near carried me off."

"I doubt that," Valdez muttered, eyeing the sergeant's protruding gut. Valdez padded across the room in his nightshirt and bare feet.

"What was that? Eh?" Morales said, glancing at the cantina owner, who was hurrying to provide clay cups and bottles of sangria to the dragoons sprawled about his tables. The soldiers were drooping from exhaustion, their limbs too sore to even think about. Morales continued to press himself against the wall, enjoying the packed earth's cooling touch.

"Nothing. Nothing," the little cantina owner replied quickly, threading his way among the tables.

The arrival of the wine brought some life back to the dragoons. They helped themselves to the bottles, carelessly filled their cups, and didn't care a whit if they sloshed some of the blood-red liquid onto their already muddy white uniforms.

The soldiers' tall, green, leather hats that made such men look so formidable on parade had been carelessly tossed into a corner. High, stiff collars were quickly unfastened, although not one of these younger men attempted to make himself as comfortable as the sergeant. Such disregard for uniform was permitted only to a man of rank. And Morales, what with the lack of any real officer in the settlement, held all the rank he needed to justify his actions.

"Drink!" he called, and stretched out a hand that Valdez immediately filled with a bottle of wine. The sergeant turned and leaned his back against the wall, tilted the bottle to his lips, and drank deeply. His capacity for both food and drink were the stuff of legend.

Valdez only hoped that this morning's early visit would prove perhaps a trifle less legendary than others he had known. Morales had been in a foul mood for days now. Just recently, word had come that a new *comandante* was on his way to St. Augustine to replace Captain Gonzalez, who had died of a fever and left Sergeant Morales in charge of the settlement's troops these many weeks. Morales had grown to love the feeling of power that came with the duties of command. He'd reveled in his newly gained authority. But now a new officer was to be stationed in the mission, and Morales would return to being a subordinate.

The notion galled him.

Still, there was nothing to be done but enjoy what he had while he had it. Morales held out the bottle and sloshed its contents. "Ah, my friend, no one has a better sangria," he told the cantina owner.

Valdez added beneath his breath, "Aye, but to my own misfortune." He walked around behind the bar, brought out another bottle, and wondered if he would be paid for his troubles. Perhaps when the sergeant was in a better mood he might approach the man with a bill.

Morales swaggered across the room, dragging his sword belt behind him like an afterthought. He paused at the nearest table and leaned on the shoulder of the detachment's corporal, Eduardo Galvez, a venerable campaigner who had spent his entire adult life in uniform. Galvez was a man of average height, with a solid build that his unremitting weariness had begun to erode.

He had been a sergeant like Morales more times than he could count. But inevitably his penchant for strong drink placed him at odds with his superiors and resulted in his demotions. At the age of forty-two, Galvez had once again attained the rank of corporal.

"Galvez, my brave corporal, how well you distinguished yourself against the *Inglés* soldiers," Morales exclaimed.

"But Sergeant. We encountered no one. I did nothing," Galvez said.

"And you have never been more distinguished," Morales said, roaring with laughter. He clapped Galvez on the back with enough force to knock the wind out of the man.

The other soldiers joined in the fun at Galvez's expense. The corporal did not seem to mind, however. In fact, except for his gasping for breath, he appeared unaffected by the sergeant's insinuations. He recognized Morales's black moods for what they were and had long ago resolved to bend with the breeze rather than resist and break.

"Now, my brave corporal," Morales said, "see that you take our horses around back of the cantina and put them in the first corral you find, eh?"

"Sí. As you wish, my sergeant." Galvez glanced forlornly at the cup of wine he would not be able to finish. Better to be thirsty, however, than to suffer a kick in the head. The corporal shoved himself away from the table and, without so much as a glance to left or right at his companions, headed straight for the door.

The younger men, thankful they would be allowed to sample the pleasure of Valdez's cantina, watched the old corporal depart. None felt pity for the man. After all, he must bear the responsibility for the treatment he received.

Morales grinned at the young soldiers surrounding him. The corporal was a forgotten incident. Morales knew these young lads hung on his every word. And he was more than willing to fill their young heads with tales of Sergeant Morales's bravery when fighting

Indians and how he routed a war party with naught but his sword and a cudgel carved from a length of cypress.

Morales had just launched into one of his favorite tales after ordering Valdez to bring them all chorizo and fried bread when a familiar figure reappeared from outside. The sergeant looked up into Eduardo Galvez's careworn features. Morales's story trailed off unfinished.

"What is it, brave corporal? Are there too many horses for you to handle? Impossible. See, you have hardly drunk any wine." Morales did not allow the corporal to make a reply. Not yet. It was easier to intimidate a man if you did not give him a chance to speak. "Yet here you stand? Have you indeed finished what I sent you to do?"

"No, *el jefe,*" Galvez said. "I have not begun."

"Then why do you disobey my orders and return to stand before me?"

"I met a boy outside," Galvez said. "One of Father Ramon's Creek Indians. He has been awaiting our arrival back in the settlement." Galvez lowered his head, bending over so that he might continue in a whisper. "He will only speak to you, Sergeant. But he says he brings important news. He speaks of *Inglés* seafarers and a treasure of yellow gold."

Morales leaned closer to the corporal. The sergeant blinked and rubbed the sleep from his eyes with a hairy paw. "Gold?"

"Sí."

"Who is this boy? What is he called?"

"His name," Corporal Galvez said, "is Esteban."

Chapter Seven

By midmorning, the hardest part of the journey, poling a raft across St. John's River, lay behind Kit and Tibbs. Father Ramon had insisted on guiding them as far as Alsino Escovar's cabin. They had left the Creek village before dawn and had made good time despite the fact that even Father Ramon had become confused as to the current whereabouts of Escovar's cabin. Tibbs had objected at first that the priest would only slow them up. But after hours spent winding through a network of forests, peat swamps, and primeval glades, even Tibbs was forced to admit that without Father Ramon's help the two Yankees would have become hopelessly lost. Now even the priest was disoriented.

Halfway across a meadow, about seventy yards from the edge of a forest of slash pines, Kit paused to take a moment's rest. His two companions were more than happy to sink down in the grass and prop themselves against a man-made battlement of cypress logs. The timber's bark was gone and the wood was worn smooth by the action of wind and rain and perhaps even fire, for one log was soot-blackened. Tibbs wiped the sweat from his eyes and helped himself to a sip of water from one of the deerskin bags they had taken from the village. Kit surveyed the placement of the logs. They were arranged in a triangle, dragged from some nearby bayou.

"Escovar has left many such primitive little forts," Father Ramon said. "He is a cautious man by nature. But I think I have him pinned down." He spoke with conviction. The priest dislodged a clump of peat from his sandal. "A man cannot have too many places to hide, Alsino has often told me." The Franciscan shook his head in resignation. "He does not trust the Creeks, even the ones around my mission. But I recognize this place. Yes, I have found him."

"Just as long as he has horses, I don't care how secretive the bastard is," Tibbs muttered, wrinkling his toes in his boots. He was wet and tired, and as the sun climbed into the sky, he was becoming increasingly uncomfortable. He adjusted the pouch over his shoulder and handed the water bag to the priest. Then he worked a kink out of his stiffened shoulder.

"You want me to carry it for a while?" Kit offered his friend.

"You've done your share of packing our gold, compadre, I can do mine," Tibbs replied, patting the pouch flap. He shaded his eyes and stared up at the hot, cloudless sky. The tall grasses seemed to droop beneath the heat and oppressive humidity.

"It isn't far now," Father Ramon said. "Just beyond those trees. See the cluster of cinnamon ferns at the base of those laurels? They mask a deer trail that will lead you right to Escovar's cabin. Just keep to the trail."

"You're sure?" Tibbs asked, arching an eyebrow.

"Yes, my son. But I will walk this last distance with you, to keep you both out of trouble. I will tell Alsino you wish to trade gold for horses. He will forgive your intrusion once he hears me out." The old priest leaned against the smooth, worn log and sighed. "I shall be glad to return to my people."

"We are in your debt, Padre." Kit had grown to like this simple man of God.

Tibbs slapped at a mosquito and left a bloody smear on the side of his neck. "God, but I will be glad to be rid of this forsaken country." He patted the pouch he carried; it contained their future.

"We are almost home," Kit said. "What will you do with your share, Bill?" It was a question they had asked one another throughout the voyage from Derna. Each time the answers changed as the men reconsidered what they wanted from life. "I don't know anymore," Kit continued. "I can't seem to think any further than a tub of hot water and a soft bed."

"Well, I can. From now on, others will risk their necks while I reap the rewards. We haven't lost so much of our gold to keep a wise man from setting himself up for life. I have plans for us, Kit. Big plans."

"I'm with you," Kit said. "Only..."

"What?"

"The talk we heard of war with Britain."

"Good God, man, that is none of our concern. We are men of wealth now. And the rich cannot afford to be patriotic."

"You're an incorrigible brigand, Bill Tibbs."

"Just trying to save you from yourself," Tibbs replied with a grin.

Kit glanced around at the priest. "Well, Father, are you rested enough to continue? The sooner we find horses, the sooner you can start back to the village."

"I am rested," the padre replied.

"Then we can be on our way." Kit scrambled to his feet. He turned and happened to check the trail of crushed grass that marked their route across the meadow. Then he froze as a troop of Spanish dragoons materialized out of the forest behind them.

At a glance Tibbs knew there was trouble. He stood alongside his friend and watched in dismay as the dragoons readied their muskets and advanced on the men in the redoubt.

"Christ! What now?" Tibbs muttered.

"Not Christ," Father Ramon spoke up. He too was on his feet and recognized at a glance the man who had tracked them down. "Sergeant Pablo Morales." The priest also knew he was in desperate trouble for having aided the *Inglés* fugitives. *Madre de Dios*, how had Morales learned of the Yankees' presence? the priest wondered.

"Get down, damn it," Tibbs said, crouching behind the makeshift fort.

"Why? He's seen us," Kit replied.

"Like a bee trapped in a spider's web, I fear we are caught, my friends," the priest said, blessing himself with the sign of the cross.

"Bees sting," Kit reminded the padre, and drew his pistols. Tibbs hurriedly readied his own weapons as he squatted under cover.

"There are too many. We're finished, damn it," Tibbs growled in disgust.

"They'll lose some of their men in the process," Kit said, facing the dragoons, who had begun to walk their mounts forward, slowly advancing on the makeshift fort. "I don't think any one of them is in a hurry to die."

"What are you getting at?" Tibbs said.

"Please. No killing," Father Ramon blurted. "I cannot allow it."

"Shut up, Padre," Tibbs said. "Kit?"

Kit checked his guns, taking care to prime each weapon. Then he looked over his shoulder at the edge of the forest beyond which Alsino Escovar's cabin ought to be. "We need horses if we're to get out of this."

"Forget it," Tibbs said. "Those dragoons would ride us down before we got halfway."

"Us. But not you, if I stay here and give them something to worry about. You go get us horses from Escovar."

"You can't stay. I won't let you," Tibbs protested.

"Do you have a better idea?" Kit waited for an answer, and when none was forthcoming, said, "Good. Get going."

"Why should you be the one to stay?" Tibbs asked, defiance in his voice.

"Because it was *my* idea," Kit retorted. "Now start off. And keep low. Crawling's slower, but they might not see you. And for heaven's sake, don't try to haggle with Escovar. Just pay him what he wants for the horses and come on. I'll be waiting right here."

Tibbs looked at the priest. "You say the ferns mark the deer trail?"

"You cannot miss it. And the path widens the closer you come to Escovar's," Father Ramon explained nervously.

Tibbs looked questioningly at the treasure bag, as if unsure whether or not to leave the gold.

"Take it with you," Kit said. "I don't want Morales to have any chance of getting his hands on what's left. He hasn't earned it."

Tibbs held his arm outstretched as Kit knelt at his

side. The two friends clasped hands. "I'll be back," the dark-haired man promised in a choked whisper. "I swear it."

"I know, Bill," Kit said. "Just hurry."

Tibbs placed one of his pistols on the ground by Kit. Then he tucked the other in his belt and crawled off through the tall grass.

"No bloodshed, please, Señor Christopher," Father Ramon pleaded.

Kit gave the man a strange look. Only his mother called him by his full name. It sounded odd, coming from the Spanish priest. Kit pointed at the soldiers at the opposite end of the meadow. "Padre, that's entirely up to them."

Sergeant Morales rolled onto his back and managed to slake his thirst with the last of the water in his canteen and that belonging to one of his troops, a slim, cautious youth by the name of Vargas. The underling watched with a mixture of anger and resignation as the sergeant consumed the last of the younger man's water. Morales passed the empty canteen back to his subordinate.

"Don't worry, little pup. You shall drink your fill once we have captured these *Inglés* sailors." The sergeant wiped a hand across his perspiring features and stared up at the cloudless void. How still and quiet... quiet! He propped himself up on one elbow. "Galvez. Corporal Galvez."

"Sí, my sergeant," Galvez said, glumly acknowledging his presence where he was hidden in the grass.

"Perhaps our friends have no more powder. Find out for me, eh?"

"Sí," came the weary reply. Grass rustled, and then the corporal popped his head up. A pistol cracked, and the corporal's hat flew from his head as he ducked back under cover.

"They still have powder, my sergeant," came Galvez's gloomy report.

"I can hear," Morales said, and added, "idiot," beneath his breath. He closed his eyes and took stock of the situation. He and his men had tried to rush the makeshift fort. It had been a halfhearted attempt. Galvez had let slip about the gold, and now each man wanted a share and no one wished to risk death in obtaining it.

Morales relived with humiliating clarity the charge his men made across the meadow. Powder smoke blossomed above the logs as the *Inglés* opened fire. Two of the dragoons dropped from horseback, and the other horsemen immediately wheeled their mounts and retreated out of range of the Yankee guns. Dismounted, the dragoons opened fire and tried a second assault on foot. It too failed, at the cost of another man. The log walls still held. The timber not only provided excellent cover, but the builder had placed his battlements on the meadow's highest point, a grassy mound that provided an excellent field of fire for the *Inglés* defenders.

A man dead, Morales thought with disgust, *and two wounded.* The sergeant dispatched his remaining men to ring the Yankees' position and then settled down to a waiting game. At least Morales could be certain the Yankees weren't going anywhere while he tried to figure out some new tactic. An hour had come and gone, and he hadn't hit on a solution except to wait for the long, hot hours to dull the senses of the *Inglés* defenders before trying another assault. Unfortunately, his dragoons were suffering as much as the men behind the barricade, maybe even more so for their lack of sleep.

"Sergeant Morales," Vargas spoke up. "You think these Yankee bastards have much gold? The boy might have been lying." The young dragoon raised up, snapped off a shot at the barricade, and as quickly crouched down and reloaded.

"The boy knows me. He knows what would happen to him and his mother and sister if he told such a lie." Morales crawled to his knees and peered above the grass at the cypress logs. He had glimpsed Father Ramon with the Yankees and began to wonder if he might be able to use the priest to his advantage.

"*Inglés!* Hey you, *Inglés*, I am Sergeant Pablo Morales. I have you trapped. Yes? You agree? Well, at least you don't disagree." Morales stroked his chin, scratched at the stubbled growth. His mind was awash with plans that he discarded as quickly as he formed them. "You throw the gold over the logs where I can see it. Then I let you leave, eh? You go north to your home. I, Pablo Morales, give you your lives. Surely your lives are more precious than the treasure you carry."

Morales wiped the back of his hand across his mouth. His lips felt waxy. It was always the same when he lied.

Safe within the walls of Escovar's fort, Kit listened to the sergeant and wanted to believe him. But an instinct for self-preservation caused him to doubt Morales's word. He looked toward the distant line of trees, hoping to spy Tibbs bringing the horses at a gallop through the pines. Kit realized with a sinking heart that he'd have to stall for more time. He hefted his shot bag and powder horn. Ammunition and gunpowder were dangerously low. He couldn't beat off another attack if the dragoons made a concerted effort.

"You hear me, Yankees?" Morales called out. "Both of you discuss this among yourselves. You see I'm right. It's the only way you have of staying alive."

"At least the sergeant thinks he's trapped us both," Kit remarked. That meant Tibbs got away. He glanced at the priest, who had become increasingly distraught as the siege lingered on and he had seen three of his own countrymen shot down.

"I guess you wish about now you had left Bill and me to the sand crabs," Kit said.

The priest shrugged. "Yes...and no. Yes, when I see men fight and kill one another and I blame myself. No, when I realize what I did was right, what the Gospel tells us to do, to treat all men as brothers."

"Yankees?"

"We're talking it over!" Kit shouted back. He studied the priest. "What about the Creek village and Father Ramon's mission?" he called back to the sergeant.

"What happens to them will happen whether I kill you *Inglés* or not."

Father Ramon lowered his head and thought of the people of the mission. He had taught them the ways of peace. And now he had betrayed them to the sergeant's vengeance. Heaven only knew what cruelties Morales had in mind. Father Ramon's converts might all be taken away in chains for harboring the men from the north. *Somehow,* the padre thought, *I must save them. But how?* Grief tore at his heart, and he was filled with confusion and remorse and an overpowering feeling of dread that there was no just way out of this predicament. Tragedy was at hand, and he stood helpless in its path. Unless—

Lead slugs thudded into the logs, showering Kit

and the priest with splinters. The two men waited out the fusillade. Kit loaded his pistols. The priest armed himself with prayer.

Kit shifted position and crawled along the cypress barricade until he reached a juncture between the logs. Here he peered through intersecting roots and waited, noticing the telltale rustle of the tall grass as some of Morales's men attempted to close in on the redoubt.

One well-placed shot might startle the soldiers and send them scurrying back. It had worked before. It ought to again.

He placed the barrel of his gun on the juncture between root and trunk. The log provided an excellent gun mount. He sighted along the barrel at the closest depression in the grass and slowly squeezed the trigger. The gun leaped in his fist and spewed a tongue of flame. A geyser of dirt erupted just inches from the grassy depression, and a man in a mud-spattered uniform leaped to his feet and scampered back the way he had come, along with three of his companions who assumed they too had been discovered.

"That's done 'em," Kit said, satisfied.

"I'm sorry," Father Ramon said from across the redoubt.

"No need to be, Padre. I just read him from the Book. I didn't plant him with it," Kit said, turning. His moment of hard-won optimism faded at the sight of the priest, pistol in hand.

"Father, no."

"I have to help my people. I am sorry. But you see, Morales will punish them all for my actions. They'll be sold into slavery, down to the last child. I cannot allow it. Maybe this will buy his mercy. I have to try."

"You aren't going to kill me."

Kit had another gun in his belt and slowly began

to reach for it. And yet what good was it? Could he shoot the priest? *If only Tibbs would return,* he thought. *Damn. What had happened to the man?*

While Kit pondered his fate and that of his friend, the priest continued to explain himself.

"No. I will not take a life. But touch your other gun and you will leave here a cripple," the padre said as he aimed the pistol at Kit's right knee. Kit sighed and did as the desperate priest ordered.

"The Yankee is my prisoner!" the priest shouted. He stood and revealed himself to the surrounding soldiers. "May God forgive me," he added beneath his breath, taking no comfort in his betrayal.

Kit simply stared at the priest. Words failed him. His world had come crashing in on him, burying him in the rubble of his dreams. Scarcely a minute later Kit was surrounded by muskets, all of them loaded, primed, and leveled at him. Then a shadow fell across Kit as Sergeant Morales stood atop one of the logs, his florid features aglow with victory.

"Well done, priest," he told the Franciscan magnanimously. Then the sweet rush of triumph melted away as the realization sank in that Kit was alone. The other *Inglés* had slipped away. And from the look of the empty clearing, the missing Yankee had taken the treasure with him. Morales leaped down and swaggered over to his prisoner.

"I am but a poor man, at your service," Kit said, meeting the sergeant in the center of the redoubt. He stood toe to toe with the heavyset Spaniard. Morales's answer was a hairy hand that seemed to come out of nowhere and caught Kit along the jaw, dropping him to his knees. But he wasn't about to play victim to the likes of the sergeant. Kit dove forward and with his head butted the big man below the belt. Morales gasped and doubled over.

"Kill him," Morales choked out through clenched teeth.

"No!" Father Ramon rushed forward and placed himself in the line of fire. He held out his hands to further impede the remaining soldiers before they could open fire. "No! I forbid this murder in the name of the Father, the Son, and the Holy Ghost."

The soldiers hesitated, uncertain what to do. Sergeant Morales groaned and struggled to his feet, one hand covering his bruised crotch. He sucked in and exhaled massive amounts of air. His eyes locked with Kit's. Something the sergeant saw made him look away.

"Very well, priest," the sergeant managed to gasp. "The *Inglés* goes with us. I shall find the other Yankee and execute them both on the spot. Then the treasure shall be ours. And that will make me happy, priest. So do not vex me. Or I will forget the good you have done." Morales glared at Kit. But the sergeant kept his distance. Then he shifted his gaze once more to the priest. "Tell me all you know, Padre. What has become of the other Yankee and the gold?"

Father Ramon lowered his head. He was unable to drive the destruction of the Christian Indian settlement from his mind. The fate of every man, woman, and child hung in the balance. The priest had no choice. He told the sergeant of Alsino Escovar and the horses and pointed out the deer trail leading through the woods.

Morales brightened. "Bring horses, my men. Bind the Yankee. Hurry! There is still time. We can still be men of wealth." Four soldiers remained to guard their prisoner while the rest left to gather in the horses. Father Ramon moved closer to Kit.

"Forgive me, Christopher," the priest said, imploring.

Kit shrugged. "Forget it, Padre." His mouth was a grim slash across his emotionless features. In the young man's eyes, something cold and deadly had been born. It lurked deep in the wellspring of his once carefree soul. "You only did what you had to do," Kit added, without a trace of warmth. "Like my friend, Bill Tibbs."

Chapter Eight

Alsino Escovar was a small, wiry little man with skin the color of a rotting peach and a face as wrinkled and hard-looking as the pit. He was garbed in native furs and wore alligator hide moccasins. A medicine bag hung from a braided leather band that circled his throat. He was missing several teeth, and those still protruding from his gums did so by the grace of God. Escovar had one other distinguishing feature: His throat had been slit from ear to ear. It was a ghastly wound left by a razor-sharp blade—no doubt the scimitar, for Tibbs did not have a knife. The dead man lay in a patch of darkened earth where the blood had been absorbed into the soil.

Kit McQueen peered down into the man's face. A look of surprise had become the poor man's death mask. He was sprawled about twenty feet from his cabin near the gate of a crudely thrown-together corral. He'd made a fence out of pine saplings and hadn't even bothered to trim the branches from the trunks. The gate itself was simply three smaller trees lashed together and then fastened to a post set in the earth. Like the corral, Escovar's ramshackle cabin looked as if he had spent as little time as possible on its construction. The walls were haphazardly chinked and fit poorly together at the corners, and one side leaned noticeably outward. Racks of animal hides cluttered the clearing and made evident what Alsino Escovar had held important in his life. Pelts of river otter, mink, and gray fox hung alongside drying alligator hides and the tawny carcass of a recently killed panther.

The dead man's cook fire was still smoldering; a chunk of roasted turtle meat had been gnawed on, then tossed aside for the ants to find. It appeared as if the trapper had been walking toward the corral when death came, taking him by surprise. He had probably settled on a price for his horses and thought there was nothing to fear. Maybe Bill Tibbs had offered Escovar the Eye of Alexander, worth a thousand times the price of a nag. Perhaps he had stood spellbound as Tibbs showed him the glittering blade and jeweled hilt. Escovar must have delighted in the bargain, not knowing he had dealt with the devil. With a quick flip of the wrist Tibbs could have slashed the trapper's throat...

"There were three horses here," Corporal Galvez called out as he knelt in the corral and studied the ground. "Or maybe two, it is hard to tell," he added with a shrug.

The other dragoons fanned out across the clearing. A few of them stumbled as they walked, their steps leaden and movements awkward from lack of sleep.

Sergeant Morales was the exception. He prowled the campsite like a wolf on the hunt. His tunic was unbuttoned now and his hat discarded for a strip of cloth tied around his head to keep the sweat out of his eyes. He looked more a pirate than a man in command of these soldiers. He carried a pistol in each hand, and as he walked his angry gaze swept the surrounding forest for some indication that Tibbs was still nearby.

Eventually Morales wound up alongside Kit, who remained under the constant guard of the two men he had wounded. They had left the third casualty to rot where he lay. Sergeant Morales drew up in front of Kit and took a moment to study his prisoner.

"What kind of fool gives gold to a friend and expects him not to run off, eh? Your friend has left you to the mercy of Pablo Morales. But I do not feel merciful. That is a weakness best left to the padre." He jabbed a thumb in the direction of Father Ramon, who was kneeling by the lifeless body of Alsino Escovar.

The priest paused a moment to look up at the sound of his name. It was plain that Father Ramon blamed Kit as well as himself for what had happened.

Sergeant Morales shifted his position and blocked the priest's view. The sergeant had just begun to regale Kit for his stupidity when one of his men called out that he had found a set of tracks. Morales indicated to Kit's guards to bring their prisoner along.

The set of tracks led out of the clearing and away from the meadow where Kit had waited, besieged and buying time for his friend. The tracks circled for a moment as if the rider had some difficulty with one of the horses (or perhaps Tibbs had been struggling with his conscience) and then cut sharply out of the clearing and on to the underbrush before heading north.

Up until seeing the tracks, Kit had been hoping for some kind of miracle that might reveal an ulterior motive for Tibbs's actions. Kit had tried to believe Tibbs was hiding in the woods waiting for a chance to help his friend escape. But the tracks pointing north dashed such hopes and left Kit with the undeniable realization he'd been betrayed.

The treasure of al-Jezzar had seduced Bill Tibbs. Kit thought of the scimitar. It seemed the Eye of Alexander cursed and corrupted whoever looked into its blood-red, jeweled orb. Alexander's luck, indeed. Kit glowered and cursed the day he had first spied the glittering blade hanging from a wall in the treasure rooms at Derna. Kit remembered how he had fallen under the scimitar's spell and watched in awe as the large, round ruby, the Eye itself, seemed to pulse with life. He had attributed the phenomenon to the flickering torchlight, but now he was not so certain. After the shipwreck, the loss of most of their booty, the death of the Trenton's crew, and now this, betrayed by his friend, Kit began to realize that the relic did indeed possess some kind of sinister power that twisted and destroyed all who came in contact with it.

A gun barrel jabbed Kit in the side. The guard who had struck him groaned and tightened the bandage around his arm to stanch the flow of blood. The fatigued Spaniard sucked in his breath and winced at the pain. He made no attempt to hide the hatred he felt for the Yankee. His lips curled back in a snarl, and he raised his musket and aimed the weapon at Kit's heart, determined to finish Kit once and for all. His finger, curled around the trigger, slowly tightened.

"No!" Father Ramon stepped in front of the gun barrel. "We are not murderers. This Yankee is a prisoner. He must be taken back to St. Augustine to await the arrival of the new *comandante*."

The dragoon retreated a step, confused by this development. Vengeance was one thing, damnation quite another. He could not shoot a priest. The sergeant's timely arrival saved him from his dilemma.

"Chico," Morales interceded gruffly. "Tie the Inglés to the cart." The sergeant indicated a two-wheeled wagon that Escovar had left in the center of the clearing. The wounded dragoon grudgingly lowered his musket, to the relief of his intended victim. Morales had shoved the pistols into his belt, and now he stood, hands on hips, his wary gaze searching the vine-shrouded forest surrounding them.

"God bless you, Sergeant," the priest said.

"Sí," the sergeant replied. "God had better bless me. Maybe the Yankee's friend hides somewhere in these woods and he comes back and sees the red-haired one is my prisoner. And this friend, he attempts to rescue Red Hair." Morales brought his face close to Kit's. "You will be my bait this night. I watch and wait. And if no one comes, I shoot you at sunup." Morales whirled on the priest, who had started to protest. "No! Keep silent, old priest, or on my oath you join him!"

And so the afternoon hours crawled past and Kit McQueen endured in silence as the moist, heavy heat settled from the stark blue sky in invisible layers. It clogged a man's lungs and made each breath a labor; he felt as if he were drowning. Kit whiled away the hours, once he realized escape was impossible, by imagining himself an osprey or any kind of falcon, one of those illustrious hunters who ride the wind's slip-stream or hang poised above the ancient land and callously observe the foolish antics, the sufferings and joys of earthbound humankind, then rise airborne to reach with feathery fingertips and brush the cheek of God.

The priest brought Kit food and water and waited with him while he ate, under guard. As soon as he was finished, his hands were quickly bound to the wheel of the cart once more.

For a long time Father Ramon had very little to say. Responsibility for the deaths weighed heavy on him; he counted Kit's imminent demise among those burdens that bowed his shoulders and shackled his spirit. Solace was beyond his reach, locked away behind doors for which he had no key. Kit assumed the priest would not wish another death on his conscience and so might find some way, under cover of night, to set the prisoner free.

Kit found a few brief seconds of privacy when the dragoon guard walked around the cart to relieve himself, and in a soft voice, audible only to the old priest, Kit suggested Father Ramon was his last chance and only hope.

The priest returned to his own bedroll by another campfire he had built for himself and settled down with his thoughts and misgivings into a troubled sleep. Sergeant Morales placed one man beneath the cart. He pitched his own blanket in the cart. He trusted no one but himself to watch the prisoner and apprehend the Yankee's partner, should the man be foolish enough to return.

The remaining men of his command settled by twos and threes around their cook fires. One by one the Spaniards succumbed to weariness. With the onset of night, the soldiers in their blankets drifted off to sleep, and their snores mingled with the night sounds of the forest and distant bayous.

Kit leaned against the wheel listening to the rush of night wings overhead and heard, somewhere beyond the black woods, the deep, bloodcurdling bellow of a bull alligator and the startled, pitiful screech of some animal turned prey. Kit noticed several of the soldiers, startled from their rest, bless themselves.

"Lord strengthen us against our enemies and deliver us from the hungry jaws of predators," Kit muttered to himself.

"And false friends," Sergeant Morales added from his bedroll in the cart. The sergeant laughed softly at his cleverness.

Kit, however, was not amused. He stretched his legs and worked the kinks out of them. His shoulders ached, and he tried to relax despite his bound hands. His wrists were securely tied to the wheel's wooden rim. Its construction wasn't all that sound, but any attempt to free himself or dislodge the rim from the spokes was bound to alert the soldier nodding off to sleep beneath the cart, not to mention Sergeant Morales, he of the immense gut and quick wit whose snores rivaled the alligators in the night. *Some sentries*, Kit thought. *Some guards*. A lumbering sot could stumble through camp and cut him loose, much less a man with skills like Bill Tibbs.

But Bill Tibbs wasn't coming. Neither was any benevolent drunkard. Kit sighed and looked up at the stars. Determined as he was to stay awake, for what might well prove his last hours on earth, he failed. Sleep mercifully overtook him. The night passed without incident.

Come the first gray hours of morning, Kit was awakened by Sergeant Morales, who told him it was time to die.

Chapter Nine

The smell of boiling coffee drifted through the clearing and mingled with the aroma of venison steaks roasting over open campfires. Kit was offered neither, though Sergeant Morales apologized with restrained sincerity. Surely, he had said, the Yankee could understand that such a courtesy only delayed the inevitable. And why waste food on a man who would soon be dead?

Kit didn't bother to reply. If these were indeed his last moments, he was not about to waste them conversing with the sergeant. As Corporal Galvez led him across the clearing, Kit studied the surrounding woods as if seeing them for the first time. Lavender and yellow butterflies lazily spread their wings upon broadleaf plants and lichen-covered rock. The moss-draped, twisted branches of a scrub oak were a miraculous display. Field mice underfoot were flushed from hiding as the men trampled a patch of ferns, and scampered off through the grass. Night would bring slithering reptiles and a blur of winged owls in search of such delectable prey.

Life and death were integral parts of an unfathomable mystery, a mystery Kit McQueen was about to grudgingly embrace if he didn't do something fast.

To everything there is a season: a time to reap, a time to sow, a time to philosophize, a time to run like hell. Heaven brought him his opportunity in the form of Father Ramon, his hands still dirty from digging a grave for Alsino Escovar. He was not about to dig another.

"No! This is wrong," the priest cried out, and stepped between Kit and Galvez. Father Ramon looked back at the dragoons halfheartedly attempting to place themselves in some sort of suitable arrangement for a firing squad while Sergeant Morales continued to berate them unmercifully for their ineptitude. "It is wrong before the eyes of God!"

"God does not see this cursed country. He has forgotten it long ago," Morales shouted back at the robed man. "I do not hear you anymore, priest." He waved his hand as if brushing off a bothersome insect.

"Come along," Galvez said to Kit. "At least you will have a pleasant place to be buried in. A less charitable man than Morales would dump you in the bayou for the alligators to feed upon."

"The sergeant's generosity touches my heart." Kit wasn't smiling.

Corporal Galvez led the way, his Yankee prisoner falling into step behind him. Father Ramon took up the rear, reciting in a gentle voice a prayer for the dying. And as he prayed, he pulled a knife from his voluminous sleeve and with a quick flick of the wrist sawed through the ropes binding Kit's wrists.

The prisoner immediately began to work the blood

back into his fingers. Feeling quickly returned, as his arms were more sore than numb. Behind Kit, the padre started back toward the cabin and the hastily formed firing squad, and in so doing masked Kit's attempted escape. Corporal Galvez continued across the clearing to the newly mounded earth of Escovar's grave.

Twenty-five feet from the cabin, where the ground was soft and easy to dig, Father Ramon had placed the earthly remains of the murdered trapper. Another fifteen yards, and the dense forest beckoned with its ancient silence and mossy gloom. Though a forbidding place to the unwary, to the eyes of Kit McQueen it offered sanctuary.

If he could outrun the dragoons and dodge their first fusillade, he just might elude them. That was the task at hand, to reach the forest without being shot down. There was no time like the present to make the attempt.

Kit lunged forward. Galvez caught a glimpse of movement and started to turn. Kit drove his hardened fist into the corporal's left side, staggering Galvez. Kit yanked the corporal about and snatched a pistol from the man's belt. He heard the outcry behind him. Morales roared the order to fire. Kit dove for the only cover that presented itself, Escovar's grave.

He cleared the mounded earth and hit the dirt as a musket volley thundered in the clearing. Geysers of soft earth erupted from the mound. That crudely fashioned cross of branches Father Ramon had erected to mark the grave all but exploded. And poor Corporal Galvez, who inadvertently had placed himself in the line of fire, choked back a scream as lead slugs ripped his bony frame and left him belly down on the grave. He shuddered, attempted to rise, then fell back, mortally wounded.

Kit scrambled to his feet and ran toward the forest. The firing squad broke ranks. Most of the men hurried to reload their muskets, while four of their number gave chase.

"Idiots!" Morales bellowed. "The Yankee is getting away. Stop him before he reaches the trees. Run, you fools. Run!" The stout sergeant made no effort to give chase. He wasn't built for speed. But four of his dragoons most certainly were. The soldiers had rested well and in relative comfort, while Kit had been bound the entire night.

Kit glanced over his shoulder, knowing such an action was a mistake even as he made it. His boots caught on a vine, and down he went, stumbling and then falling forward. He twisted and landed on his shoulder, then immediately rose up on one knee and leveled the pistol he had taken from Galvez. Kit's pursuers had just passed the grave where the unfortunate corporal lay dying.

A well-placed shot might slow them up and give Kit time to reach cover. He sighted on the lead runner, a lithe-looking Spaniard in a rumpled green and white tunic. The dragoon was armed with a pistol and chanced a shot at a dead run. His aim was wild.

Kit fired, and the corporal's pistol bucked in his grasp. Galvez must have loaded his weapon with a heavy charge, for the gunshot sounded unusually loud.

Even more surprising, two of Kit's pursuers, running several feet apart, dropped and doubled over, one staggering a few steps and falling backward, clutching at his throat. The other two Spaniards spun around on their heels and retreated at a dead run toward the cabin. Kit stared in disbelief at the gun in his hand. *What the devil?* he thought. Then he ducked as another volley of gunfire rippled from the emerald shadows behind him. A bugle trumpeted like the horn of Roland as powder smoke blossomed in the underbrush, and war cries filled the air as if a horde of banshees had been loosed among the pines.

Kit hugged the ground and gripped the pistol by the barrel, ready to use the weapon like a war hammer if need be. The army in the forest was no friend of Morales's. The Spanish dragoons bravely held their ground, but their muskets were no match for the rifles of their hidden enemies. Sergeant Morales looked on, furious, as first one, then another of his men yelped in pain and staggered off, wounded. The skirmish line began to waver.

"Hold bravely, now," the sergeant roared above the gunfire, sensing his dragoons' growing panic.

"We are outnumbered!" one of the men shouted.

"It is the Yankee army! They'll kill us all!" a second soldier exclaimed.

"Then we must drive them—ahh!" Morales's words were cut short as a slug ripped his shoulder and knocked him on his backside.

Seeing the sergeant fall was the last straw for the remaining Spaniards. Sergeant Morales's presence alone had held them in place. Leaderless now, three men bolted for their horses, and then the rest of the skirmishers followed suit. They rode past the cabin, raced across the clearing, and galloped into the woods.

Morales, struggling to his feet, cursed them through his clenched teeth and ordered his men to stand and fight. But his bullying commands fell on deaf ears. The dragoons were routed. Morales groaned and clutched at his shoulder. He could stay and probably die—or join his men in flight and live to battle another day. The choice, though obvious, was no less bitter. Sergeant Morales was a proud man. Defeat did not come easy to him.

He turned slowly, ignoring the lead slugs spattering the earth at his feet. With the bugle taunting him from across the clearing, the sergeant lumbered off toward his own mount.

"Come along, old priest," he said, glancing at the robed figure huddled in the shadow of Escovar's cabin. "I see your hand in this."

"Not mine, but the hand of God," said Father Ramon, sagging against the wall.

"Well, your heathen bunch of Creeks shall feel the hand of Morales for all the trouble you have caused me, and there is no one to blame but yourself," the sergeant growled as he caught the reins of his frightened stallion. The animal had been tethered to a tanning rack. It only took a second to free the animal. "I'll take the rest of the horses, and you can walk back to the damn village—that is, if your Yankee friends let you live."

The sergeant steeled himself against the pain and prepared to swing up into the saddle. The firing behind him had ceased, which only filled him with a deeper desire to get the hell out.

Back in the clearing, Kit scrambled to his feet. He had watched the Spaniards break rank and flee. He saw the sergeant fall and rise again like a wounded whale. The sergeant was attempting to escape, the same man who had taunted him and would have shot him down in cold blood. Fury filled him, perhaps for the treatment he had received at Morales's hands. Then again, it might have been the hate that welled in his heart for Bill Tibbs, the supposed friend who had abandoned him to die here among the bayous. Suddenly Kit McQueen could stand aside and watch no longer. Oblivious to the slugs whirring past, he stood and, armed with his unloaded pistol and the rage burning in his veins, charged the cabin.

"Morales!" he roared, and his challenge rang above the din of battle. It was at that moment the rifles in the woods behind him fell silent. "Morales!"

Sergeant Morales hesitated at the sound of his name. He recognized the voice and the challenge in its tone. He smiled then, and instead of lifting himself astride his horse, he took the pistols from his saddle holsters and faced the clearing yet again.

"Let there be an end to this, Pablo," Father Ramon pleaded from off to his right.

"Sí. There will be an end...the end of this troublesome *Inglés* whelp," the sergeant assured. He wiped a forearm across his perspiring features and winced as pain coursed through his wounded shoulder. "Even with a clipped wing I can still handle the likes of Señor McQueen," Morales added. He tucked one pistol inside his tunic. The other he calmly raised, sighted on Kit, and fired...and missed as Kit dodged.

Kit heard the slug whine past but never lost stride in his race with death. The Spaniard's smooth-bore pistols weren't very accurate at a distance, but at close range the next shot could cut Kit in half.

Fifteen yards became ten as Kit drew near, his every muscle working with fluid, feline grace. Morales drew the second pistol from his tunic, cocked and leveled his weapon. Kit threw the pistol he had taken from Galvez in an overhanded toss that sent the weapon spinning toward the sergeant. Morales held his fire and crouched to avoid the missile. He momentarily lost his footing as he stepped back into a shallow depression in the earth.

Kit tensed and leaped the remaining few feet as

the sergeant recovered and tried to center his aim on his airborne attacker. Kit landed like a battering ram with a vicious, stiff-legged kick to Morales's chest. The sergeant's pistol discharged into the air in a tongue of flame and billowing black smoke. Morales, for all his mass, was knocked off his feet by the impact, and he landed hard, arms open and legs akimbo as he sputtered and gasped for breath.

Kit leaped onto the man's upper torso. The sergeant huffed and groaned in agony as his attacker pinned him to the ground. Morales's eyes bulged in his head, and he knew his death was at hand.

Kit reached over and tore the still smoking pistol from the sergeant's grasp. He gripped it by the barrel and raised the gun like a hammer, its iron-embossed stock now a lethal bludgeon. Kit glared at the sergeant. His hand trembled; then he slammed the pistol down with enough force to bury the weapon several inches into the soft earth a hair's breadth from Morales's skull.

Mud spattered the sergeant's face as blood drained from his features. It took Morales several seconds to realize he was still alive.

"By the grace of God and that good man yonder" —Kit nodded toward the cabin and Father Ramon— "I'll not kill you." Kit stood and hauled the disheveled sergeant to his feet. Morales made no reply; his brush with death had left him momentarily humbled.

Kit glanced aside at Father Ramon. "Take your sergeant home. Hurry. Leave while you can."

"God bless you, my son," the Franciscan said. He mounted up, as did Morales.

"I don't understand you, *Inglés*," the sergeant said. "Now I am in your debt. Pablo Morales always pays his debts!" The sergeant shook his head in confusion, pointed his horse toward the trees, and rode away.

"May the Lord speed you homeward, my young friend," the priest said. He made the sign of the cross in blessing over Kit.

"Be well, Padre." Kit slapped the rump of the padre's horse and sent Father Ramon Saucedo galloping off toward the forest behind the cabin.

Kit inhaled the aroma of the venison steaks the Spaniards had left sizzling over a pair of cook fires. Escaping execution had worked up an appetite. He squatted down and began to eat, waiting for his mysterious benefactors to join him.

They weren't long in coming.

Chapter Ten

"We are the Army of the Free Republic of Florida," said Iron Hand O'Keefe as he gnawed the chunk of meat he'd skewered on the hook that served for his left hand. He swallowed, then leaned back and roared with laughter. The "army" consisted of two dour-looking Choctaw warriors and O'Keefe, a giant Irishman who was dressed much like his red-skinned companions.

The long-haired warriors had followed O'Keefe across the clearing from the woods where they had fired on the Spanish dragoons. Thanks to the eighteen rifles now strapped to the back of a nasty-tempered mule, three men and a bugle had been able to create the illusion of a much larger force. O'Keefe had kept his men under cover until the last of the Spaniards was long gone. Then he and his two companions had packed the rifles and warily approached the campsite, drawn by the irresistible aroma of hot food. Like the Choctaw warriors, Iron Hand O'Keefe was garbed in buckskins and carried a tomahawk. His lantern-jawed face was painted for war. His silver hair hung past his shoulders. By their deference to him it was obvious the warriors considered the Irishman their leader.

"I be Patrick O'Keefe, but my people call me Iron Hand."

"Your people?" Kit asked, looking up from his cup of coffee.

"The Choctaw," O'Keefe explained. "Took me in many a year ago when I wandered into their village, sick and lost and damn near crazy with fever. Nursed me to health. Hell, I had no place to go. I was just an ignorant Irishman who'd jumped ship in Charleston. I come inland so's the damn British press gangs would never find me again. I stayed on and learned the ways of the Choctaw and made 'em my ways." O'Keefe plopped a morsel from his hook into his mouth. "Gun carriage crushed my hand aboard ship. Damn thing never healed. When it started to rot, the ship's doctor— butcher, I calls him—sawed it off. That's something else I owe the British for. Smithy in Charleston made me a hook. First class work he did, eh?" He held out the iron hook for Kit's inspection. "Injuns are a super- stitious lot. The hook sort of set me apart as something special. So I wasn't among 'em for long when these lads made me a chief. Of course, the Choctaws ain't nobody's fool. Their chiefs have a habit of getting killed off, by Creek Red Sticks, mostly. But I reckon these here rifles will even things up."

The Irishman turned and said something to his companions, and the warriors nodded and walked off to load up the dead Spaniards onto a couple of horses.

"We'd better plant these poor lads before they ripen," O'Keefe said. "Young Otter and Stalking Fox will tend to them."

"I'll help." Kit stood and walked toward the grave of Alsino Escovar. The padre had left a shovel by the mounded earth.

"My braves could drop them in the bayou yonder," O'Keefe suggested.

"They died doing what they felt was right," Kit said.

"Killing you?"

"I'll see them buried proper. I'm not asking you to help," Kit snapped back.

O'Keefe chuckled. "You're a stubborn one. Do things your own way, even if it means charging into battle with naught but an unloaded gun. By heaven, you remind me of me."

They buried the dead men in a row alongside Escovar. Young Otter and Stalking Fox seemed anxious to be done with the job. Not that it was a pleasant task by Kit's standards, but still he wondered if the warriors expected the men to return to life to give battle. O'Keefe cleared up the mystery.

This was Creek country—Red Sticks, as the Irishman called them. He went on to explain how the Red Sticks and Choctaws were mortal enemies. It was this animosity that led the Choctaws to act as guides for a volunteer militia sent to invade Florida, part of the territory claimed by the Creek tribes. The militia had been reassured that U.S. troops would quickly follow once an insurrection had begun in the Spanish colony.

Unfortunately, the troops never came. Perhaps the Washington politicians had gotten cold feet concerning the invasion, what with the possibility of another war with Britain. No doubt more cautious heads had prevailed. Whatever the reason, O'Keefe, his Choctaws, and the volunteers from Georgia, Tennessee, and the

Carolinas were left on their own. Without reinforcements, they soon found themselves outnumbered. Decimated by death and disease, the militia fell apart into smaller groups of desperate men, struggling to escape not only the Spaniards but the vengeful Creeks as well.

O'Keefe and his scouts had made the best of a bad situation. Salvaging the rifles and gunpowder their companions had abandoned, the Choctaws were heading back to the hills of Alabama. The extra rifles would help their people prevail against the Creeks, who outnumbered them almost two to one.

Kit found himself liking the Irishman. Despite his silver hair, Iron Hand O'Keefe was only in his early forties, but he'd spent almost half his life among the Choctaws. He was a bit of a braggart, and no doubt the man was not above a little larceny if the cause was right. But he had saved Kit's life. And from the way O'Keefe and the Choctaws had fought, Kit doubted he'd find any better company to ride the trail with, especially if they ran into trouble.

Of his own background, Kit spoke little. He recounted how he'd been shipwrecked and captured by the Spanish, who obviously had been looking for the likes of Iron Hand O'Keefe and the other remnants of the military expedition. Kit made no mention of the treasure or Bill Tibbs's betrayal. It was a private matter, to be locked away deep in his heart until another day.

A swarm of glossy bronze ibises cleared the treetops and momentarily blotted out the stark blue sky. The beat of their wings was like some great rushing wind, and their lofty cries rang out over the forests and marshlands like the voice of nature itself. Theirs was a song older than the dreams of man.

It was time to leave, Kit thought as he shoved a brace of pistols in his belt and took up a rifle from O'Keefe's supply of firearms.

Stalking Fox, the younger of the two Choctaws, watched the birds with a mixture of awe and dread evident in his coppery features. He was roughly the same height as Kit but leaner limbed. He carried none of the extra muscle the white man had developed after a year at sea.

Though he had been part owner of the *Trenton* and could have enjoyed an easy berth, Kit McQueen had often worked right alongside the crew until he had mastered the art of seamanship, for such had been his father's teaching: that a McQueen took nothing for granted and earned his way in the world. Going to sea had provided Kit an opportunity to learn something new, and he had made the most of the opportunity.

The treasure he had stolen from the Corsican bandit, al-Jezzar, was lost to him; a friend's betrayal had given him cause to hate—yet that too was in the past. At hand in the here and now, he had a pair of sturdy horses, pistols, a rifle, and a tomahawk O'Keefe had presented to him along with the sound advice that a tomahawk made a sight better weapon than an unloaded gun. Kit had the clothes on his back, a full belly, and the promise of a tomorrow. What more could a man ask for in this world?

He glanced at Iron Hand O'Keefe, who was rechecking the rifles and ammunition they had loaded on the pack mule. The Irishman draped his bugle over the tied-down rifles.

Young Otter rode up on Kit's left. He also had been watching the ibises as they winged their way north. Young Otter was a husky, long-armed young man who after an initial suspicion seemed to accept

Kit. The warrior had never seen a man with red hair and kept wondering if perhaps Kit had somehow managed to set his head afire. He gestured toward the birds and spoke in his native tongue.

Kit looked to Iron Hand O'Keefe for help.

"He's telling you them birds we seen are the spirits of our enemies. They go before us," the strapping Irishman explained. "Kind of like a procession, you might say. The enemies we make . . . and the friends, too, we're bound to meet 'em farther down the trail." He scratched his belly with his hook hand. His buckskin shirt was worn smooth in spots, and it bore the stains from a month of meals.

O'Keefe was no nosegay, to be sure—but then again, Kit thought, they weren't standing around at a church social, either.

"Choctaws have their own peculiar way of seeing things," O'Keefe continued. "They figure it's all like a man standing at midcreek. No matter which way he moves, it sets up ripples that touch each bank, the one he's left and the one he's going to."

O'Keefe noticed the Choctaw had already mounted. They had the right idea. It was time to quit this place of death.

Kit shaded his eyes and looked up as the last of the ibises vanished beyond the treetops. The spirits of his enemies, the ghostly memories of his friends. What lay ahead for him now? Home? Retribution? Time was supposed to heal all wounds. But not this cold hatred that clawed at his heart and caused him to shudder even as it filled him with deadly resolve. No, this would could only be cauterized with vengeance.

Kit leaped astride his mare and walked the animal a few paces out into the clearing, away from O'Keefe and the Choctaws, and faced north. When at last he spoke, it was in a soft yet ominous voice, words of warning for his betrayer.

"Look over your shoulder, Bill Tibbs. I'm here. You son of a bitch, I'm still here!"

PART TWO

Home

Chapter Eleven

Almost two years later, Kit McQueen again had reason to think of Iron Hand O'Keefe and his Choctaw allies and their escape from Spanish Florida. It was the Fourth of July and the good people of Springtown, Pennsylvania, had chosen to have a celebration despite how badly the nation was faring in its war with the British. Kit had traveled to the Springtown Fair with his mother Kate, his sister Hannah Louise, and Hannah's two daughters. Thirteen-year-old Penelope loosely held Kit's right hand while eight-year-old Esther Rose kept a tight grip on his left.

The girls took after Grandmother Kate with their yellowgold hair and skin the color of freshly poured cream. Penelope, who gently pulled free of his grasp, was the independent one and obviously more interested in a fourteen-year-old boy who was standing alongside his father in the limner's tent. Esther Rose, however, was riveted to the paintings surrounding her as the limner, with a decided flair for the dramatic, uncovered yet another of his battle scenes, this one a horde of Choctaw braves swarming over a keelboat stranded on a bar in the Mississippi. The boatmen were putting up a valiant fight but were hopelessly outnumbered and doomed. Several had already fallen to knife and tomahawk.

Almost everyone in the tent gasped. Even the scenes of Revolutionary War battles had failed to elicit such a response. Grisly massacres at the hands of red-skinned heathens were the limner's most popular renditions. There was something especially awful about such depredations. And the audience was suitably horrified and thrilled. It was at that moment Kit remembered Iron Hand O'Keefe, Young Otter, and Stalking Fox, all who had saved his life. He had fought side by side with the Irishman and the Choctaws and driven off a Creek war party near the Tallapoosa River, and they had proved more faithful comrades-at-arms than Bill Tibbs.

The limner, Patrick Blackwell, gestured to the painting with a sweep of his hand. "Here you see, goodly neighbors, my own depiction of the dangers to be found when traveling the Father of Waters. Behold these poor, brave souls who battle bravely against such savages. I have remained true to the accounts personally rendered unto me by riverboat men come all the way from St. Louis to petition our government for aid and assistance against such attacks as what I have depicted."

Kit snorted in disgust as he studied the painting. Blackwell had portrayed the supposed Choctaws as half-naked savages with shaved skulls and faces hideously tattooed.

"Uncle Kit, those are awful men," Esther Rose gasped, her strong little hand tightened, and her eyes were wide with a mixture of fascination and fear, much like the other people in the tent.

"And now, dear ladies and gentlemen, another painting, if you will, showing the aftermath of this murderous rampage." Blackwell, with a great deal of dramatic flourish, indicated an easel to his left. The painting was hidden behind a coverlet of scarlet satin. "Please. If you will, cover the eyes of any children present. Quickly, now, for what you will see is for the eyes of grown men and women. I dare not wish to ruin the sleep of our innocents."

"Oh, no. Uncle Kit—" Esther tried to protest, but Kit covered her eyes with his hands. He glanced at Penelope, who returned his look with a "don't even think of it" glare. She was thirteen, a child no longer and determined to prove it.

"The keelboat men are at last overcome and killed to a man, but alas, the women and children aboard the boat are not so fortunate," the limner entoned. "Pity the women and children, my friends, for theirs is the cruelest fate of all. Behold!"

Blackwell yanked the satin cloth away to reveal an ornately framed canvas on which the limner had painted a scene of unparalleled brutality, at least to the eyes of the audience. In the background the keelboat from the previous picture was in flames. Upon a curiously barren riverbank, three rather buxom women were struggling as their garments were torn from their bodies by the savages. Another woman, with her bodice ripped asunder, lay sprawled upon the ground, her hand clutching the dagger she had plunged into her naked breast. She had taken her own life rather than submit to the indignities these red devils had in store for her.

As for the children, ropes had been tied around their necks, and they were being led off into a captivity that Blackwell began to describe in such lurid detail that several of the farmers were reduced to tears, while others knotted their fists and muttered empty, angry threats. Two women swooned and had to be taken from the tent, which was certain to provoke the interest of those still waiting to pay their dimes and enter the limner's exhibition. Several of the women in the audience openly wept as Blackwell continued his tale of woe.

Kit had to admit that what the limner lacked in artistic talent he made up for in showmanship. His oratory was descriptive, flowery, and full of passion. His voice quavered as he regaled his listeners with an account of the tragedy he had so "humbly" sought to present.

Kit noticed that Penelope, whose features had grown pale, had drawn closer to him as if for protection. She chose well. Two years had not softened Kit McQueen in the slightest. He possessed no rank, nor was he a man of inordinate stature, yet his compact frame was sleek and powerful and there was in his eyes the look of a man who had faced death on more than one occasion.

He was dressed in a loose cotton shirt, nankeen trousers, and worn leather boots and carried a double-edged knife whose foot-long blade rode in a sheath on his left side. His pistols he had left tucked away beneath the seat of the phaeton he had driven into Springtown from the family farm. His mother and his sister Hannah were elsewhere on the Springtown Commons, no doubt prepared to give him a tongue-lashing for sneaking off with his nieces to the limner's exhibit.

"And now, my dear friends, the last but hardly least of my canvases," Blackwell intoned, demurely covering the scenes of massacre. He hurried over to the last of his works. This painting he had framed in cherry wood embossed with gold highlights. "On this joyous day of our nation's celebration, even in this time of war, we pause to remember the glory that was and ever will be, the triumph of freedom!" With one last flourish the limner swept the coverlet from this final masterpiece, a thirty-six by thirty-six-inch painting of Cornwallis surrendering to Washington at Yorktown with the British troops and the continentals looking on in a vast sea of bodies. The crowd in the tent erupted into a thunderous applause and cries of "Well done" and "God bless these United States."

Kit noticed Colonel Tim Pepperidge, a stout, gray-haired gentleman standing with his wife Mercy, edge close to the historical painting. Tim was one of the heroes of the Revolution. As a young man he had fought alongside Daniel McQueen, Kit's father, against Tory raiders at the Battle of Phoebe's Farm. The Daughters of Phoebe, a religious order of unmarried women, had worked a farm an hour's ride from Springtown. The Daughters eventually abandoned their calling, and the farm was sold to Tim and Mercy. Colonel Tim Pepperidge had followed Washington to Yorktown and been present at the surrender.

Tim's eyes misted over and his lower lip trembled as he studied the picture that, for all its probable inaccuracies, brought back a time of strife and struggle and glory the colonel would never forget.

Blackwell seemed pleased with the reactions of the people in the tent. But another audience awaited. The limner quickly made his way to the door flap and held back the canvas panel to allow the townspeople to pass through. They filed past an assortment of merchants and farm families who were excited about entering the exhibition. They had heard the cheers and outcries of horror and were eager to discover for themselves what their friends and neighbors had experienced.

To Kit's relief, Kate and Hannah Louise were nowhere around. He commended himself on his luck and hurried Penelope and Esther away from the limner's tent so he would not even be suspected of misconduct. He heard a round of applause from across the Springtown Commons and noticed the crowd that had gathered around the tables on the opposite side of the Green. No wonder Kate and Hannah weren't close by. The judging of the pies had begun. Hannah was convinced that her sweet cherry cobbler was going to claim one of the prize ribbons this year. Kate had come along to give her daughter moral support.

"I'm going to find Mother," Penelope said. "I want to be there when she wins."

"You want me to walk with you?"

"No," Penelope replied breezily. "There's Matthew Schraner." She pointed at a solid-looking young man whom Kit had noticed in the limner's tent. "I'll walk with him."

The shy boy had been unable to give his attention to the paintings in the presence of such a beauty as Penelope. Kit noted with amusement that Matthew was standing a few yards away, staring with mock interest at a potter busily hand-building pinchpots in the shade of a gaily striped three-sided tent.

"Are you sure he's up to it?" Kit asked. "You are a handful."

"Oh, Uncle Kit," Penelope said, exasperated. Then she hurried over to Matthew Schraner, who almost fainted dead away that his lady love should speak to him. He glanced at Kit, who nodded his permission. Then Matthew walked off, arm in arm with Penelope, who led him along.

"Gently, girl," Kit said in a wistful tone. "Gently."

Kit felt a tug on his sleeve. Esther Rose looked up at him, her cherub cheeks a blushing pink. "Now we're alone."

Kit looked down at his eight-year-old niece and

thought to himself that in another ten years she would be quite the temptress. The boys of Springtown had better beware. He knelt in the dust at her side. She wore a calico dress with a blue lace cap upon her head and blue slippers that were smudged from all the dust and dirt.

"And what, my pretty, did you have in mind?" Kit asked. "Shall I ask the fiddlers yonder to play us a merry two-step, and we'll dance a jig for the amusement of the crowd? And I insist you promise every dance to me."

"Oh, Uncle Kit, you're so silly." The little girl laughed, then showed him a handbill she had hidden behind her back. "I want to see *him*."

The handbill was an advertisement for the Trenton Titan, a man of uncommon strength and ferocity, at least according to the handbill's author. Beneath the caricature was an open challenge to all hardy souls to try their luck against the Trenton Titan. Any man forcing the Titan beyond the boundaries of a circle drawn in the earth would win five shiny silver dollars for wagering one.

Kit had just finished reading the handbill when the Titan's partner, a short, sly, weasel-faced man, began calling out to one and all to gather around. A crowd had already begun to gather as he completed the circle he had drawn in the dirt.

"Esther Rose, this isn't for you," Kit said.

"I want to see. I want to see."

"Your mother would skin me alive."

"I want to see!" Esther Rose said. Then she changed her tone and stared up at Kit with a doe-eyed expression that would melt the heart of a Hun. "Please? I won't tell. Just for this much minutes." She held up her thumb and forefinger barely an inch apart.

Kit reached over and narrowed the gap even farther.

"For this much minutes," he corrected. Esther seemed satisfied. Kit gathered her into his arms.

"I love you, Uncle Kit," she said close in his ear.

"I love you, too, my pretty."

Kit entered the crowd and made his way to the edge of a circle about twenty feet in diameter. Kit was soon surrounded by the nervous and daring. He sighed. A dollar was a fool's wager, even to win five. This Titan no doubt was an experienced brawler and undoubtedly knew every trick in the book.

"Oh, look, the hairy man, the hairy man! From the picture!" The child's voice served to galvanize the crowd's attention, and all heads turned and voices stilled as the Trenton Titan brushed through the townsmen.

He stood just under six feet tall and wore boots and woolen trousers. He was bare-chested and his upper torso was covered with coarse, black hair on chest, back, and sloping shoulders. He was stout with a hard, round belly. His legs were slightly bowed, his thighs and arms heavily muscled. His features were hard and bunched, and he peered out at the world through a visage of gristle and bone that had taken one too many hammerings.

He looked around at the crowd, placed his hands on his hips, and rocked back on his heels with loud, raucous laughter that was thick with contempt. For in truth, the man emanated such meanness that quite suddenly a dollar seemed much too precious to wager for the chance at five dollars and a broken back.

"Come one, come all," the Titan's partner continued to exhort. "You need only force my man out of the circle. Step up, you flower of Springtown's manhood, and cover yourself with victory laurels on this glorious Fourth."

"You mean funeral columbines," Jonah Greene, a

storekeeper's son, muttered. A brash, handsome youth of eighteen, Jonah had lost his nerve at the sight of the ruffian, much to his lady's disappointment. The girl beside him pouted and looked away as if her escort had disgraced her. The storekeeper's son could not bear her scorn. A big, strapping lad, he reached in his pocket, withdrew the coin, and held it aloft. Now his lady fair beamed as Jonah stepped out into the circle and faced the Trenton Titan, who grinned and charged.

Jonah tried to brace himself. He was young and strong and had a girl to impress, which might have helped him carry the day. But stopping the Trenton Titan was like trying to halt a wild bull.

Kit winced at the crunch of bone and flesh as the Titan slammed into Jonah. He tried to cover Esther's eyes, but she was too slippery for him. As for the action in the center of the circle, it was mercifully brief. With a *woof* of expelled air, Jonah seemed to cave inward as the Titan smacked into the youth, lifted him in a bear hug, continued on a few paces, then hurled the storekeeper's son from the circle. The girl who had incited him to his fate stifled a cry, grew pale, and ran to the youth's side, where he lay stunned and gasping for breath.

"Ha—ha—ha." The Titan threw back his head and roared. "Is that the best Springtown can do?" He stooped over, retrieved Jonah's dollar coin from the dirt, and made a great show of flipping it to his partner.

Half a dozen riverboat men who had come up from Trenton in hopes of earning a little wager money on their champion joined in and continued to deride the crowd in hopes of stirring up enough civic pride that a host of townsmen would step forward and add to the Trenton winnings. Kit stood aside, bemused at the riverboat men's antics. Esther noticed his expression.

"You think the hairy man is funny, too, Uncle Kit?" the little girl asked as she was lowered to the ground.

"Well, lass, he's a formidable champion, all right, but he's either too proud or too stupid a blowhard to play this crowd for a profit," Kit replied. "He's intimidated folks. Now they're afraid of him."

He glanced at his niece and grinned. She was trying to understand, but the Titan had distracted her. One of his cohorts began to play upon a pipe, and the Titan, in taunting the crowd, had begun to dance a jig.

Suddenly, big Abram Hawthorne, the town blacksmith, tossed a dollar into the circle and advanced on the Titan. The chorus of cheers that greeted his arrival soon turned to cries of dismay as he met a fate similar to Jonah Greene's. A head butt to the chin knocked him senseless, and the Titan had only to drag him out of the circle right in front of Esther Rose.

The brawler dripped with sweat as he hauled his latest conquest out of the ring. He noticed the girl watching him. He was surprised to find such a small one among the crowd. He wrinkled his features and snarled to startle her, but Esther held her ground, reassured by the presence of her uncle behind her.

"What do you think of that, missy?" the Titan said with a wink.

"I think you're a stupid blowhard, just like my uncle said," she said quite sweetly.

Kit, who had been about to scoop her up into his arms and take her away from the crowd, froze, his arms outstretched. For a moment he considered pretending he didn't know the tousle-headed child. But his actions had already branded him as her relative.

"Blowhard, is it?" The Trenton Titan straightened up. Then his lips curled back to reveal a row of broken teeth, and he backed away, waving Kit into the circle.

"Come, then, little man, and prove your words, or by heaven I'll feed them to you along with your liver."

Kit grimaced. He could feel the eyes of the crowd upon him. He felt a tug on his trouser leg. Esther beamed up at him with her beatific smile.

"Did I do something wrong?"

"No. I did," Kit said. He knew he ought to just turn and carry his niece off to the rest of the fair. But pride held him in place, foolish pride.

Esther winked at him and said, "Let's get him, Uncle Kit." The fearless child stepped forward, and the crowd broke into laughter. Kit caught the girl beneath her arms and deposited her outside the circle. He slipped the sheath from his belt and handed the girl his knife in its buckskin scabbard.

"Esther, hold this for me. And a minute from now, if I'm alive, I'll take it back."

Kit advanced to the center of the circle as all through the crowd money exchanged hands and wagers were laid as to how long he would last. The outcome, after all, was inevitable. The Trenton Titan had the advantage of height and weight.

"So you show some spunk, eh?" the brawler muttered.

Kit didn't bother to reply. Fights weren't won with words. He sized up his chances and knew if he was to leave the circle in one piece he'd have to use brains as well as brawn. The Titan was a bull, and like a bull he fought only one way, hard and head on.

Kit's thoughts drifted back to Young Otter and Stalking Fox. On the trail up from Florida, Kit, the Choctaws, and Iron Hand O'Keefe had encountered a Creek war party and fought a brief but furious skirmish during which Kit had observed his Choctaw allies in hand-to-hand combat. They fought with wild abandon and used their whole bodies to trip and kick and bludgeon their opponents. Kit had watched, and he had learned.

The Titan brought Kit back to the present with a feint. He lowered his shoulder and lumbered forward. Kit retreated and maneuvered himself around the circle until his back was to the men from New Jersey. The riverboat men tried to distract Kit with catcalls and insults. Kit turned a deaf ear to them; such men did not matter. The only one who mattered was preparing to attack.

With a grunt and a growl the Trenton Titan charged, all two hundred and eighty pounds of bad temper and meanness. Kit waited a second and then, to everyone's surprise, lunged forward, but just as he closed with the big man he turned sideways and hurled himself into the Titan's legs in a body block that caught the heavyset man in the shin.

The Titan grasped empty air and went flying, landing on his face in the dirt and skidding to the edge of the circle, spattering his cohorts with dirt in the process. The Titan cursed and lumbered to his feet in time to glimpse a blur of motion as Kit leaped up and planted both feet square in the Titan's chest.

The brawler flew backward out of the circle and landed spread-eagled atop his companions, sinking a couple of them to the ground in the process.

The crowd erupted into cheers and Kit was suddenly transformed into the hero of the hour. However, a hero's life is a risky business. Even as he turned to wave to his neighbors, the riverboat men, showing poor sportsmanship as well as the effects of the prodigious amounts of rum they'd consumed, plunged forward to avenge the Titan's defeat. Jonah Greene, the blacksmith, and a half a dozen of the townsmen around the circle rushed forward to Kit's defense.

Kit sensed the danger too late. He turned as one of the riverboat men, Weasel-Face, struck him full on the jaw. Kit stumbled, caught off balance, and fell. Weasel-Face leaped onto him and momentarily pinned Kit's shoulders while the brawl erupted all around the circle.

Kit managed to squirm from side to side and free one arm as Weasel-Face grabbed a fist-sized stone and tried to bash Kit's skull. Kit moved quicker and caught the stone-wielding hand. Weasel-Face cocked his free hand to batter the man he had pinned. Kit steeled himself, tried to shove free, and braced for the blow.

To Kit's astonishment Weasel-Face screamed, scrambled off to one side, and clutched at the bloodied seat of his trousers. Kit sat upright and saw Esther Rose standing close by with Kit's long-bladed knife in her hand. The tip was dotted with crimson where she had jabbed the shiny steel point into Weasel-Face's posterior. The riverboat man scrambled to his feet.

"You little whelp," he roared, and took one step forward. Kit dropped the man in his tracks with a single well-placed left hook that twisted the man's head halfway around.

"Whee!" Esther Rose exclaimed as the battle raged about her. Kit grabbed her up, tossed her over his shoulder, and raced through the churned dust and bloody, battered souls who were having one hell of a fine time whipping these louts from Trenton. Kit had to dodge a few punches and returned in kind what came his way as Esther squealed with the excitement of it all.

At last Kit stumbled clear of the melee, and when he had trotted a safe distance from the combatants he set Esther down and collapsed wearily beside her to wipe the blood from his bruised knuckles. They were both quite grimy from the experience, and Esther's dress was torn at the hem.

Uncle and niece stared at one another for a moment. Esther kissed him on his battered cheek.

"I knew you'd beat the hairy man," she said.

"How did you know that?" Kit sucked in a lungful of air. The fighting had already begun to die down, ending as quickly as it had begun. The riverboat men were being led away, shown to their horses, and escorted out of town.

"'Cause I was there to help you," the girl replied tenderly.

Kit thought of Weasel-Face and the look on the man's face as Esther stuck him.

"I guess you were, at that." He chuckled. "Why should I ever have worried?" Then he appraised her smudged cheek and soiled dress and had to sigh. "How am I ever going to be able to explain this to your mother?"

"Don't even try," Kit's older sister sounded in an ominous voice. Her shadow draped across them both, man and child. Kit McQueen, the conqueror of titans, flashed his most winning smile and slowly turned. It was a game try, but one look at Hannah's livid features, and he knew the cause was already lost.

Chapter Twelve

Kate McQueen did her best to make lunch a pleasant experience. She led her quarreling family to a comfortable spot beneath the shade of a weeping willow down in front of the Friends' House. She had spread a worn, wedding-ring-patterned quilt on the ground and set out pewter plates and cups, then unwrapped a platter of cold chicken she had roasted the previous night, a quarter wheel of cheese, and a loaf of bread. There was sweet cider to drink and, for dessert, ample portions of Hannah's cherry cobbler with the "second place" ribbon still affixed to the cheesecloth and draped over the golden crust.

Time had not dimmed Kate's beauty, but had only mellowed the fiery spirit behind her still striking features. Her yellow hair was highlighted with silver strands, and laugh lines wrinkled the flesh around her eyes and mouth. Hers had been a life full of love and laughter interspersed with sorrows that no one ever escapes with the passage of time. She had seen war.

She had buried a daughter and a husband. But Kate refused to allow life's pains to darken her spirit.

There was much to be thankful for, not the least of which was being here on this summer's afternoon with Hannah and Kit and Kate's own dear granddaughters, Penelope and Esther. It felt good to have her family together again. They only needed Captain Clay Burgade, Hannah's husband, to complete the family. But Clayton Burgade had resumed command of a schooner and joined the fledgling fleet of American ships hoping to wrest control of the Great Lakes from the British. Hannah could only guess as to her husband's whereabouts. His absence had taken its toll on her. So Kate could understand her daughter's moods, the temper that flared as quickly as a firecracker and stung like a hornet.

"Enough, daughter," Kate finally remarked, and Hannah, whose features were flushed from her most recent outburst, looked around at her mother and her mouth dropped open.

"But . . . surely you aren't taking his side. Look at Esther, she might have been killed!" Hannah angrily tucked a brown curl back beneath her bonnet, but the errant strand worked loose and lay upon her rounded cheeks.

"I am taking the side of peace and quiet and proper digestion," Kate said, reaching over to pat her daughter's hand before withering Kit with a single, scathing glance. "Christopher is guilty of dreadfully poor judgment. I wholly agree. And you have said as much. So let there be an end to it. Esther is unharmed and there is nothing so wrong with her dress that a proper needle and thread won't mend."

Kate handed a chicken leg to Esther, who sidled over to her uncle. Kit sat with his back to the tree trunk and his legs outstretched and crossed at the ankles. The eight-year-old reached up and gave his nose a gentle bop with her chicken leg, then grinned and began to eat.

Kate noticed that Penelope and Matthew were seated close together. Matthew's stomach growled as he positively beamed at the platter of chicken, all thoughts of romance and courtship put on hold until he had appeased the gnawing hunger in his belly. Penelope seemed more than a trifle miffed at his lack of attention to her. Kate managed to hide her amusement. Men were so much alike, appeasing their needs in strict priority, oblivious to the effects of their conduct on the women in their lives. Still, it was best Penelope became acquainted with these traits. At thirteen, she was still young enough to learn to make them work for her.

Kit went straight for the cobbler and helped himself to a dishful of the cherry-laden, syrupy concoction. "Hannah, I cannot believe this cobbler came in second. To what? There could have been nothing better." Kit scooped a mouthful and sighed with contentment as he chewed and swallowed and smacked his lips. "By heavens, this is food for the gods, you mark my words." He enjoyed another mouthful and winked at his sister.

"You keep your false compliments to yourself, Christopher McQueen," Hannah replied, still peeved.

"Constance Oesterle won first place," Kate added.

Kit sat upright, indignation on his face. "The judge's sister? On my life, I'll call him out, and we'll settle this on the field of honor. His sister, too! The cheat! Never you fear, Hannah, I'll right the wrong, be assured."

"The only thing I can be assured of is that you

will make a horse's—" Hannah glanced around at the children, "uh—*backside* of yourself and embarrass me!" Hannah's mouth was drawn into a taut, bloodless slash, more like a grimace. Kit thought she seemed to swell and then settle in on herself.

She shook her head, buried her face in her hands, and began to shudder. Kate looked alarmed. Kit set his plate aside and rose up on his knees to put his arm around Hannah.

"There, there, big sister. It's all right," Kit gently comforted. His voice sounded warm and full of compassion.

"Not if you have your way, you silly ox," Hannah replied, and tilting her head back gasped for air as she subsided into laughter. Kit was caught off guard. He had expected tears. Then he realized the joke his sister had played on him, and he scowled with mock anger and returned to his place against the willow.

Kate had to smile. Everything would be fine now. She began to relax and enjoy her family, secure that the crisis had passed.

Kit looked down at Esther. "You know, I forgot to claim my winnings," he suddenly realized. And the Trenton men were long gone. Hannah pointedly cleared her throat. Kit caught the hint. "Just an observation," he added quickly. "In all innocence."

He might have continued to place his foot in his mouth, but a string of exploding firecrackers interrupted him. The young boys responsible for the attack scampered off across the commons. By the time Hannah had regained her composure, she had forgotten her brother's last remark. The weeping willow hung like a canopy around them. Kit's thoughts drifted back to Barbary and the tents of the desert nomads. He had seen such sights, taken such risks, only to return empty-handed.

Bill Tibbs. No, don't think on him. Let those memories sink under their own bitter weight. There. That's better. Empty-handed? No. The pressure against his palm felt warm and reassuring. He lowered his gaze to Esther, dozing against him. Her hand had wormed its way into his fist as she nodded off.

He let her sleep.

By evening, the celebration had just about run its course. Every exhibit, from the silversmith's to the potter's, from the quilt exhibit to the limner's tent show, had been visited. All the pies had been judged, a horse race had run its course, and livestock had been shown and auctioned off. Old Archibald MacIllhenny had entertained the crowd with his bagpipe tunes, and the Springtown fife and drum corps, though sorely depleted by the current hostilities with Britain, marched through the commons and circled the wildly cheering throng. "Yankee Doodle" brought the farmers and townsmen to their feet, and on the spur of the moment the populace followed the fife and drum corps in an impromptu parade around the Liberty Tree, a grand old oak that dominated the center of the Green. The tree had served as the focal point for many a patriotic rally during the Revolution. It remained an important symbol for the town and the surrounding community.

With the onset of night, campfires were started and dinners were prepared as families settled down to wait for the celebration's final act to commence.

Esther woke in her uncle's arms as Kit led the rest of his family back to where they'd left the carriage, on the south side of the commons. She was ecstatic over the prospect of spending the night out under the stars.

Many of the farm families shared her sentiments. Just being in the center of the bustling little town with its many shops and stores and taverns was a thrill. Tavern doors were propped open to permit a steady stream of traffic. Merchants who normally closed up at sundown kept their shops well lit to attract the curious customer with a penny to spend.

There were rooms to be had in town; Kate alone had several friends who had offered a place at their hearthsides for the widow of Daniel McQueen. But Kate had promised her granddaughters a night under the stars. And as tent after tent rose up, a great feeling of cheer and well-being spread throughout the families. Perfect strangers visited one another and chattered away like old friends. At last it was time for the pyrotechnic display, and though the assemblage of rockets, fire wheels, fountains, and flaring candles could not hope to rival the displays concocted in the larger cities, still, each starburst, each eruption of some miniature Vesuvius, was greeted with a hearty round of applause and cries of approval.

Kit watched the fireworks and marveled at how different from war these bomb bursts were, blossoming into flowers of iridescent fire and falling back to earth in a myriad of colors. *Nothing like exploding shells and grapeshot and shrapnel that could shred a man to doll rags,* he thought.

Yes, the struggle with Britain was going badly, despite the war hawks' vain predictions. British troops were no doubt massed in Canada preparing to invade. By the time the next Fourth rolled around, these harmless pyrotechnics might be interchanged for the more real and utterly deadly display. The very idea of British troops marching up the Trenton Road filled him with dread.

He longed to do his part, to defend the country of his birth. And yet, for more than a year he had held himself in check. With Clayton Burgade gone there was no one to look after Kate and Hannah, no one to tend the inn and work the farm. He couldn't abandon his mother and sister and two nieces in the hour of their need. So Kit leaned back against the wheel of the phaeton, and with Esther Rose riding his shoulders he pretended to enjoy the fireworks, all the while seeing through this grand parody of battle to the truth of the matter, where his duty lay like a hurled gauntlet waiting for him to accept its unstated challenge.

Kate noted the look on her son's face. Even in the sharp, sudden glare of the rockets and the flash of miniature volcanoes spewing crimson sparks she recognized her husband, revealed for an instant in Kit's features. And her heart raced at the thought of losing him to the war. He was as reckless and bold and quick-tempered as his father. There burned in him that same determined love of country that had dominated the life of Daniel McQueen.

Having Kit for a year had been a selfish happiness. She wanted it to continue. It seemed like only yesterday he had returned from Derna, haggard and weary, with only the buckskins on his back and a pair of horses to show for his privateering. He had been content to labor in the fields, to work his father's forge, and to be a loving uncle to Esther and Penelope.

No, she wouldn't let it end. Kate McQueen had buried enough of her family. But having her son again had eased the burden on her. Indeed, she had known peace these past months. And she would allow no one and nothing to interfere with her happiness. She drew closer to Kit and, reaching out, placed her hand on his arm. He looked at her.

"I'm just glad you're here," Kate said. "I don't know what I'd do without you." There, a simple gesture, an inflection of voice, and the web of her affection tightened its hold. Now if only she could lose the guilt, if only she could cast it aside like some threadbare, tattered cloak, buried in the bottom of a trunk and at last forgotten.

Chapter Thirteen

The Hound and Hare Inn looked much the same as it had in 1776. Its white oak plank facade wore a recent coat of whitewash. The stone walls of the courtyard were overgrown with ivy, and those same verdant vines had worked their way upward to obscure the wrought-iron arch beneath serpentine strands. Sunlight glinted on the windows along the front of the tavern that faced the east, and a gentle breeze stirred the branches of the apple trees that surrounded the two-story structure. Kit drove the phaeton onto the circular drive, leaving the wheel-rutted Trenton Road for the last fifty feet of their trip. He continued past the courtyard and around to the north side of the inn where the barn stood, closed and shuttered, and a gaggle of geese and chickens flapped their wings and scattered to the safety of their pens, whose gate stood ajar.

Kit frowned and glanced around for Miles Grauwyler, the handyman he had left to watch over the place. Kit had taken a liking to the young immigrant and hired him to help give the Hound and Hare a fresh coat of paint. Kit had given Grauwyler an extra two days' wages to watch over the grounds and keep the tavern open for business. The Trenton Road was a heavily traveled thoroughfare, and Kit had anticipated showing a goodly profit despite their absence from the inn. The absence of any patrons and the fact that no one stepped forth to greet the phaeton's arrival implied the Hound and Hare had been left untended.

Kit halted the carriage, and as Esther leaped out and scampered off to play, her uncle headed straight for the barn, where he had glimpsed a fluttering piece of paper tacked to one of the barn doors. Off to his left, he heard Abigail, their milk cow, bellow her greeting. The animal had managed to knock down a section of the knee-high picket fence that separated the family garden from the pasture and was busily eating her fill.

"My carrots!" Hannah exclaimed as she noticed the intruder. "Oh, no. And the peas. Not the peas!" She lifted her skirt clear of her ankles and ran off to save her garden. Penelope started to follow, but Kate called her back to help unload the bolts of cloth Kate had purchased before leaving Springtown.

Kit didn't bother calling out. If Miles Grauwyler was on the premises he would have heard the clatter of the carriage on the cobblestone drive. He reached the barn and found the crudely scrawled note Miles had tacked to the door with a nail.

I am gone to seek my fortune elsewhere. A wagon has came by bound for the Ohio country and there is a place for me. I taken some food.

> *Your obedient servant—Miles G.*

"I'll be damned," Kit said with a wag of his head as he tugged on the door and pulled it open. He walked back to the carriage and led the mares by their reins into the barn. He unhitched the horses from the singletree and led the animals out the side door to the corral, working quickly, going through the motions from habit.

Using the pitchfork he shoveled out a mound of hay for the hungry animals to feed on. Flies circled a puddle of fresh manure, and a crow on a nearby fencepost cawed its raucous cry, informing the wild things that man had returned. Kit had a special fondness for crows. It was something his father had once told him, that crows could not be tamed. Nature burned too deeply in them. They would never relinquish their freedom and live caged and subservient to man.

Years ago, Kit, as a young lad, had found a crow with a broken wing and carried the injured bird to his father. Daniel McQueen had set the wing and kept the poor, frightened creature in a cage to speed the healing process. Once, when Daniel was chopping wood, he brought the cage along, thinking to give the injured creature a little fresh air and sunshine. He had barely begun at the woodpile when one crow after another began to dive at the cage and strike it. The other birds were willing to sacrifice themselves in an effort to kill the caged bird rather than allow it to remain imprisoned.

Kit, just a boy and as stubborn as his father, spent day after day with the bird, feeding it, trying to win the creature's trust. But when the wing had healed, the crow began to refuse its food. No matter what young Kit brought the bird, from captured insects to bread soaked in milk, the crow remained resolute, impervious to temptation and slowly, irrevocably dying.

Kit continued to stare out into the corral and

beyond the fence to the grove of apple trees, where he had at last carried the cage and freed the bird he had wanted so badly to keep. Despite his tears, young Kit had felt elation surge within him at seeing the valiant little bird rise to become a black blur against the steel blue dome of sky, swirling, diving, soaring in ever-widening circles and scolding the clouds. Suddenly Daniel McQueen was there, standing alongside his son, his hand upon young Kit's shoulder as he gently said: "This is what it means to be free. This is how it feels. Don't ever forget, son."

Kit could still feel the pressure of his father's hand here in the familiar stillness of the barn. He crossed the interior to stand by the cold forge where Kit had watched his father, mallet in hand, standing like some demigod, bathed in the glare of the fire as he pumped the bellows and sent a column of sparks whirling up the blackened chimney. He closed his eyes, touched the stone-cold ashes, and shuddered as if some ghostly hand had reached through his body. Was that the rustle of a mouse in the straw or a spirit whispering in his ear? The wind's song or his father calling in the stillness? "Never forget..."

Chapter Fourteen

Kit felt Esther's hand clutch at the sleeve of his hunting shirt as he steadied his rifle against the tree trunk they had used for a blind. The hunter sighted on the whitetail buck, aiming at a spot just behind the shoulder where the animal's matted coat darkened. Esther had insisted on coming along. Three days after the Fourth of July celebrations and weary of helping her mother tend to the garden, the little girl was eager to escape the duties of home life for a walk in the woods with one of her favorite adults. But she hadn't counted on this. To her, the whitetail was a creature of magic, appearing miraculously out of a shadowy grove to drink from a sweet, clear stream.

Thirty yards away from the deer, Kit's finger curled around the trigger of his long rifle. He had the animal dead center. He could already picture the deer's carcass draped over his horse. Hell, he could already taste the hindquarter roast, fresh from the oven and ready to carve. His stomach growled. *Steady, now,* he cautioned, *take your time. This buck isn't going anywhere but to the smokehouse. Slowly, squeeze the shot off, squeeze—*

"Run! Run! Run!" Esther shouted, bolting to her feet. She jumped and waved her hands, and the startled deer bolted to the right as Kit fired to the left. He watched, helplessly, through the billowing powder smoke, as the whitetail bounded back into the forest. Kit wrinkled his nose. He'd traded the imaginary aroma of a venison roast for the acrid smell of his wasted shot. It was hardly a bargain.

"Yep . . . you missed," Esther said, as if criticizing his marksmanship. "Here, Uncle Kit, you better wear these." The little girl brought out a pair of spectacles she had fashioned out of vines. She slipped the woven green strands over his ears, the lens part resting on the bridge of his nose, and he peered over the wildflower rims.

"That's much better," he said. There just seemed no way to lose his temper with the child. Her smile thwarted him at every turn. He looked back at the forest and the trembling underbrush the whitetail had cleared as it escaped to the safety of the pines. Kit stood and proceeded to reload his rifle, ramming home another charge of powder and shot and priming the weapon. Esther Rose watched him with interest.

"When I get bigger, I'll hunt, too," she said.

"You'll have a lean diet, my pretty," Kit muttered. "Better marry a storekeeper or a butcher or any wealthy man, eh? Then you'll always have something to eat and will not have to rely on the harvest of your compassion."

Esther frowned as she tried to make sense of this latest comment. Then she tsked-tsked and climbed up on the log, the better to face him.

"Uncle Kit. You are always saying things I don't

understand. And besides, I'm gonna marry you when I grow up."

"Is that a fact, young lass?" Kit chuckled.

"Yes." Esther nodded. "I've already told my mother, even."

"And what did she say?" Kit brushed a leaf from her moppet's cap of curls.

Sunlight surrounding them forced a continuously changing pattern of shadows and light here in the forest. Another child might have been overawed by the immensity of the woods. They were a good hour's ride from the Trenton Road. But Esther did not seem worried in the slightest. The blood of the McQueens flowed in her veins, to be sure.

Kit's niece struggled a moment to remember. Then her expression brightened. "I remember. Mama said we deserved one another." Esther pursed her lips and turned serious. "Is that good?"

"Sure it is, my pretty," Kit said, scooping the girl into his arms. He started back down the trail to the grove where he had left his dun mare. It was easy enough for Kit to retrace his path through the forest. After all, now he was wearing his "spectacles."

Kit and Esther reached the Trenton Road in the waning hours of the day. He urged the dun into a gallop, much to Esther's delight. The girl loved the feel of the wind in her face and the spring of the horse's powerful muscles beneath her. She squealed with delight as Kit kept a reassuring hold on her and guided the mare onto the cobblestone drive. Immediately he saw there were three extra horses tethered to the corral fence. On closer inspection he noted the military saddles the animals wore. He reined the mare to a slow walk and rode up alongside the new arrivals. The mounts lowered their heads to the water trough and after a perfunctory glance at Kit resumed drinking.

"Oh, my," Esther said. "Maybe somebody has come to stay. I better go help Mama." Esther squirmed free of Kit's grasp and dropped to the ground. "Good-bye, Uncle Kit. Thank you for taking me hunting," the girl called over her shoulder as she hurried across the yard and disappeared through the back door of the inn house. Kit dismounted, unsaddled the dun, and led the animal into the corral. He gave the mare a slap on the rump, and the animal trotted through the gate and headed straight for the mound of hay beneath the shed roof overhang Kit had attached to the outside wall of the barn. The low roof protected the hay in inclement weather.

Kit had reshingled it himself a couple of weeks ago. Esther had insisted on helping him. He grinned at the thought of her, hammer and nails in hand, standing at the foot of the ladder and awaiting his instructions. She was something, all right.

Kit smiled and then returned his attention to the three horses. The animals had come a long way. Their coats glistened with perspiration. Kit cradled his rifle in the crook of his arm and headed for the main house.

Premonition dogged him like a shadow. From something unnamed, he sensed a change in the wind, but for better or ill, the answer waited within.

Colonel Gain Harrelson was a slim, balding, forty-year-old officer whose features even in repose were sharp and tightly drawn. He wore civilian clothes, as did the two capable-looking lieutenants who acted as his aides. A passerby might take the travelers for frock-coated gentlemen and think no more of them.

The notion that their military saddles and arms might give them away had apparently escaped the soldiers. Kit would have mentioned as much, but Colonel Harrelson was not the kind of man to accept criticism. The colonel waved a hand toward the chair opposite him, inviting Kit to join him at the table.

Penelope arrived with a platter of pork roast sandwiches. Hannah followed with a pitcher of hard cider. Esther carried the pewter tankards and made a grand show of setting one before each of the men. Penelope rolled her eyes and muttered a silent prayer that Esther wouldn't embarrass her.

"Thank you, dear lady," Harrelson said with a half bow.

Esther curtsied and managed a gracious smile that dissolved into an embarrassed laugh as she hurried back across the room.

The lower floor of the Hound and Hare consisted of a spacious tavern room dominated on one side by a black walnut bar and an assortment of kegs and bottled spirits. The air was redolent with the smell of tobacco smoke and roasting pork. The pale blue walls were draped with battle flags and adorned with paintings.

Indeed, the tavern was a veritable gallery of works depicting incidents from the Revolutionary War. Itinerant artisans and artists were known to stop at the inn and leave a sample of their craft or handiwork as payment for a meal and a night's rest. Near the fireplace the shelves of an enormous walnut hutch were crammed with stoneware plates and cups of varying sizes and shapes.

"Lovely children," Colonel Harrelson remarked, helping himself to one of the sandwiches as Penelope stopped by his table and filled his tankard. Harrelson allowed Penelope to walk out of earshot before adding, "They might have been mine." He glanced over at Hannah, who blushed at the remark. They were old friends, having known each other since childhood.

"Gain . . . how you talk," she chided.

"It's true. Every word," Harrelson protested. "They'd be mine save for one terrible mistake. I introduced Hannah to my closest friend, Clay Burgade—and condemned myself to bachelorhood."

Kit's sister continued to blush, the red in her cheeks spreading down to her throat. She leaned forward to refill Harrelson's tankard. Her breast brushed his shoulder, and for a few brief seconds, as long as it takes to sharply inhale and slowly release one's breath, Hannah and the colonel gazed into each other's eyes.

Kit held his tankard out below the pitcher Hannah held suspended above the table. At last he reached up and tilted the pitcher, and dark gold cider poured from the spout. His action broke the spell of the moment. Harrelson cleared his throat and assumed once again a more military bearing.

Hannah left the pitcher on the table and hurried off to shoo her two daughters outside. Esther and Penelope had begun to quarrel; the youngest girl was determined to prove she knew every bit as much as her older sister. The argument's net result was that both girls were banished to the garden with instructions to weed every row.

Colonel Harrelson folded his hands and studied the young man seated across from him. They were not strangers, for Gain Harrelson had been a frequent visitor to the Hound and Hare, and before moving to Washington he had entertained Hannah and Clay whenever the couple were in Philadelphia. Since his assignment to the War Office, his visits had been infrequent, and even less so with the onset of hostilities between the United States and Great Britain.

"Ahh...but I have not come to relive the past or capture a memory of what might have been," Harrelson said.

"No?" Kit said, still suspicious. The feeling he had out in the yard lingered.

"No." Harrelson washed a mouthful of sandwich down with cider. That was enough to take the edge off his hunger. "The war goes badly. Even Clay and his war hawks have begun to have their doubts. And the initial overtures of peace have been made." He glanced aside at his two subordinates, who had already wolfed down one sandwich each and had each started on another. "Station yourselves outside. Allow no one to disturb us."

"Now, see here—" Kit protested.

"I have already secured Kate McQueen's permission," the colonel interrupted. "You see, I must be able to speak freely. No one knows I have left Washington, save General Wilkinson and my superiors. With British spies skulking about, my uniform might have brought trouble to your mother and Hannah. And that is the last thing I want."

"Agreed," Kit replied. He watched the two lieutenants, food and drink in hand, leave by the front door, and when they were gone, Kit leaned forward on his elbows and his boyish facade faded as his eyes took on an icy glint. The time for pleasantries had passed. Kate's absence bothered him. Where was she? It wasn't like his mother to avoid the tavern's visitors, even ones whose behavior was as strange as Harrelson's. Then again, perhaps Kate had already discovered the colonel's motives.

Now it was Kit's turn.

"Colonel Harrelson—my sister's already married, so I know you didn't come to propose."

The colonel sat back, surprised by the remark. Then he realized the meaning behind Kit's statement of fact.

"Quite so, my young friend. To business, then, eh? And the reason I have come." Harrelson took a sandwich off the platter and placed it on the table. "Here are the British, in Canada poised to strike our northern border. And this tankard is a second British force that we feel is preparing to strike at the underbelly of our country. We are prepared to meet the threat in the north, but our efforts in the south have been a failure. Andrew Jackson has twenty-five hundred Tennessee Volunteers stationed in Nashville. We could move those men to the coast were it not for all the Indian unrest. Alabama and Georgia are aflame. Every courier brings word of new depredations. Jackson's men cannot move unless the Red Sticks Rebellion is crushed."

Harrelson sat back, brought out a pipe and tobacco pouch from his coat pocket, and proceeded to fill the bowl as he continued. "The Indians are receiving rifles, probably transported out of New Orleans by British agents. But that is only part of the problem. One man, a white renegade, has organized the Choctaw and Cherokee and created a reign of terror that must be stopped. I believe you know the traitorous rascal. The Choctaw call him Chief Iron Hand." The colonel saw he had piqued Kit's interest.

"What makes you think I know him?" Kit asked warily.

"I've known of your escape from Florida for some time now, including your encounter with a man called Iron Hand O'Keefe. The very same renegade that has put himself in the middle of things, I might add." The colonel emphasized his point by removing a Choctaw medicine pouch from his coat pocket. Harrelson placed the bag between the tankard and the sandwich. "Right in the middle," the colonel repeated. "And we cannot worry about the British until something has been done about Chief Iron Hand O'Keefe."

Kit looked up and met the colonel's steady gaze. "What do you want me to do?" he asked, unwilling to commit himself.

Harrelson drew a dagger from his boot sheath. Steel glittered in the sunlight as the colonel buried the pointed blade in the tabletop, skewering the medicine pouch in the process. The implication was all too clear.

"Iron Hand O'Keefe is my friend."

"That's what I'm counting on. You know the man. And he probably still trusts you enough to let you get close."

"O'Keefe saved my life."

"And he has been responsible for over a hundred deaths—men, women, and children. Shall I read you a litany of names? Find O'Keefe and learn who is supplying his redskins with rifles. Kill him or lure him into a trap and let Jackson's Tennesseans capture him."

"And if I refuse to go?" Kit asked, testing the waters.

"I will see O'Keefe a prisoner or dead." Harrelson sternly replied. He exhaled a lazy cloud of tobacco smoke. His tone grew gentle. "Son, your loyalty is commendable. But our country is in peril. We must be free to defend our southern flank. O'Keefe has made his alliance with the British. This is war. And sometimes in war a friend must be betrayed."

Kit abruptly stood, knocking over the chair behind him. The colonel had unknowingly struck a nerve, his fatalistic remark like salt trickled on an open wound.

Harrelson was taken aback. For a fleeting moment he thought Kit had been about to attack him.

Much to the officer's relief, Kit turned away and walked across the room to stand by the soot-darkened maw of the fireplace. He leaned upon the hearth and looked up at the brace of pistols hung from iron hooks driven into the gray stones. He reached up and placed his hand upon the guns, his father's finely balanced weapons.

"The 'Quakers'?" Harrelson asked, remembering the stories he had heard of Daniel McQueen's exploits during the Revolution and the pistols he wryly called his "Quakers" because they brought peace whenever Daniel drew them from his belt—an everlasting peace.

Kit nodded. "Yes." His hand lingered on the walnut grips and the black iron barrels, so cool to the touch.

"Kate has graciously invited us to stay the night," Harrelson said. "Against her better judgment, I'm sure. She knows why I'm here. I respected her too much not to tell her. She and your father have given of themselves whenever their country called. Now I've come asking for her son. I have been authorized by President Madison to offer you a commission as a lieutenant." The colonel rested his hand on Kit's shoulder. "I'll see to my men and have them stable the horses for tonight. Tomorrow morning I'll start back to Washington. Come with me, lad. You are needed."

"To help kill a friend?" Kit asked bitterly.

"To help save innocent lives," the colonel gravely replied. He patted the younger man's shoulder. "I don't envy your decision, friend. But I know you'll make the right choice."

Colonel Harrelson started toward the front door. He walked with clipped, quick strides and held himself erect and proud. He opened the door and looked out at his men, waiting in the sunlit yard, his two lieutenants. Harrelson hoped he would leave with three.

Chapter Fifteen

He was leaving. That was all there was to the decision. One moment Kit McQueen's mind had been full of turmoil as he struggled to choose between his sense of duty to his embattled country and loyalty to his own family. And then, like a fresh gust of wind after a cloudburst, the answer came to him, the way was made clear and he knew what he had to do. But telling his mother was not going to be easy.

It was midnight, yet he could not sleep. And so, alone in the barn, he had put these sleepless hours to good use. As his father before him, Kit, too, found solace and a kind of peace among the tools of Daniel McQueen's trade. Kit stoked the forge until he had a suitable fire. In a matter of a few hours, Kit had replenished the barn's supply of horseshoes and nails, and replaced an iron rim on one of the carriage's wheels. He had even repaired the latch on the barn door.

His ironwork completed, Kit shifted his attention to the grindstone. Right foot working the pedal, he set

the wheel spinning. He hunkered over the grindstone
and gingerly held the foot-long blade of his hunting
knife to the wheel. Sparks flew from the blade, and the
steel turned warm in his hands until it carried a
razor-sharp edge. He shifted the blade and honed the
opposite edge until he could shave the hairs from his
arm with either side of the blade. So intent had he
been on his work, Kit had not noticed his mother until
he straightened to wipe the sweat from his features.
Then he spied her, alone among the flickering shadows, a solitary woman of simple, solemn beauty.

Kate had not announced herself. She was content
to wait and watch her son as in the past she had
watched her husband, Daniel McQueen, laboring at
his forge, lost in thought.

Like father, like son.

She had never pressed him on what had happened
with the *Trenton* and how he had come to be in
Florida, or for that matter, what had become of Bill
Tibbs, who had been like an older brother to Kit and
who had often stayed at the Hound and Hare as an invited guest. The errant second son of well-to-do Philadel-
phians, Tibbs had been a likable young man who
shared Kit's passion for fast horses and excitement.
After Kit's return from the sea, alone, with nothing but
his weapons and the clothes on his back and a hard
glint to his eyes, Kate had questioned her son only
once as to the fate of his friend. Kit would only tell her
that he and Tibbs had gone separate ways. But the
bitterness in his tone had been impossible to miss. She
sensed his anger and his hurt. Still, whatever had
occurred was shrouded in secrecy, and she respected
her son too much to pry.

Kate closed her eyes and pictured the tousled-
haired child he had been. At ten years, Kit had been

full of mischief, wild and daring, with a fearlessness that propelled him from one predicament to another. Once, he had climbed the inn's steep roof. At twelve, Kit had come close to burning down the barn while trying to forge his very own knife.

Kate pictured the lad as he emerged from the smoke-filled barn, his cheeks streaked with soot and tears, his shirt singed. He wore the red welt on his forearm and the blisters on his knuckles like badges of honor, and he gripped in his hands the crudely formed knife he had fashioned all on his own.

Another memory overshadowed the image of the boy. She saw again the open grave, felt again the pain as Daniel McQueen's coffin was lowered into the ground. And there was Kit, fifteen years old and too proud to cry in front of the people who had come to pay their last respects to a brave man.

Kate remembered how her son, no longer able to stand idly by while all the world was coming to an end around him, had strode purposefully to the edge of the grave. All eyes turned to watch him. Even the minister ceased his prayers and watched with curiosity, his solemn visage momentarily relaxed. Kit drew the knife from his belt, the blade he had crafted as a boy of twelve. Despite the near catastrophe, his father had been so proud. Kit had cherished that crudely honed weapon.

In her mind's eye Kate watched her son kneel on the mounded dirt and gently, reverently, place the childhood blade upon the wooden coffin, like a Viking prince paying final homage to his liege and lord, a warrior's weapon for a warrior king.

Rest in peace, my darling Danny, one day we'll be together again.

"Mother?"

The sound of Kit's voice brought her back to reality. He held up the blade and inspected the edge, then hefted the weapon to see if he had altered its balance. He had weighted the hilt to offset the weapon's broad blade. Despite its size, the knife could be thrown with accuracy if need be. Kit returned the blade to the sheath at his waist. He pulled on his linsey-woolsey shirt. She had caught him off guard, yet he was glad she had come. Putting off a confrontation never solved anything or benefited anyone.

Arguments, considerations, all the reasons and decisions he had struggled with hit him at once and left him speechless. Where to begin?

"You'll be leaving, won't you?" Kate said, stealing his initiative.

"Yes," he replied, amazed at her perception.

"Colonel Harrelson is like a thief in the night: When he leaves, life is never the same."

Kate walked over and embraced her son. She pressed her cheek to his and then kissed him. Kit held her in his arms, knowing this might be the last embrace from her he might ever have. It was a morose thought, but one that had credence. If he had learned nothing else from his experiences, it was that life was full of the unexpected.

His mother opened his hand and placed something round and hard in his palm.

Kit opened his fist and looked down at a coin, and not just any coin, but a British crown sterling, a large silver coin with the initials G.W. carved on one side. He knew the story behind the coin: General George Washington himself had presented it to Daniel McQueen in recognition of his courage and service to the newborn nation in the early hours of its struggle for survival. Daniel McQueen, Kit's father, had hung the coin from a cord of braided leather and worn the makeshift "medal" all his days. Kit had assumed the Washington medal had been buried with his father. He was surprised to find it in the palm of his hand.

"Your father wanted you to have it," Kate explained. "He left it up to me to choose the day and time. I believe he would want you to have it now, when you are leaving."

"Then you knew—"

"From the moment Harrelson told me his reason for being here."

Kate stepped back to drape the braided leather cord over her son's head. The coin gleamed against his chest. Kit studied the medal (How often he had seen it dangling from around his father's throat!), then tucked the coin inside his shirt, where it would remain, close to his heart.

"I tried to think of something to say, words to compell you to stay," Kate confessed. "But the damn medal kept countering every argument."

She chose a bale of hay near one of the front stalls and sat down. A blur of motion caught her attention up near the rafters, and she looked up to see a barn owl flutter in through a loft window. The owl held a field mouse in one mighty talon. It lighted on a rafter, worked its way over into a shadowy corner where the roof sloped, and began to feast on its kill.

"How did you know I'd be leaving with the colonel? I scarcely worked it out for myself just a while ago."

"You are your father's son, aren't you?" Kate smiled. She folded her hands on her apron. "Dan wouldn't have been able to pass up Harrelson's offer, either."

Kit sighed in relief. He had expected a torturous scene. He thought he knew Kate McQueen better than most, but she was still able to surprise him. He walked across the barn, dragged a stool over with his toe, and sat down beside his mother.

"You are full of marvels, lady." He grinned. "But will you be all right? You and Hannah and the girls?"

"Of course we will. Just because I like having my son around, don't go thinking we're helpless." Kate reached out and touched his hand. "What of you? There is so much hidden behind those eyes of yours. Are you healed?" Kate patted his hand.

"As much as I'll ever be until I set something right," Kit replied coldly. Then he brightened. "I have my roots under me now. That's what my time here has brought me. I've walked in my father's shadow, stood where he stood, and I am better for it. When I first came back, I thought, maybe if I filled his shoes, took his place here, I could make up for past failures."

"You followed your own path," Kate said. "That is all your father ever wanted for you. He knew the price of freedom better than most. He treasured his own."

Kit stood. He looked up as his dun mare poked its head over the gate of its stall and whinnied. Kit ambled over to the animal and scratched its nose. Then, taking an apple from a nearby barrel, he rewarded the dun with its favorite treat. Kit looked around at his mother.

"I never understood why Father felt the way he did about...well...about the country—our country— until I thought I'd never see it again. I don't rightly figure I can ever say it the way it ought to be said. But during those long days, home and country became like a precious dream, something to live for, to hold on to, and, if need be, to die for."

Kate studied her son's features as he spoke what was in his heart. His face seemed to glow as if illuminated from within. There was fire in his highland blood, so what else could he do but burn? She rose from the bale, straightened her apron, and started toward the barn door.

"I have packed your provisions for tomorrow's journey and have left them on the table in the kitchen." She smiled bravely. "Sleep some. You've a long journey before you, son."

Kate had done what she had to do, and later she could feel proud of herself and take comfort in that decision. But tonight, she was a mother whose only son was riding off to war. She had a right to her tears.

Chapter Sixteen

DANIEL CHRISTOPHER MCQUEEN
Born August 25, 1742
Died December 1, 1800
Beloved Husband and Son of Liberty

He could have been buried in a plot in Springtown, but Daniel had loved this spot behind the inn, beneath the shade of oak and walnut, here on the edge of the forest and overlooking a meadow where the livestock grazed and a narrow cornfield where deer were wont to explore in the gray hours of a summer dawn.

Kit had been the one to discover his father on that bitter cold day in December, slumped over an anvil, dead as the iron he lay across, a blacksmith's hammer in his hand. Daniel McQueen had died at the trade he loved, the trade that gave him peace when he wasn't risking his life for his country. The memories of that wintry morning were etched in Kit's mind and came flooding back as he stood by his father's grave on the morning of departure. There were good memories, too, of a strong and loving father, easygoing, full of humor, compassionate yet, in times of conflict, indomitable and unyielding as the steel he'd forged.

Kit was dressed in a blousy, coffee-colored shirt and black breeches tucked into calf-high boots of supple leather. A worn black belt circled his waist and secured a pair of pistols, butt forward, holstered one above each hip. The "Quakers" had drawn Kit to the mantel in the early hours of the morning, and he had brought them to his room and fallen asleep.

His had been a fitful sleep, full of disturbing images and fragments of dreams, some that caused him alarm, others that brought him a momentary peace. One in particular lingered after he awoke in the silence of his bedroom. He had seen his father, shrouded in the mists of dream time. A big, rugged man in homespun clothes, Daniel opened his shirt and stared down at his chest. He no longer wore the initialed British coin that had become his own private medal of honor.

"So you wear it now, eh, lad?" the dream ghost said. "Then you'll be needing these." And with that, Daniel McQueen held out the matched pair of guns he called the "Quakers."

Standing at his father's grave now, Kit drew one of the pistols from his belt. It was a fine weapon, with a ten-inch heavy bore and a hexagonal barrel encased in a burled walnut stock. Each gun fired a .50-caliber lead ball, capable of leaving a fist-sized hole in an enemy. Each gun butt was tipped with molded iron. The weapons made excellent war clubs should a man not have time to reload in a close fight.

"Thanks for the guns, Father. And the medal—I'll take care of them." Kit gnawed on his lower lip a moment, trying to find the words. He shifted his stance, returned the gun to its holster, and hooked a thumb in his belt. "When I came back, after losing everything to that bastard Tibbs, well, I guess maybe I just felt sorry for myself. I just wanted to be here and let the rest of the world go to hell without me. It's taken a while, Father. But I reckon I've sorted things out. And now this Harrelson's come, with a job that needs doing. So it's time I go. I know you understand." He knelt by the grave and placed his hand upon the grass-covered earth at the base of the headstone. "Goodbye," he whispered.

Then he stood and started back across the meadow, where wildflowers bloomed in the wind-rustled weeds and dragonflies hovered and darted and soared in acrobatic splendor, their airborne dance of glory on a lazy summer's morning.

Esther Rose was waiting by the cornfield. She held a bucket filled with half a dozen roasting ears, fresh picked while waiting for Kit to notice her. Sunlight played upon her golden-yellow curls and her cherub's cheeks, and the breeze ruffled the hem of her sleeping gown, whose white lace trimming was wet from dew. Allowing Kit his privacy at his father's grave site was almost more than the eight-year-old could manage. The minute Kit started across the meadow, Esther's control quite simply dissolved, and the girl rushed toward her uncle as fast as her bare pink feet could carry her.

Soon she was in his arms, swept off the ground by her Uncle Kit, who lifted her high above his head, then held her close.

"Good morning, princess."

"Nothing good about it." She choked back a sob. "You're leaving."

"But I'll be back."

"How do I know? Papa's gone. He hasn't come back."

"I've never lied to you," Kit said, lowering her to the ground. He knelt at her side, yanked a pouch from his belt, and emptied its contents into her outstretched hand. Polished silver gleamed as she beheld a delicate flower Kit had crafted from a silver spoon he had melted and poured into a mold.

"A rose for Esther Rose."

Yes, a rose with its petals in bloom and its serpentine stem tipped with tiny thorns. The little girl's eyes widened with delight.

"Oh, Kit, it's so beautiful. I will keep it forever."

"Then you'll have me with you forever," Kit told her. He kissed her cheek. She kissed his nose and laughed. Tears glistened in her gentle eyes.

"But what can I give you?" she asked plaintively.

"You already have," he said as a lump slid upward into his throat. Sweet Jesus, this wasn't going to be easy. As he held her close, one of the rose's silver briars pricked his neck and drew blood. Having her love and her trust was worth the pain.

"Watch me while I saddle the mare," he said. "C'mon, Lady Esther."

"Queen Esther," the girl corrected in a whimsical tone.

"Your wish is my command," Kit declared. He took her by the hand and started toward the barn.

"Then I command you not to leave," the little girl replied regally.

Well, I blundered into that one, Kit admonished himself, *and no way out.* But the child was wise beyond her years, and she knew a lost cause when she saw one. Esther dragged on his hand until he stopped

by the corner of the house, where a flock of tame
ducks nibbled insects from the shortened grass and a
pair of goats idly grazed nearby. They kept the yard
cropped around the inn. Esther tugged her uncle to a
stop. She motioned for him to squat down where she
could whisper a secret in his ear.

"I'll miss you, Uncle Kit. More than anything in
the world. But we mustn't let the queen hear." She
straightened and continued toward the barn, this time
bravely leading the way. After all, she was Queen
Esther. And she had a silver rose to prove it.

PART THREE

Alabama Uprising

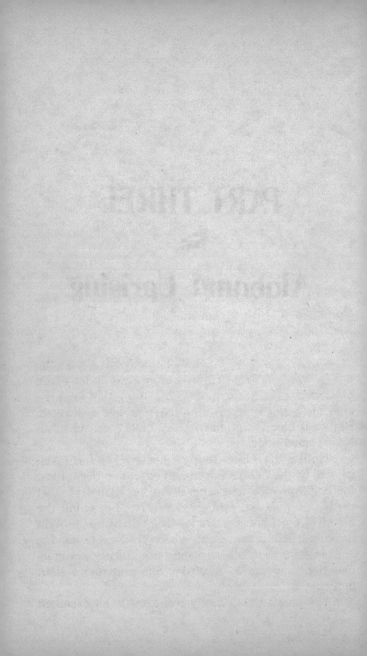

Chapter Seventeen

September 1, 1813
Alabama Territory

The first day of September might have been the last for Raven O'Keefe. Lithe and tawny, with long hair, black as a pirate's heart, the only thing that kept the eighteen-year-old Choctaw alive was her quickness. Her Irish blood wouldn't let her quit, even when all had seemed hopeless.

Unlike the other young Choctaw women taken captive by the Creeks, Raven had not for an instant lost her determination to escape. It was her Irish pride that made her stubborn enough to survive, but credit the blood of her Choctaw mother that taught her to fight back and fight mean, using whatever came to hand.

She crouched behind a shagbark hickory, her muscles tight and poised to strike. She clutched a stout branch.

The gnarled and knotty wood made an excellent

club that at close range could be just as effective as the rifled muskets of her pursuers. The Creek warriors who had followed her through the winding, shadow-shrouded hollows of the Appalachians were certainly at close range.

Raven scolded herself for the brief rest she had snatched in the hours of morning. But she had been winded and tired from the moonlit run. After slaking her thirst on the spring water seeping from the hillside, the half-breed woman had been unable to resist resting her weary limbs. She was battered and bruised and had needed the hour's sleep. A cracking twig had awakened the fugitive. Raven now flattened herself against the hickory and gripped her makeshift club as the near silent pad of moccasins drew closer.

Wolf Jacket wasn't going to take her alive, not this time. Her resolve was firm. Another twig snapped. Did the Creeks hold her in such disregard they were careless in their approach? She would teach them the price of cornering a Choctaw woman, mixed blood or no.

Her heart began to pound in her chest. Her breathing was ragged; she sucked in air through her clenched teeth. Suddenly a Creek warrior stepped past the hickory, a British rifled musket carried in the crook of his arm. It wasn't Wolf Jacket, but he'd do. Raven wanted the man's firearm. She was a crack shot, and a gun would sure lessen the odds against her.

The man spied Raven as she swung the club with every ounce of her strength. He tried to raise his short-barreled gun to protect himself. He moved too slow. The branch caught him full in the face, cutting short his warning cry as he choked on a mouthful of his own teeth and blood. The warrior flew backward into the underbrush and discharged his British flint-lock into the air.

He tried to shove himself upright, but Raven bludgeoned him again. She broke the club against his skull and then grabbed for the wounded man's rifled musket and tried to drag it free from his grasp. But even dying, he managed to cling to the weapon, his finger tightly curled around the trigger.

Raven didn't have much time. The shot would bring the others. She tugged and pulled, and the Creek flopped toward her, his eyes filled with hatred beneath a mask of blood from the grievous wound she had dealt him. Dying, he denied Raven her prize.

A lead slug clipped the branches overhead, and a second thudded into the hickory she had hidden behind. She released the rifled musket and raced off downslope, losing herself in the mist.

Wolf Jacket emerged from a cluster of trees and approached his wounded companion at a dead run. He was quickly followed by four other Creek warriors.

They were all men of average height, well muscled, with their black hair cropped short and their faces streaked with the crimson and yellow markings of war. Each man carried a rifled musket of British origin and a finely honed tomahawk whose iron blade had been forged in the furnaces of Blackwall outside of London.

Unlike the buckskins of his companions, Wolf Jacket's attire included the red coat of a British officer. He had adorned the garment with the pelt of a red wolf he had killed. The coat's brass buttons were dull now and the scarlet fabric faded. Still, the coat was Wolf Jacket's mark of authority, and he wore it proudly. Among the people of his village stronghold, the word of Wolf Jacket was law. He had proven himself a wise and cagey leader, utterly fearless in battle. And as he hated his enemies—the Cherokee and Choctaw and the white Americans who continually encroached on the Creek hunting lands—so did he love his own people.

He knelt by the side of the man Raven had killed and placed his hand on the dead warrior's chest.

"Sleep well, my brother," said the war chief of the Red Sticks. Of all the Creek nation, the Red Sticks were the most warlike and the fiercest in battle. Death was no stranger to them. Still, Wolf Jacket was full of grief. He and Yellow Knife had played as children, hunted together as young men, fought side by side along the warrior's path.

"Your great heart is stilled. Your strong life is taken by the half-breed whelp of Iron Hand." Wolf Jacket reached over and took the dead warrior's tomahawk. "With this you will be avenged. She will die by your own 'hawk.' I have spoken."

He straightened and turned to his companions. The man closest to him was a dark-eyed warrior whose lower jaw had been cruelly ripped by a ricocheting slug during the attack on the Choctaw village three days past. The wound had crusted over but would leave a frightful scar. His name was Runs Alone, an ambitious warrior, who was dutifully loyal to the red-coated brave as long as it suited his purposes.

"Take the gun of Yellow Knife and the medicine pouch from around his throat. Bring these things to his mother, that she might weep for her son."

"It will be done," Runs Alone replied.

Wolf Jacket turned to the other three warriors. "We will hunt this half-breed down and bring her head back on a pole so that when Iron Hand comes to free his people he will lose heart."

"There is no trail. She must have run into the creek," said Little Badger, the youngest of the three. He was anxious to prove his worth to Wolf Jacket, a warrior he held in the highest esteem. The man had continued down the slope for a few yards, following the runoff. Farther downhill the spring's flow branched off into two directions. Raven might have followed either of them. Little Badger began to reload his weapon.

The rifled muskets of the Creek braves were short-barreled weapons that the Red Sticks found to be excellent for use in the thick forests of northeast Alabama. A man did not need a long gun so much as a gun that was easy to carry, maneuverable in dense foliage, and simple to care for. And with the success of the raids on both the Choctaw camp and the looting of Hope Station, Wolf Jacket had plenty of furs, pelts, and stolen silver and currency to bring to the gunrunners who supplied his people with the British-made firearms.

Wolf Jacket stood aside as Runs Alone unfastened the medicine pouch from around Yellow Knife's throat and tucked it inside his buckskin shirt. He also removed the dead warrior's powder horn and pouch of rifle balls. He straightened, nodded to Wolf Jacket, and started up the hillside. If he was lucky, Runs Alone might even be able to catch up to the main war party before they reached the Tallapoosa River.

Snake, an elder warrior who had remained silent throughout the pursuit, at last spoke up as Runs Alone headed south over the ridge.

"Wolf Jacket, this is a foolish quest. One Choctaw woman is of little importance. We ought to follow Runs Alone and rejoin our people." Snake squatted in the dirt and fished a chunk of pemmican from a pouch on his belt. The invisible fingers of a breeze tugged at his silvery hair. Age enabled him to criticize Wolf Jacket without incurring the war chief's wrath. Snake had been a warrior as long as Wolf Jacket had been alive. His counsel was often sought, for there was much he had seen and done, and his travels had taken him throughout the land of the Mississippi and the Tennessee. But his counsel was not sought today. And Wolf Jacket as much as told him so.

"Raven is the daughter of Iron Hand. With her in my lodge, the Choctaw chief will be like a mad animal and lead his people to ruin."

Snake listened. But he was careful to read between the words of the war chief. Perhaps what he said made sense. Still, a man could have his doubts. A man could also lose his head by expressing those doubts. Snake was no fool. He had voiced his concern, and if his arguments did not sway Wolf Jacket from his intended course, then there was nothing more to be said.

Wolf Jacket knelt by the spring and cupped a handful of the bubbling, cold water to his lips. He was thirsty and tired from the chase. But the 'breed girl had shamed him. His pride was wounded. She had escaped him, and by all the sacred spirits, she would pay. He studied how the watercourse widened as it meandered downslope. She was clever to keep to the water. But he was a relentless hunter and had never returned to the Red Stick village empty-handed.

Wolf Jacket took a steel-bladed hunting knife from his belt and dug the point into the tip of his thumb until the blood flowed. Then he placed his thumb in the water and watched as a ribbon of his blood blended with the stream. His features impassive, his gaze dreamlike, the war chief began to softly sing in a monotone:

> "Water spirit, hear me.
> This is my blood.

I give it freely.
Blood of the earth, now we are one.
Guide me. Lead me.
Bring me to the one I seek.
Do not let me walk in shame.
I will be your drink.
Now I am wounded.
Bind me with the one I seek.
Iron Hand's daughter.
Water spirit, hear me."

He straightened and stood, and there was a glimmer of triumph in his eyes. The magic was made, it was finished. He could sense the power.

"Little Badger will go with me. We will follow the right fork of the stream below." He indicated the spot where the stream branched off in two directions, divided by a fallen tree. Farther below, sunlight glimmered on the surfaces of twin streams that wound their way through the oak and hickory forest. "Snake and Blue Kettle will follow the left fork. Fire a shot if you discover where she has left the stream. We will do the same. If we have not found her by nightfall, we will start back."

Wolf Jacket hefted his rifled musket, checked the load, and then motioned for Little Badger to come along. The young warrior was only too happy to comply. He beamed with pride at being chosen to accompany the war chief.

He flashed a grin at his companion, Blue Kettle, a sullen-faced warrior who shrugged and busied himself with his own rifle. Blue Kettle had fired the first shot at the Choctaw. But he had been off balance and had wasted the shot. In retrospect, Blue Kettle was glad he had missed. Wolf Jacket seemed to have a personal interest in the 'breed, and killing her might have cost Blue Kettle his life.

As for honors, let them fall to Little Badger. Blue Kettle wanted only to rejoin the war party. There were plenty of other women. But all the pretty ones might be claimed before he and the other warriors returned to the village at Horseshoe Bend. Blue Kettle kept his feelings to himself until Wolf Jacket and Little Badger had started down the hill. Then he turned to Snake, who began his descent along the watery path. Blue Kettle quickly fell into step alongside the Red Stick warrior.

"You spoke the truth, old one. I heard your words, and they were good counsel. We should abandon this chase. Let the girl go. She is unimportant. If Iron Hand comes against us, we will destroy him. Our guns are many, and his are few."

Blue Kettle glanced at the man alongside him to see if his words were having any effect. Snake continued on in silence. He seemed oblivious to Blue Kettle, who only echoed the older brave's earlier sentiments. Blue Kettle sighed in despair and ceased to protest. What was the use?

His mood turned black as they entered the emerald shadows of the forest. It was there, where the spring-fed stream branched and one fork was lost from view of the other, that Snake unexpectedly halted. Blue Kettle continued on alone for a few paces before he realized what had happened. He turned and found Snake stretched out against the trunk of a weathered sassafras.

The old warrior had broken a twig from a low-hanging branch and was proceeding to fill his pouch with the tree's mitten-shaped leaves. He took care to add pieces of root bark to the mixture. Dried, it would provide a nourishing tea. He crushed one of the leaves in his palm and inhaled the fragrance. Blue Kettle's shadow fell across him. The old brave did not bother to look up.

"Rest," Snake said. "Even the young need rest. And our village is many days' walk from here."

A broad grin spread across Blue Kettle's face. Suddenly the world seemed brighter.

"Truly you are the wisest of all," the younger man said.

"Take care that Wolf Jacket does not learn of my 'wisdom.' Else our heads will hang before the gates of our village and our bones rot beyond the walls," Snake warned. He stretched out his legs, closed his eyes, and allowed the weariness to seep from his limbs. He fell asleep reliving the raid on the Choctaw village and the wholesale slaughter of men, women, and children. Snake saw the faces of those he had killed and then a parade of the women and children taken captive. He saw one woman in particular, a fiery-tempered, black-haired 'breed with startling green eyes. Ah, yes, Raven. She who had escaped. But she was only a woman, unimportant. Just one woman.

What could she do?

Chapter Eighteen

Raven O'Keefe had never thought about dying until now, on this rain-washed afternoon, when she came stumbling out of the shadows of the stately oaks lining the banks of flood-swollen Turkey Creek, a tributary of the Coosa River. Raven gingerly hobbled to the water's edge. She had twisted her ankle earlier in the day but had continued on in a desperate effort to reach Hope Station. The settlers there were on good terms with the Choctaw, and she could count on sanctuary within the station's stockade.

All that had changed now, and her hopes faded as she hobbled out onto the creek's sandy bank. For almost an hour Wolf Jacket and Little Badger had played cat and mouse with their quarry, herding Raven with well-placed shots that sent her stumbling through the rain toward the impassable creek.

Healthy, with two strong ankles, she could have easily outdistanced her enemies. Hampered as she was with her injured ankle, Raven was soon at the mercy of the Red Sticks. As she paused, a gun fired off to her right, shattering a nearby limb. She slipped and slid down the mud-slickened walls of a ravine. Another gunshot, and a geyser erupted from the rain-covered ground barely inches from her leg as a slug carved a furrow in the earth.

Toying with her, yes, and driving her on, wearing her down until the woman stumbled out of the trees and staggered toward Turkey Creek. With Hope Station just another couple of miles away, all Raven had to do was ford the creek and follow a deer trail east through the trees for another hour at the most and she'd be safe. She'd have a place to rest and recuperate before setting out to find her father and the other warriors he had taken with him to the council houses of the Cherokee.

Raven's hopes faded as she stared at the torrent that blocked her path. There was no crossing Turkey Creek until the flooding subsided. To attempt such a crossing was akin to suicide. And yet, such a death might be preferable to capture.

She stared at the raging waters where once a placid stream had gently ambled among the emerald hills, and in that moment rejected self-sacrifice even as Wolf Jacket stepped out from beneath the draping branches of a willow. He parted a leafy curtain and approached his cornered captive.

Raven knelt and scooped up a chunk of shale bigger than her fist. Wolf Jacket snapped off a shot and blasted the rock from her grasp. She half spun and cradled her arm and numb fingers. Then the woman faced him again. Hurting, yet undaunted. Wolf Jacket didn't bother to reload. He tossed aside his rifled musket and pulled a tomahawk from his beaded belt. Rain had begun to mottle his war paint, transforming his features into an even more grotesque mask. He held out the weapon he had taken from the lifeless body of his friend Yellow Knife, the warrior Raven had killed.

"You have tried me, mixed-blood," Wolf Jacket said. "But the chase is ended. And I have won." He warily approached. "First I will take you; then I will bring your head to my village, to hang about the walls of our council house."

He unslung his powder horn and shot pouch, the better to free his limbs for action. The tomahawk was all the weapon he needed now. Let her struggle. Ah, yes, he wanted her to struggle. It made the inevitable all the sweeter.

Raven flexed her fingers and tried to shake some feeling back into her hand and arm. Her black hair was plastered to her skull and neck and shoulders. Droplets of rainwater mixed with sweat stung her eyes.

She made a feint as if trying to bolt past him on the left side, then altered her course and tried for the right, but the footing proved too treacherous and her strained muscles weren't up to the feat. She slipped and fell to one knee before the Red Stick chief, and like a cat she rose with bared claws, her hands ready to tear into Wolf Jacket with the last of her strength.

He retreated a step and reconsidered his intentions, deciding the woman had become more trouble than she was worth. He raised the tomahawk and prepared to strike. A rifle barked from back up the wall of the ravine and the tomahawk exploded in half as a lead slug shattered the wooden shaft. The iron blade plopped into the racing brown waters of the creek.

Wolf Jacket spun around and reached for his rifled musket, then remembered it was empty. He had needlessly shot the rock from Raven's hand. He glared up at his assailant. The Red Stick's look of surprise mirrored Raven's own startled expression. She had been seconds from death. Now, one accurately placed slug from a Pennsylvania rifle had won her a reprieve.

On the slope overlooking the creek bank, fifty feet from the edge of the floodwaters, Kit McQueen steadied his dun mare and returned his smoking rifle to its beaded buckskin scabbard. He had heard the gunfire on his way to Hope Station and tracked the shots to Turkey Creek. He'd spied the Choctaw woman and watched in admiration as she attempted to face down the Red Stick warrior.

Kit had reacted on instinct and didn't regret his actions one bit, though he had undoubtedly made a mortal enemy of the Creek.

Wolf Jacket started toward his rifled musket, figuring to reach the weapon and load it before the white man could ready his own gun.

"I wouldn't," Kit said. His eyes were shadows beneath his broad-brimmed hat. But Kit's voice was strong and filled with warning.

Wolf Jacket stopped and peered around at the man on horseback. To his dismay he noted the flintlock pistol Kit held. Where had the white man come from? Was he one of the spirits of the dead? But the pistol he held was real enough. And the man had already proved himself Wolf Jacket's equal with a gun.

The warrior's mind raced through his options. There weren't all that many. He could try a bluff, stall for time until Little Badger arrived. Or he could run like a bear with a swarm of bees at his tail.

"White-skinned fool," Wolf Jacket called out in Kit's own tongue. "Know that I'm Wolf Jacket, chief of the Red Sticks, the people of war. Run while you can. Flee to the safety of the northlands, where your people are many. Leave the land of the Creeks, or you will die."

"I'm called Kit McQueen. And you, sir, have wasted your chance," Kit replied laconically. He gestured toward the Indian's discharged weapon. "Bold words won't buy you another. Call me a fool, eh? Why, I've eaten boiled mush with more brains than you show." Kit cocked the "Quaker" he had pulled from his belt. So much for options. Wolf Jacket spun on his heels, dove into the raging waters of Turkey Creek, and was instantly borne away on the onrushing brown current.

Raven watched, open-mouthed, as Wolf Jacket was swept out of sight around the bend, beyond a hillock covered with hickory and oak. He was gone, the danger momentarily past. But Raven had the feeling she'd not seen the last of the Red Stick. He was a dark and dangerous man, larger than life; his deeds were spoken of in the camps of his enemies. Such a man was born to die in battle. She did not think even the raging waters could kill him.

Kit dismounted and led the dun mare down the incline to the mud-slick creek bank. When Raven turned to face him, her comely features took his breath away. All the other women he had known, from the ballrooms of Philadelphia to the harem halls of Araby, paled before this mixed-blood lass.

Raven brushed a strand of her lustrous black hair away from the corner of her mouth. Her startling green eyes had a luminescence all their own, sparkling like twin emeralds, filled with daring and mirroring a wild, free spirit.

Kit puffed out his muscular chest, threw back his shoulders, and swaggered up to the young Choctaw woman, who continued to study him, her features filled with curiosity. Kit knew he was probably behaving like an idiot. But by heaven, she left him feeling utterly inadequate. He was forced to rely on pretense.

"Well, then, my darlin'," he began in English. "Yours is the prettiest life I've saved all day." He slapped the barrel of his pistol against the palm of his left hand. "What say you?" he asked with a wink. He wasn't prepared for what came next.

One moment Raven was hesitant, suspicious, edging back toward the floodwaters that had blocked her escape. Suddenly her wary expression was transformed into a look of alarm, and she dove forward into Kit and knocked him off his feet, slamming him back into the muddy bank. She landed on top of him, knocking the breath from his lungs.

A gunshot sounded barely a second later, and a lead slug whined through the space where he had been standing.

"Hey!" he gasped, and worked his arm free as she rolled aside. It took him a moment to realize what had happened then he twisted around to face his attacker. Little Badger stood about twenty feet away. The warrior had just worked his way through a stand of dense timber and undergrowth now threatened by high water as the creek was a good six feet out of its banks. The warrior had seen Wolf Jacket's desperate attempt at escape and was determined to avenge the possible death of his chief. But his first shot had missed, thanks to the cursed half-breed woman. It was a race with death to chance another. His fury gave him the foolish courage to try. The young warrior pulled the plug from his powder horn with his teeth and poured a charge of gunpowder down the shortened barrel of his rifled musket.

Kit rose up on one knee and raised his pistol,

sighting the heavy octagonal barrel on the Red Stick's chest.

"Drop your gun," Kit said in English, and then repeated the command in broken Choctaw, which the young warrior understood.

Little Badger did not even bother to patch the rifle ball as he rammed it home. Speed was more important now.

"Drop it, I say," Kit repeated. Trying to catch his breath made his gun hand waver. He sucked in, held the air, slowly released it.

The Creek warrior never slowed or wavered. He tapped a trace of black powder in the pan, cocked the weapon, and Kit shot him. The "Quaker" boomed like a hand cannon, and the impact of the slug sent the Red Stick flying backward, smashing him against the trunk of a hickory and dropping him as broken as a cast-off puppet. He fired his rifle on the way down, blasting a hole in the rain-soaked sod. The gunshot echoed, following the distant, dying reverberation of the pistol shot. The warrior made a horrible noise, that of a man struggling for air, for life. He shoved himself off the ground. Blood dripped from his mangled chest and mingled with the mud beneath, forming a puddle the color of burned gravy. Then Little Badger's strong arms failed him, and he settled back to earth and lay still.

Kit scrambled to his feet and quickly reloaded his flintlock pistol. Cockiness had come near to costing him his life. He studied the creek bank, both sides going and coming, and then gingerly approached the dead warrior. He knelt and pried loose the man's grip from the rifled musket. He hefted the weapon and studied the buttplate. It was only a moment before he realized he was holding a British-made firearm.

"And I'll just bet the other one is exactly the

same," Kit muttered, and, putting the first weapon down, turned to examine the weapon Wolf Jacket had dropped.

Raven picked up Little Badger's rifled musket, steadied the weapon in her hands, and aimed it directly at Kit's midriff. Kit froze. The Red Stick's weapon he held was useless, and his own brace of pistols were tucked in his belt.

The Choctaw woman cautiously advanced on the white man until her rifled musket almost touched his chest. Then she raised the weapon and placed the muzzle to Kit's forehead.

"I was hoping the Choctaw were still a people of honor," Kit spoke in the woman's own tongue.

Lifting the gun's barrel, Raven tilted back Kit's hat, revealing his thickly curled, shaggy red mane. Her green eyes widened with renewed interest.

"You do...uh...speak the language of your people?" Kit asked, struggling with the dialect.

Raven stepped back and appraised the man standing before her. The she stunned him as she finally spoke.

"Well and again, my darlin'," she said. For all her Indian attire, the lilting tone of an Irish-bred lass rolled off her tongue. "And yours is the prettiest life I've saved all day!"

Chapter Nineteen

Wolf Jacket should have died there in the raging current: crushed by an uprooted hickory tree, smashed to lifeless ruin against shale outcroppings, or skewered on a mass of bristling roots that thrust out of the riverbank like dragon's teeth—he should have died.

A couple hundred yards down from where he had leaped into the creek, the sodden warrior struggled out of the churning brown waters. He had caught hold of a low-hanging oak branch and hauled himself hand over fist from the flooding creek. Once clear of the water he had managed to swing over to the bank, drop to safety, and then dig into the mud to keep himself from sliding back into the creek.

Bruised and battered, he crawled up the rain-slick bank. He vomited up the silty contents of his stomach, and when the spasms had ended, the Creek forced his arms and legs to dig into the soft earth and propel him farther from the water's edge, crawl a yard, slide back a foot, scramble forward another few feet, alive because he had willed it, alive because the spirit of the water had tossed him back, alive because he had already mingled his blood with the waters of these ancient hills, bursting with foliage in the brief, sweet days before autumn.

A fine mist began to fall, then the low, heavy clouds loosed their burden as they drifted up and over the rolling foothills and steeper ridges of the Smoky Mountains. Wolf Jacket rolled over on his back and allowed the droplets to wash his torso. With outstretched arms he lay still, as if asleep or dead. But he was neither. The warrior was merely allowing the steady downpour to soothe and massage his weary limbs and get the blood circulating again.

At last he stood, climbed the few remaining feet, and lost himself in the forest. There was nothing to mark his passing save a furrow in the green earth and a trace of war paint. His features might be washed clean, but his heart was still filled with rage. He could do nothing but vent his anger on the uncaring timber and the lowering sky. When that was spent, Wolf Jacket started south to rejoin the war party he had abandoned to pursue the half-breed daughter of Iron Hand O'Keefe. Failure did not sit easy with him. But he was alive. And he would make a sacred offering to the Above Ones that one day he would again cross paths with the white man who called himself Kit McQueen.

Chapter Twenty

The Alabama sky melted down around the blackened remnants of Hope Station. The stockade walls lay in ruins, although here and there a single charred wood post thrust upward from the rubble. The blockhouse had caved in on itself about the base of a stone chimney, set square in the center of destruction like a headstone for this place of death.

As for the dead, the ravens and scavenging red wolves had had their day, feasting on the burned and butchered inhabitants. Beneath the droning rain, bones and blood and soot and mud mingled, formed pools and rivulets to catch more of the sky's steady tears. If the dead defied identification in their present state, not so their killers. Kit spied a tomahawk whose shaft bore the Turtle Clan markings of the Choctaw. He noticed another buried deep in the remains of a post. A flintlock rifle also lay nearby. The Turtle Clan markings were burned into the weapon's walnut stock. Yes, the perpetrators of this tragedy had been careless in what they had left behind—careless, or cunning as a fox.

"I feared this," Raven said solemnly, drawing up alongside Kit. "One of the Creeks guarding me wore a tall, black hat with a blue feather in the crown. I recognized it. I had seen Jonas Talbot wear it many times. But I hoped the Red Sticks had taken it from his homestead and that the station was safe."

Kit and Raven stood just inside the stockade, where the gate would have been. Perhaps the Red Sticks had tricked their way inside the stockade. Or maybe they had stormed the walls and overpowered the defenders by sheer weight of numbers. The reasons didn't matter now—not to the dead, nor to the watchers in the rain.

The dun was eager to be away from this grim and silent place. The overpowering stench of death had alerted the animal and made the mare skittish as a colt.

Kit shared the dun's sentiments. He hadn't the time or strength to dig all the graves that were necessary. And there was no one but the girl to hear a parting prayer. Kit spoke the words in his mind and sent the souls of the deceased on their way.

The woman at his side began to chant softly in a melodious voice:

> "We are gone.
> We have become people of shadows.
> The Grandfather Above has built a fire
> in his lodge. We are gone.
> And enter into the warmth."

Kit reappraised the woman, marveling at how quickly she shed her father's culture and became as a full-blood Choctaw. It was an appealing combination, one that left him unsettled yet awakened his interest. He swung around and faced her. Then, without speaking, they both turned as one and quit the burned-out remains of Hope Station.

"We need to get out of this rain," Kit muttered, slogging back toward the forest.

"I know a place," Raven said, and gestured toward an area of the forest where the timber thinned and an outcropping of shale formed a shallow cave that would provide a serviceable shelter from the elements.

Kit was in a hurry. He remounted his horse and offered a hand to Raven, who hesitated, then shrugged and allowed Kit to haul her up behind him. The heat of her body passed through her water-soaked garment and warmed his back. Kit, trying to keep his mind on the business of survival, pointed the dun toward the thinning trees but kept the mare to a walk.

He might be drenched to the bone, but he wasn't crazy. After the grisly discovery he had made, the touch of Raven's hand, her warmth, the flutter of her breath on the back of his neck offered some small balance to the horror.

They rode away then from Hope Station and did not look back.

Rain singing to the ground, a lovely sound, drop by drop in the dark. Who can tell them apart? Who can capture the wind or ride the thunder or hold the last days of summer in his hands and steal time or reel in the past like a ship hoisting its anchor and preparing to sail? Some things are unattainable.

Rainstorms brought out Kit's pensive nature. It had been a day filled with discovery and death. Kit leaned on his flintlock rifle and stood near the lip of the overhang ledge beneath which he and Raven O'Keefe had built a fire to dry themselves out and capture a little warmth. The ledge was large enough to accommodate the man and woman at one end and still provide shelter from the elements for the dun mare ground-tethered a few yards away.

Kit stared out into the dark. Hope Station was hidden in the blackness of the forest, and it was just as well. Let the earth accept its dead, let them nurture the soil, and in the spring let wildflowers grow where ashes have been.

He turned back and found Raven watching him. There had been little time for talk—what with gathering enough dry wood for a fire and scouting the surrounding countryside for any of Wolf Jacket's friends. He held out his hands to the blaze.

Raven spooned boiled meat into a wooden bowl for Kit and helped herself to an equal portion.

No dainty eater here, Kit noted with amusement, comparing the Choctaw woman to the ladies in Philadelphia he had known. Raven ate with gusto, relishing each bite. Her wooden spoon clattered on the sides of the bowl as she scooped the broth into her mouth. Her appetite was going to make some serious inroads into his supply of jerked venison.

If they didn't find Iron Hand O'Keefe in a couple of days, Kit would have to restock his saddlebags with fresh game. Still, it pleased him to watch her. She seemed so open and honest and free of any pretense. Most women would have been numb from undergoing such an ordeal as had almost claimed her life.

They passed the meal in silence. Raven finished first, looked longingly at the remaining few morsels of meat in Kit's cook pot, and when the man nodded his go-ahead she helped herself to seconds and quickly finished the last of the food. Only with her hunger appeased did she become self-conscious of how quickly she had devoured her meal.

"My father has always said that hunger is the best seasoning," Raven told the man sitting alongside her. "Never has deer meat tasted better." She dabbed sheepishly at her mouth with the sleeve of her buckskin shirtdress. She settled back against the shale wall, which radiated the warmth of the campfire.

Talons of gray smoke curled over the rock shelf to dissipate in the singing downpour.

"It was raining like this the morning Wolf Jacket raided our village," Raven said, her smile fading as her thoughts drifted to the past. "My father and most of the men had gone to the village of the Cherokees to decide what to do about the white soldiers preparing to make war on us. The Creeks to the south. Colonel Jackson's Volunteers to the north. Wolf Jacket planned his raid well. Though a few escaped, many were captured. The old ones were killed outright." She lowered her gaze to the flames, and her eyes smoldered with green fire. "Wolf Jacket has had his day. But we will have ours."

"Of that I have no doubt," Kit said. He set aside his empty bowl, filled two blue tin enamel cups with strong black tea, and handed one cup to the Choctaw. "Here, Fire-seeker."

Raven glanced up, surprised by Kit's knowledge.

"So you know why the Raven's wings are black?" the woman asked.

"In the early days the Father Above hid fire in the heart of a hollow sycamore," Kit said. "Raven discovered the hiding place and crawled down into the tree. She retrieved the fire and brought it back for the world to have. But her beautiful plumage was burned black by the flames."

"Poor Raven." A smile tugged at the corners of her mouth.

"Not so," Kit countered. "Raven showed she had courage. And goodness. Her dark wings mark the beauty within and without. And men still sing of her deeds and tell her story about their sacred campfires."

Raven lowered her head and looked out past the veil of her long hair. Her voice was silken soft as she spoke. "And what of Kit McQueen? Is there one to sing of his deeds?"

"Maybe," Kit replied gently, his thoughts drifting back to a little girl and how she stood in the center of the road and watched her uncle ride out of her life. She had bravely managed not to shed one tear, but had raised her hand to wave good-bye.

Good-bye. I will never forget you. I will always love you, Uncle Kit. Good-bye.

He wiped a hand across his face and blinked the memories from his mind's eye, returning his thoughts to the present, where there was beauty and danger enough for this man's life. "But the song is long ago and far away."

He yawned and stretched his legs toward the comfortable blaze Raven had built. Then he snuggled down in his blanket. Raven shivered in her damp clothes and slid over toward Kit. Commandeering the left side of his bedroll, she reclined beside the white man.

Kit studied her a moment, appraising her actions. She had moved, not out of passion but practicality. He understood and pulled the other blanket up to Raven's shoulders and lay back, listening to the pattering chorus of the rain and the quiet, steady rhythm of her gentle breath. They were both sweet music to his ears.

Kit closed his eyes and let the downpour lull him into a deep sleep that lasted well into morning.

He took no notice when the rain ceased.

He was oblivious to the sunrise.

He never heard the heavily armed, war-painted men as they circled the shale overhang to cut off escape and then cautiously closed in for the kill.

Chapter Twenty-one

"The only reason I don't shoot you outright," Iron Hand O'Keefe said as he cocked his big .56-caliber rifle, "is 'cause maybe I've misread what looks to have happened here!" He centered the weapon on Kit's spine. Kit's eyes popped open. He was turned toward Raven and had his right arm draped across the woman where she lay against him. Sunlight glimmered off the rock walls.

It took him a moment to recognize the voice. Presuming on the mercy of an old friendship, Kit slowly rolled over and sat up to face the war chief of the Choctaws.

"You'd finish what the Spaniards tried to do back in Florida?" Kit asked.

Iron Hand O'Keefe brightened and retreated a step. "Well, kiss the Blarney Stone, if it ain't Kit McQueen!" O'Keefe grinned and started to lower his rifle, then snapped it up again. "See here. What be you doin' with my daughter?"

Then he softened as Raven got up and came to

him. A look of relief washed over his features as he hugged her.

"Oh, father, can't you see we were both hiding from the Red Sticks?" Raven said. "This white eyes needed protection, so I kept him with me."

O'Keefe looked anxious for a fight. The Irishman and his war-painted followers wanted their people back. And they wanted revenge.

"A hunting party of Cherokees brought us word that the Creeks had crossed the Tallapoosa and were raiding north. I figured they'd hit our village." O'Keefe turned and looked off in the direction of Hope Station hidden beyond the wooden hillside. "We tried to cut them off." O'Keefe kicked at a rock and sent the stone rolling downslope. "We failed."

Using his forearm, the Irishman brushed his shaggy, silver hair back from his face, taking care not to gouge his face with his iron hook. He tapped the hook against the horn dangling from the braided hair rope he wore around his throat. "I'll not sound my horn again until I see Wolf Jacket dead before me on the ground."

Kit searched the red-skinned faces of the warriors surrounding him. They wore their hair long, unbraided, and unadorned like their buckskin shirts and leggings. Their faces were streaked with the white and red markings of war. Kit noticed that the men were haphazardly armed. Some carried Pennsylvania rifles, long-barreled trade guns that had no doubt seen action during the American Revolution. A few of the warriors carried muskets, also left over from the glory days of the Continental Army. The rest brandished bows and knives and tomahawks. There wasn't a British-made weapon in the bunch.

These were hard and implacable fighters, who

once wronged would not rest until they had exacted vengeance for the misdeeds of their enemies. Kit had no trouble reading the determination in the eyes of such men. Hatred was an emotion he knew only too well.

"We are to gather at Willow Creek by the night of the first full moon. Then my Choctaws will hold council and decide what course of action to take." Iron Hand related his decision to the men around him, who responded enthusiastically to their war chief. Kit managed to understand just enough of the Irishman's instructions to know that O'Keefe had told his followers Kit was a friend and was to be trusted...up to a point.

Another five heavily armed warriors emerged from the woods behind the shale outcropping. The man in the lead stopped short in surprise. He was a stocky, round-faced individual, who after recognizing the white man hurried forward to join O'Keefe and his daughter and stand proudly before Kit.

"Young Otter!" Kit said.

"Kit McQueen! So the white man's world could not hold you," Young Otter replied. "Have you also come to make war on us, as the white soldiers to the north prepare to do?"

Young Otter's question hung poised in the air, unanswered. O'Keefe noted Kit's lack of response. Kit turned to the Irishman.

"We must talk, Iron Hand, and before the first full moon."

O'Keefe said, "Tonight, then, when we make camp. You can have your say. We'll hold our own council, eh, lad?"

"The sooner the better."

O'Keefe motioned for the men to follow him and

then looked at his daughter. "I'll have a couple of men escort you to the village of the Cherokees."

"I will not go," Raven stated flatly.

"What's this?" the Irishman glowered. But his daughter refused to be cowed. O'Keefe glanced sheepishly at the Choctaws around him, many of whom were old friends and bemused by his daughter's obstinacy. Raven's stubborn ways were often the talk of the village; but then, so was her courage. Iron Hand O'Keefe took the young woman aside. "Now, see here—"

"I am as good a shot as any man." Raven patted the rifled musket she held. "And I shall have my own revenge against the Creeks. The spirits of those I saw murdered demand this of me."

O'Keefe shook his head and snatched at his beard with his hook hand. He sighed, a sign of grudging acquiescence. "If your dear mother were alive—"

"Star Basket would tell me to follow the path of my destiny," Raven concluded.

Ah then she had him. Images of the charred remains of the Choctaw village flooded the Irishman's thoughts. The sight of such ruin, the ground littered with the bodies of the aged ones and the young warriors who had been killed defending their home ground, the blackened wreckage of the longhouses, Raven's capture, all had left him sickened and filled with dread.

But she was alive and unharmed and with him. What father wouldn't want his daughter safe from the dangers that lay ahead? Yet her words were weighted with a truth he might once have been able to deny as a lad of County Kerry—but he was a Choctaw now. He was Iron Hand. And only a fool ignored the spirits of those who had gone above.

"Come," he said to her, and started off toward the forested hills that crinkled the southern horizon.

Kit caught up the reins of his dun mare and walked up beside O'Keefe's daughter as she fell into step behind her father.

Chapter Twenty-two

Fireflies whirled and darted like a spiral of exploding stars that burned bright and winked out, only to be reborn elsewhere in the deepening shadows of the forest. Raven leaned against the trunk of a white oak and watched a red-bellied woodpecker tap-tap-tap out a cadence in his unceasing search for food. Elsewhere among the branches, a trio of gray squirrels quarreled over rights to a cluster of acorns. Eventually the threesome began a series of feints, chittering insults, and guarded attacks that soon became a madcap chase among the spreading branches of the oak and carried over to a shagbark hickory. The combatants disturbed a nesting of scarlet tanagers that swarmed into the air with a wild *chip-chiree, chip-chiree* that lingered on the breeze long after the birds themselves were lost from sight.

O'Keefe's daughter glanced over her shoulder at the campsite he had chosen to spend the night. It had been a tiring day.

O'Keefe had led his men on an irregular course

that criss-crossed the hills and cut across ever-winding valley and hollow. By late afternoon, they had met up with another party of Choctaw warriors whom Iron Hand had sent off to the west. These new arrivals brought eight children, Choctaw boys and girls from eight to twelve years of age who had eluded capture.

There had been much celebration as some of the children were reunited with their fathers. Though a great and terrible challenge lay ahead, at least these children were safe. In the morning the boys and girls would be sent with an escort back to the Cherokee village. Once again Iron Hand had hinted at the notion of sending his daughter along with the children. Raven had walked out of camp, refusing to hear of such a thing.

She returned her attention to the deer trail faintly visible among the trees. She started along the path and disappeared among the tall timber. About twenty-five yards from camp she located a small spring bubbling out of the ground, a pond no larger than six feet across. The cool, sweet-tasting water was ringed with animal tracks. A fawn darted into the brush as Raven stepped around a tree and out onto the trampled leaves and grass. Removing her shirt she knelt by the spring and cupped the cold water to her breasts. When she had washed, the young woman redressed and settled back on her heels.

A twig snapped, announcing Kit's presence. From the look on his face Raven suspected the man with the flame-red hair might have been standing back in the woods watching her.

He seemed to read her thoughts but wasn't about to admit his guilt. Yes, Kit had stood off among the shadows, uncertain whether or not he should intrude on the young woman's privacy. Then Raven had partly disrobed and he had done the gentlemanly thing . . . and *slowly* turned away. *My God,* he had thought, *it's like stumbling upon Eve in Paradise.* The sight of her left him breathless.

Now that he stood before her, damned if he wasn't as tongue-tied as a schoolboy at a church social. He doffed his broad-brimmed hat and knelt by the spring. "Pardon me. I thought I'd just fill my water flask."

"But you don't have it with you," Raven told him. Her sharp eyes missed nothing. And she was not about to let him off the hook. It amused her to see this cocky intruder wriggle in discomfort.

"I must have left it on my horse," Kit offered lamely.

"Then drink of the living water while you can," Raven said. "For you will not be able to carry it with you when we leave."

Raven stood and skirted the edge of the pool as she drank. Her limp was less pronounced now. She had ridden the dun mare throughout the day and her ankle was rested.

"I am grateful for the use of your horse today," she said, drawing up alongside Kit.

Kit straightened and stood. "The animal is yours for as long as you wish."

"A generous gift," Raven replied. "But mine are a proud people. We always reciprocate, worth for worth. Now, what could I give you in return?" A faint smile touched her lips. Her striking green eyes seemed to twinkle like twin stars.

Kit gulped and was about to make a suggestion when Iron Hand O'Keefe barged into the clearing, noticed how close Kit and his daughter were standing, and shattered the idyllic moment with a brusque clearing of his throat, a noise as melodic as a toppling tree.

"Well, bless my soul, the resiliency of youth. Even in the face of tragedy and bloodshed the young find time to sneak off together!"

Kit jumped back, color in his cheeks. Even Raven seemed to be caught off guard, but she handled it better than Kit. Then again, being headstrong and unhampered by propriety, she felt no need to defend her behavior. This gallant, flustered stranger awakened her interest, and she wasn't ashamed to admit it.

Raven wasn't blind, however. She could read the look in her father's eyes and knew he wanted to talk with Kit and wanted to talk alone. The young woman held her ground. O'Keefe fixed the girl in a stare as icy as the spring-fed pond, but it failed to dent her resolve.

"By heaven, lass, you've too much of your father in you," the Irishman muttered. He shrugged and waved a hand toward the trees and Young Otter joined them, along with Stalking Fox, who had been among the new arrivals, and a powerfully built older warrior named Abram, who had been baptized by a missionary up on the Tennessee. The aroma of roasting venison trailed the men out of the woods along with the noise of playing children.

"We will hold our council here, and you may stay and listen, daughter, but try to keep that tongue of yours still for once."

Kit hooked his thumbs in his belt while the other warriors slaked their thirst at the spring. O'Keefe lit a pipe. Stalking Fox, who also recognized the white man, had made no overture toward Kit. He did not give his trust so easily as Young Otter, whom he considered a foolish man.

"All right, McQueen." O'Keefe puffed on his pipe as the other men squatted in the trampled grass a couple of yards from the water's edge. The glade was not large enough to accommodate the entire war party, but it would do for this council. "Now, tell me why you've come to our hunting lands."

Another man might have lied, fearing to turn friends into potential enemies. But Kit McQueen owed Iron Hand O'Keefe his life. More than that, he owed him the truth.

"I am a lieutenant in the army of the United States," Kit answered. "And I have been sent to bring you back a prisoner or see you dead."

Stalking Fox reached for his tomahawk. The other warriors stiffened at Kit's reply. Iron Hand O'Keefe nodded sagely and continued to smoke his pipe as if nothing had happened. He exhaled a cloud of smoke that billowed between him and the red-haired officer.

"That may be easier said than done. But may I ask why?" The Irishman looked up at Kit. The younger man had made no move toward his pistols. There was obviously something more to what the lieutenant had to say.

Kit ignored Stalking Fox's open hostility and knelt by O'Keefe.

"The army thinks the Choctaw have allied themselves with the British and are responsible along with the Creeks for these attacks on the Alabama and Tennessee settlements. Even now Andrew Jackson is in Nashville putting together a force of militia. When he's ready, Jackson will head south to wage war against the tribes he thinks are working for the British."

"Working for the British? Me!" O'Keefe exclaimed. He held up his hook. "They took me away from home and hearth! They cost me my youth and my good left hand." The Irishman snorted in disgust.

"That's why I'm here," Kit said. "I came to warn

you. And to find out for myself just who is supplying the Red Sticks with their weapons.''

Iron Hand O'Keefe sized up the smaller man. He had to like Kit, for his courage and his brash resolve. But before O'Keefe could ask just how the lieutenant planned to accomplish all this, Raven interrupted them, for she too had information to share.

"The *Alejandro*," she said.

The men all turned to her, wondering why a young woman would speak in council.

"Wolf Jacket is expecting to rendezvous with a boat called the *Alejandro* where the Tallapoosa joins the Alabama. I heard him brag about the many guns he would receive, enough for every Red Stick who follows him."

Kit smacked his fist into his open palm. His eyes burned with excitement. "Well done!" he exclaimed. She beamed at his compliment. Kit squatted alongside O'Keefe. "I'll beat the Creeks to their rendezvous if I can by heading downriver. All I have to do is find the boat, sneak aboard, and capture the British agent."

"Is that all?" O'Keefe grunted. "That ought to be a romp in the tulips for a fire rocket like yourself. Maybe I'll send a few of my men along just in case you need help."

"They might come in handy." Kit grinned. "I'm unfamiliar with the country along the Alabama."

"I know the way," Raven spoke up.

O'Keefe puffed himself up. "Now, see here, daughter—" he sputtered.

"None of the other warriors here have traveled the length of the Alabama," Raven explained to her father. "Only you and I. And you must gather our people at Willow Creek. That leaves me."

"I should never have taken you to Mobile," O'Keefe

said with a sorrowful wag of his head. He glanced at Kit. "I just figured to give her a taste of civilized culture and such." He emptied his pipe, tapping it against his hook. Then he tucked the pipe back in his possibles bag, a leather pouch that held flint, lead balls, patches, and his pipe and tobacco.

"I don't know..." Kit began.

"That's right," Raven said. "But I do. I remember the way. There are marshes and swamp farther south. A person could easily get lost."

"I also shall go," Young Otter blurted out. He was eager for adventure. Kit turned and clapped Stalking Fox on the shoulder. "Join us, my brother?"

The dour-looking warrior fixed his brooding gaze on the white man. His features were dark with mistrust, his brows knotted in a frown. Then he nodded in agreement, but the look on his face made it clear he was going along more to keep an eye on Kit than to raid a riverboat.

Kit didn't give a damn how the man felt toward him as long as Stalking Fox knew which way to point his rifle in a fight.

"So be it," Iron Hand O'Keefe said. He held out his hand to Kit, who clasped it firmly. "I'll gather my Choctaws and keep clear of Colonel Jackson and his volunteers. For as long as I can." The Irishman frowned, and his voice took on a tone of warning. "But there is bloody war a'coming, lad. And we might yet find ourselves staring at each other through smoke."

Chapter Twenty-three

Miles to the north of the Choctaw hunting grounds—just outside the settlement of Nashville in the Tennessee country—an army of militia had settled in along the banks of Fox Creek. Choosing an abandoned farmsite on land recently purchased by their commander, more than a thousand volunteers had erected makeshift shelters, log cabins, and tents. They impatiently bided their time, enduring days of boredom and inactivity while more frontiersmen and farmers came into camp, eager to join up with General Andy Jackson and wipe out the marauding savages down in Alabama Territory once and for all.

Dominating the center of the encampment was a ramshackle farmhouse whose log walls were in dire need of rechinking before the winter winds began to blow. Andrew Jackson had commandeered the house for his headquarters.

This afternoon in early September found him reclined upon a daybed that his orderlies had brought out on the front porch. From this vantage point he oversaw the encampment, issued necessary orders, settled disputes between the rough-hewn woodsmen gathered in the meadow, and endured a bout of dysentery and the recurring pain of an old wound. A pistol ball was lodged in his side, the legacy of his most recent duel. The nagging pain had put him in a foul mood.

He'd tried to shift his thoughts and concentrate on something else, like his dear wife Rachel, waiting for him back at the Hermitage. He missed her more than he thought possible.

A horseman riding at a fast clip through the encampment caught the general's attention. He shaded his eyes and at last recognized Captain Marcus Bellamy. Being born in the "Garden of the Waxhaws" in South Carolina, the same as Jackson, had ensured young Bellamy a place of rank in this army of volunteers. The captain kept his horse at a gallop through the camp, skirting breakfast cook fires and cabins and tents and leaping a makeshift barricade of barrels to the cheers of a trio of buckskin-clad hardcases. They waved to the horseman as he dashed past.

It was obvious that Bellamy was bound for the farmhouse. There wasn't a militiaman who envied the captain, for it was common knowledge that General Jackson was in an especially ugly mood, what with his poor appetite and the nagging discomfort of his wound.

Bellamy halted his charger in the shade of the farmhouse, leaped down from the saddle, and slipped to his knees in the dirt. He cursed and dusted off his blue woolen trousers, then straightened his short-waisted jacket and adjusted his leather cap.

"A poor dismount, Marcus," a voice from the porch admonished.

Bellamy's cheeks reddened, but undaunted by the criticism he hurried up onto the porch. The captain

was proud of his uniform and his ranking, though both
had been earned not by deeds but by a happenstance
of birth. Bellamy was certain he would prove his
mettle on the field of battle, given the opportunity.

"General Jackson, I have come from Nashville!"

Jackson raised up on his elbows and stared at the
officer he had created. The general was a tall, gaunt
man with a bold, unyielding gaze burning from his
sallow features. His hair was silver and unkempt. But
his voice was steady and cut the air like a whip crack.

"All the way from Nashville, you say? By heaven,
Marcus, you *have* had a trip. Let me stir myself from
this chair and let you rest your weary bones."

Jackson swung his long legs around and sat upright.
But instead of continuing his charade he poured himself
another brandy and managed a tentative sip. "Must be
nigh on to five miles." He took a corncob pipe off the
table and clamped the stem between his teeth. A few
strikes from his tinder box, and the tobacco was lit.

Bellamy ignored the commander's caustic sense of
humor. He reached inside his coat and brought out a
leather packet.

"A dispatch. I encountered the rider in Nashville
while procuring supplies for the camp. I left the wag-
ons to make their way at their own speed and hurried
this along to you." Bellamy held up the packet. His
boyish features beamed with excitement. "It is from
Colonel Gain Harrelson of the United States Army. Perhaps these are the commissions we have been hoping
for." A captain of volunteers was not nearly as prestigious as a rank recognized by the War Office of the
federal government. Jackson frowned at the captain's
implication that the commander of the Tennessee Volunteers was in any way anxious to be commissioned. In
truth he was, but damned if he intended to show it.

"Well, hand it here, man. Hand it here," Jackson growled. Then as an afterthought he nodded toward the bottle on the table by the daybed. "Help yourself, if you've a mind to."

"Thank you, General," Bellamy exclaimed, and hurried to pour a drink before Jackson changed his mind.

The general's nature was often mercurial—fiery one instant, cordial and polite the next. A man never knew when he might step from the tulips into a beehive around the likes of Andrew Jackson.

The general opened his dispatch and positioned himself so that a ray of sunlight fell across the handwritten page. "What the . . . this dispatch should have reached here a month ago," Jackson complained.

Bellamy shrugged and continued to wait in respectful silence, hoping for good news yet uncertain whether he ought to inquire as to the contents.

Andrew Jackson slowly stood, one hand rubbing his abdomen as he continued to read. He walked to the edge of the porch and raised his hawk's eyes to the encampment, the meadow, and the blue hills beyond. He inhaled the aroma of frying salt pork and cornmeal mush and wondered how long it would be before he could eat again. Jackson seemed an irrevocably lonely man at this moment, an intense and solitary figure poised on the edge of greatness.

"By thunder, do they think me some journeyman who has never heard the war whoop of savages?" he blustered.

"Sir . . . uh . . . bad news?" Captain Bellamy inquired haltingly.

To the captain's relief, Jackson did not reproach him. Instead, he leaned against the pole supporting the porch roof and crumbled the dispatch in his hand.

"Colonel Harrelson has informed me that I can

expect one Lieutenant McQueen. Colonel Harrelson believes this upstart lieutenant can be of great help to me in making peace with that renegade white Choctaw Iron Hand O'Keefe. Make peace? I have gathered over a thousand men, furnished them with weapons and clothing paid for by myself. And yet, with such a superior force and my own considerable experience, I cannot hope to prevail without the aid of this...this...Lieutenant McQueen."

Bellamy gulped his brandy. The liquor flowed like a rivulet of fire down his throat. Warmth spread to his limbs. He glanced longingly at the bottle and licked the last drop from his glass. *No commission yet.* He sighed to himself.

"Well, General, this McQueen fellow must be quite the hotspur," Bellamy said.

Andrew Jackson glanced over his shoulder at his subordinate. "You are ever the optimist, Marcus."

Any day now he was expecting another hundred men from over in the Cumberland country. They'd come hungry and ready to fight. *They'll get their fill of sowbelly and savages before I'm through,* Jackson thought. He glanced at the dispatch crumpled in his fist. According to the date of this missive, Kit McQueen was overdue. The lieutenant should have arrived days ago. He swept the distant hills at a glance. General Andrew Jackson had a campaign to launch, and he wasn't about to wait for some lieutenant.

"Hrumph," Jackson grumbled. "Quite the hotspur, eh? Just where the hell is he?"

Chapter Twenty-four

Paddles rhythmically dipped into the muddy waters of the Alabama. The two dugouts shot forward, propelled by strong arms and backs and aided by the current of the river. Kit McQueen glanced over his shoulder at the woman seated at the stern of the craft that had carried them for the past three days toward a rendezvous with the mysterious riverboat, the *Alejandro*. Young Otter and Stalking Fox, in a dugout of their own, kept pace with Kit, keeping a few yards behind the lead boat.

Kit returned his attention to the river ahead. Raven used her paddle as a rudder and steered the boat around the obstacles she remembered, and where the river split occasionally to isolate a hillock of land and create an island of tangled greenery, she chose to cut across certain shallows, keeping in mind which short-cuts to take and which to avoid.

Kit trusted her judgment. After all, Raven had certainly been right about where Iron Hand had cached the dugouts and concealed them on a riverbank below the Coosa. It had taken almost a week to reach the boats. Rain had slowed their progress south of the hills, and twice they had almost blundered into Creek war parties.

Stalking Fox was of a volatile nature, and it had required a great deal of persuasion to keep him from attacking the Red Sticks, who outnumbered Kit's party by never less than three to one. Kit lauded the warrior's courage, but their mission was to locate the riverboat, not commit suicide in such a futile display of bravery. Young Otter understood and helped to keep his friend in line. There was a time for war and a time for vengeance, but this was a time for stealth.

River water splashed the back of Kit's neck, and he looked around and noticed Raven trying to suppress a grin. He dug his paddle below the surface of the river and sent a wave of water exploding over the rear of the boat. Raven stifled a scream and ducked forward, laughing as the water missed her by inches. They were traveling close to the west bank of the river. The shadows of the trees stretched across the glassy surface, reaching to join with the opposite bank and cloak the waterway in darkness.

The afternoon hours had passed swiftly on this fourth day of river travel. Arm muscles were growing accustomed to the stretch and pull of paddling—and after all, the river itself was doing most of the work. Returning upstream was going to be another story, and Kit didn't look forward to that.

Raven spotted a suitable inlet and steered the dugout toward a low, grassy bank where a natural barrier of fallen timber had collected enough silt to channel a fraction of the Alabama into a U-shaped cove fringed with a dense stand of cattails and, beyond them, a thicket of willow and oak to further conceal their campsite. The dugouts glided through the rushes. Kit leaped out of the boat as the bow slid up on the bank. Raven climbed over the stern and helped her partner haul the dugout halfway up the bank. Young Otter and Stalking Fox followed suit, though Stalking Fox slipped to his knees in the mud and muttered to himself.

Kit cradled his rifle in the crook of his arm and walked off from the river to enter the deepening shadows of the forest. His eyes ranged the timber, searching for any sign of intruders other than himself.

Blue jays darted among the trees and protested his presence. He sensed movement near his boots and glanced down in time to see a smoke-gray cottonmouth slither beneath a rotting branch and burrow beneath the leaves and underbrush carpeting the forest floor. Kit shivered. The damn snake must have been five feet long. A lethal, venomous killer on the hunt. And Kit had missed stepping on the reptile by a stride.

A breeze stirred the branches and set the limbs of the oaks swaying. The treetops were burnished gold by the slanting rays of the late afternoon sun. It was a world of fragile beauty and sudden death.

"All depends on where you stand," he said softly.

"And where do you stand?" Raven said, coming up the trail his footsteps had left in the soft earth.

The breeze tugged at her long black hair. She had braided one length and tied the end with a patch of tanned rabbit hide adorned with tiny amber shells. She carried a rifled musket and moved with an air of casual grace. She fixed the white man in her green-eyed stare.

"Stalking Fox does not trust you. He thinks your army will turn on us when you no longer need our help."

"I understand a man like Stalking Fox. He does not trust because he loves his people."

Raven scoffed—a brief, bitter laugh—and then continued what she had come to say. "Then you do not understand Stalking Fox at all. He does not trust because he has a great desire in his heart for me."

"I don't understand," Kit said.

"And he sees me in your dugout," Raven finished, and cocked her head, a wry, playful smile on her face.

"Oh, well, I suppose I could..." Kit was about to suggest he change dugouts and partner with Young Otter. But the words wouldn't come. He enjoyed her company and wasn't about to exchange it for some stocky Choctaw warrior, even one as good-natured as Young Otter. "I suppose that's just too bad for Stalking Fox." There, he said it.

By heaven, O'Keefe's daughter left him tongue-tied!

Raven walked past Kit to stand in the shade of the oaks. Soon it would be the Leaf-Changing Moon, painting the forest foliage with brown and gold and vermilion. And after the season of harvest, the tree limbs would shed their colorful mantles (save for the pines) and stand stark before the wintry breath of the hard-faced sky. The wilderness frontier was all the home Raven had ever known. Her father had spoken to her of the villages to the north, and though she had cajoled him into the trip to Mobile, that port wasn't really the same as visiting the places a man like Kit had seen.

"Tell me of the great villages," Raven said to the man standing behind her. "Tell me of your Philadelphia and Washington and Boston."

Kit smiled, and taking care to skirt the underbrush that might still conceal the snake, he drew close to the Choctaw woman. "Well, there're lots of people—too many, if you ask me. And they have rules to go by, to tell them what to do and when to do it."

"And there is music? And libraries? My father has told me of such things. And some people live in lodges tall as these hills."

"Maybe not quite as tall," Kit told her, gently amused. "Yes, I have walked the streets of the white man's villages. But the music I have heard pales in comparison to the wind in the branches of the oaks. And I have learned as much from forest trails and meadows and the wild sea spray as I have from books." He shook his head and thought, *Listen to me. I sound like some bloody cavalier.*

Raven glanced aside. "Still . . . one day I shall see for myself."

"I imagine you will," Kit said. He kicked at the ground, examined the depression he'd left in the dirt, cleared his throat. "I'd be honored to show you those places, sometime." He looked up and into her warm green gaze.

Silence reigned; it was a comfortable quiet that the two of them enjoyed. Raven found herself liking her companion more and more. Though Kit had not been raised among the Choctaws, the All-Father had most certainly touched him and given him the vision to see the truth of things. She heard his stomach growl. Moments later hers answered, and she laughed.

They reached the same conclusion and started back to the riverbank. Kit glimpsed movement off to the right and noticed Stalking Fox leaning on his rifle, keeping watch from a nearby thicket. The warrior, once discovered, stooped down and began to gather firewood.

Kit wasn't fooled. The flesh crawled on the back of his neck as he turned his back on Stalking Fox. Kit had a gut feeling one of them wouldn't be returning from this river run. Sweat trickled down his neck; the back of his blousy shirt was matted, soaked through. He was beginning to feel like a walking target. He checked his rifle. Yes, it was loaded and primed. Stalking Fox better take care. This was one target that intended to shoot back. In civilization, as in the woods, a man must step carefully and keep watch for the snake in the grass.

Chapter Twenty-five

Moonlight shimmered on the river's surface, and the moon itself was a pale disc of silver overhead, afloat upon an obsidian sea. Stark, somber shadows rose up from the river to form the opposite bank. The rush of owl's wings cut through the stillness. The inevitable night stalkers were prowling the forest. Somehow, man stood between, striding the frontier as both hunter and prey.

Kit studied the moon's reflection, and then reached inside his shirt and lifted the medal until it caught the glare and shone in the palm of his hand. He heard footsteps—a twig cracked behind him. Kit tensed briefly, then relaxed as Raven approached with a gourd bowl filled with boiled meat and corn and the starchy stalks of the cattails she had harvested from the river's edge. Behind her and several yards back, Young Otter and Stalking Fox squatted by the campfire wholly involved in their own meals, though Kit had the feeling Stalking Fox was keeping watch on him no matter how absorbed he seemed in his dinner.

Raven was looking at the British crown bearing the initials G.W. scratched upon the surface, the medal given to Daniel McQueen in another time and another war.

"A gift from my father," Kit explained.

Raven nodded and studied the coin. "Your father is a warrior?"

"He is dead now," Kit said. "Yes, he was a warrior. But he thought of himself as a blacksmith and a farmer...a man of peace who liked to build and to watch things grow."

"It is good you keep his spirit with you," O'Keefe's daughter replied.

"Yes. I keep it with me—and him."

He tucked the medal back inside his shirt and gratefully accepted the bowl of venison stew. The cattails tasted something like potato, and the plant's green shoots were sweet as wild asparagus.

He looked out over the river. They were making good time, at least so it seemed. The breezes off the river were cooling, which eased the day's labor, and though he watched the riverbank with a wary eye, Kit still had time to appreciate the beauty of these woods. He'd heard wild turkeys call from the depths of the forest.

Just that afternoon while rounding a bend, the dugouts had startled half a dozen whitetail deer as they drank at the water's edge. The startled herd had fled from the river and vanished among the oaks and climbing bittersweet.

Kit marveled at the countryside. It was a good land, blessed with all manner of foods to sustain the varied wildlife, a land whose rich soil offered a bountiful harvest to those willing to clear the field and sow the seed. But the land's richness was its own curse as well as its blessing. For a place worth having was worth fighting for. The dogs of war had come to the territory's smoky, cloudswept hills and verdant valleys, to its lush, grassy meadows and sparkling creeks and rivers.

The fight for land was an ages-old conflict, one that Kit figured had been going on since Cain slew Abel. As for Kit's part, he had to believe his cause was just. He intended to do whatever needed to be done to help peace return to this territory. And that meant convincing General Andrew Jackson and his army that the Choctaws weren't their enemy. Visiting Jackson at his Tennessee encampment with a British agent in tow seemed the best way to sell the sharply opinionated general on the idea of just who his enemies really were.

"Your thoughts," Raven said, "do they travel upriver or down?" Kit was a curious man, one moment outgoing, pensive the next.

"Maybe a little of both."

"Be careful that they do not become lost in the night," the woman cautioned.

"As long as you're here," Kit replied, "they'll find their way back." By God, he'd said it. He couldn't believe his own courage.

Raven uttered a little embarrassed laugh. "I think perhaps you are like my father. Such words come easy. But is it bold talk or the truth?"

"Maybe you ought to wait around and find out."

Raven did just that.

Young Otter helped himself to another bowl of stew, then returned to his place by the campfire. Stalking Fox had barely touched his food. He'd set his bowl aside and was honing the iron blade of his tomahawk on a sharpening stone. The blade made a rasping sound as the metal edge ground along the flattened surface of the palm-sized rock. Now and then, he lifted his eyes from his work to stare out at the darkness where Raven had gone to bring food to Kit. That she failed to immediately return left him seething.

"She does not see you with her heart, my brother," Young Otter said.

"And who does she see? The white-skinned one who will betray us?" Stalking Fox snapped back.

"Your spirit is poisoned against him. Your words fly like arrows to strike him down." The normally jovial Young Otter frowned and shook his head in dismay. "But I have also walked the trail with this man and found he speaks straight."

"Then you are as easily tricked as the foolish daughter of our chief."

"And does not Iron Hand also have white skin? Do you say he will betray us?" Young Otter challenged.

"It may be so," Stalking Fox retorted. His friend had pinned him there, for in truth Chief Iron Hand had proven himself a devoted and capable leader. Still, he did take the warriors of the village off to the Cherokee stronghold, permitting the Creeks to mount a successful raid against the Choctaws. "When the white general, Jackson, brings his army against us, who can tell where Iron Hand O'Keefe will stand?"

"I will not hear it," Young Otter scolded. "Because Raven has not come to your blanket, you strike out like a wounded panther."

"And you have become fat and foolish as an old woman," Stalking Fox said.

He rose and, taking up his rifle, muttered he would take the first watch. Then he stamped off in the direction of the river.

Young Otter started to call his friend back to the campfire, then reconsidered. *No, the Choctaw thought, it is better for Stalking Fox to be alone where he will only have himself to argue with and no one's appetite to sour.*

Moonlight, and bittersweet, and the splash of a fish breaking the surface of the river, and the faint perfume of distant pines mingled with woodbine and wild geranium. The world was steeped in magic this night. For a brief moment, for Kit McQueen, it all seemed to stop. The silver moon, and the clouds, diaphanous as starswept bridal veils, froze in place. The forest creatures, the night wings, halted in place as if rooted by a sudden gap in time.

He turned to Raven, who was sitting beside him on the riverbank, and pulled her into his arms. To her own surprise, she did not resist as his mouth covered hers in a hungry kiss. And when it ended, the world wheeled onward, unchanged. But for two people, it wasn't quite as dark or empty as it had been before.

Kit inhaled slowly, then exhaled and tried to make some sense out of what had just happened. There were no words to explain his actions. Alone by a riverbank with a beautiful young woman beside him and a silver moon overhead, what man wouldn't have thrown caution to the wind and taken his chances? No, sir, a comely lass on a warm late summer's eve, alone . . . damn!

"By my oath, him again, is it?" Kit glowered as he stared upriver, where a familiar figure spied on them from about fifty feet away. "Enough is enough. I'll not have him sneaking around behind my back."

"Kit, no. Let me." Raven protested. She had never been kissed before. It had been a pleasant experience, one that seemed right with this stranger who had come riding into her life. Stalking Fox was no man to take lightly. She reached for Kit's arm, but he shrugged loose and strode along the bank toward the intruder.

Stalking Fox saw him coming. He'd wanted this all along. There was no need to offer a challenge. Kit his risen to the bait. Stalking Fox set his rifle aside and pulled the tomahawk from his waist. Kit unbuckled his belt and the "Quakers," holstered butt forward, dropped to the ground.

As the distance closed he could hear Stalking Fox laughing softly. Twenty feet separated them, then fifteen. At ten Kit charged. His sudden speed caught Stalking Fox off guard. The warrior raised his weapon. But his timing was off as Kit dove toward him and knocked Stalking Fox backward onto the sand.

Both men rolled over and over along the muddy bank. Kit caught hold of his opponent's wrist and slammed it against a rock until the warrior lost his hold on the tomahawk. Stalking Fox momentarily kicked free. The two men traded blows, then locked together again, this time toppling into the river.

Kit managed to catch his breath as he was dragged under the surface. Stalking Fox tried to pin him beneath the surface. Kit twisted, reached out and caught a handful of hair, and pulled the warrior over on his side. He sputtered clear of the water and caught Stalking Fox with a hard right to the jaw. Kit shoved him back into the mud and kneed his opponent in the gut, then held him under long enough for the Choctaw to gulp river water. Kit dragged the man back onto shore and left him sprawled and gagging among the rushes.

"We have a job to do. But so help me, you come prowling around me again and I'll settle this proper," Kit gasped, his features dripping and flushed with anger.

Stalking Fox crawled up the bank, wiped the mud from his eyes, and staggered toward his rifle. The fight wasn't over.

"Son of a bitch," Kit muttered, and made for the

pistols he had dropped along the way. Where the hell were they?

Young Otter emerged from the shadows. He'd heard the commotion and come to investigate, rifle in hand. He took in the situation at a glance. Stalking Fox altered his course and reached for his friend's long gun.

"No." Young Otter tried to retreat. Stalking Fox had a viselike grip on his companion's rifle and wrenched the weapon free. Young Otter called out a warning. Kit turned, unarmed, to face the Choctaw. Then, from out of nowhere, Raven stepped between them. She held a pistol in each slender hand and pointed them at Stalking Fox.

"No," she said.

"Stand aside," the man with the rifle snapped.

"Will you kill the daughter of your chief? Has the heart of Stalking Fox become so poisoned he will do the work of the Red Sticks?"

Kit tensed his muscles and prepared to spring toward Raven and knock her out of harm's way. If he was lucky, maybe he'd be able to catch one of his pistols and defend himself.

Suddenly the game changed, and the odds, too, for that matter. A long, wailing shriek sounded on the night air like a lost soul spinning into hell. Stalking Fox paled and lowered his rifle. Young Otter, behind him, muttered a prayer to the Master of Life. Raven slowly turned, looking to Kit for confirmation.

Kit nodded. That shrill, piercing whistle could only belong to a riverboat. They'd found the *Alejandro*.

Chapter Twenty-six

Kit squirmed his way through an emerald netting of vines and underbrush and raised a spyglass to his eye to study the *Alejandro*. The craft was a shallow draft sternwheeler, about ninety feet from bow to stern, with twin stacks that should have been trailing banners of gray smoke as the capable-looking craft forged its way upriver, its steam-driven engine driving against the Alabama's steady rush to the Gulf. But the riverboat wasn't going anywhere, not for a while. The sternwheeler had run aground during the night. Its bow tilted up where the boat had tried to plow a furrow through a sandbar that jutted out from the east bank. Concealed beneath a foot of muddy water, the sandbar held fast its prey. The main deck was aswarm with activity as the *Alejandro*'s crew worked to extricate the riverboat. Other men were repairing the boiler and engine, damaged when the boat came to its violent stop. Kit took a moment to check the hurricane deck and pilot house, but these decks were devoid of activity. No one needed to be at the ship's wheel. The

Alejandro wasn't going anywhere until its crew dug it loose from the river's sandy grasp.

While half a dozen hardcases labored at the bow, another group had been assigned to replenish the sternwheeler's supply of firewood. No doubt the *Alejandro's* captain had ordered the boat's engine kept under pressure and ready to work. That meant keeping the hungry boiler well fed as soon as it was fixed.

One of the crew hurried along the hurricane deck and stopped at the captain's cabin located just below the pilothouse. The crewman knocked at the door and a few seconds later entered.

Kit kept the spyglass trained on the cabin door in hopes of discovering the *Alejandro's* captain. A few moments later the crewman emerged from the cabin, this time bearing a tray laden with plates, a thick wedge of cheese, a coffeepot, cups, and half a loaf of crusty bread. This crewman, whom Kit took to be the ship's cook, was immediately intercepted by two mean-looking guards who were armed with rifled muskets.

The guards helped themselves to the remainder of the bread and cheese before resuming their rounds, patrolling the hurricane deck as they kept watch over the forested riverbanks.

The door to the cabin beneath the pilothouse opened once more and Kit shifted his spyglass yet again. A man in a black frock coat and a short-brimmed cap stepped out onto the hurricane deck. He was a tall man with stringy black hair that fell to his shoulders. In contrast to the riverboat's swarthy-looking crew and his own dark clothes, the captain's features were pale, as if the sun's fierce rays had no affect on his white skin.

Kit adjusted the focus on his spyglass, his pulse quickening. There was something uncomfortably familiar about the man in the frock coat. Features took form in the lens, the blurred image defined itself, becoming the one face that Kit McQueen would never forget.

"Bill Tibbs," Kit said beneath his breath.

It was all he could do to keep from charging down the riverbank and roaring out a challenge to the "friend" who had left him to rot in some Spanish dungeon.

Tibbs walked to the edge of the hurricane deck and bellowed orders to the men on the sandbar, exhorting them to greater effort. The crewmen gestured toward the sandbar, where a jagged log had ripped a hole in the hull. The sternwheeler needed to be patched as well as dug free. Tibbs finished with his crew and started back toward his cabin. But he slowed and then turned to look across the river, as if sensing he was being watched.

Kit lowered the spyglass. Sunlight glinting off the lens would be a surefire giveaway. Tibbs continued to study the opposite riverbank. A breeze sent the branches shuddering overhead.

A gray fox appeared out of the shadows not five yards from Kit, who remained motionless despite the blood pounding in his veins. The fox picked its way to the water, and after checking the commotion surrounding the riverboat for any indication of a threat, the animal lowered its head and drank.

Tibbs shrugged and went into his cabin. Kit gasped for air, realizing he'd been holding his breath. He tucked the spyglass into its case and with trembling limbs crawled into the forest and clumsily retraced his steps back to his Choctaw allies.

Raven noticed the change in the lieutenant the moment he arrived in the clearing. Curiosity etched her features. She and the other Choctaws had watched the *Alejandro* from a distance, leaving Kit to chance a closer observation. What had he seen?

His features were tightly drawn, and his eyes filled with grim resolve. The transformation wasn't lost on Young Otter or Stalking Fox. The two warriors exchanged glances and then peered at the white man with renewed interest when he spoke.

"The riverboat's hung up and damaged," Kit said in a leaden voice. "And there seems to be a problem with the engine. Maybe something broke when the boat ran aground. I can't see them going anywhere today."

"And tonight?" Raven asked.

"We'll need a fire raft," Kit told her. He looked at the two braves. "Bring it downriver under cover of dark and set the paddle wheel afire." He kicked at a small mound of twigs at his feet. "We'll blow it to kindling."

Kit started down the path that led to their campsite, but when he drew abreast of Stalking Fox he turned and faced the warrior. Both men were bruised from their altercation. Stalking Fox met the white man's eyes, then faltered and broke contact.

"Is the trouble finished between us?" Kit said. "I want to know. Now."

The warrior looked at his companions, then at the ground, at the shadows, everywhere but at the man before him, in whose burning gaze the Choctaw had seen death.

"It is finished."

Chapter Twenty-seven

Bill Tibbs woke with a start. Perspiration beaded his features, but his mouth felt dry as a discarded flask. He cleared his throat, working up enough spittle to aim into the spittoon by his bed. He rubbed his chest, hoping to ease the pressure. It was always this way after a dream, after the same cursed nightmare that had plagued him for these many months. He thought they'd played out, for he'd enjoyed a good five months of uninterrupted rest. Now it was back, the same blasted dream.

He was stumbling through a forest, the sword clutched to his chest. Someone was chasing him. He did not know who and was afraid to find out. Panicked, he continued to slog his way from bayou to bayou, pursued by the sloshing steps of an unseen enemy. His guns were gone. All he had was the sword.

At last, unable to run another step and knee-deep in the primordial muck of the swamplands, he turned to face his enemy. And waited. Waited. Just as his spirits began to rise, lichen-encrusted arms shot up out of the bog to imprison him in their ghastly hold, closing about his throat.

Tibbs could not even scream as he stared in horror at the decayed remains of Kit McQueen, reaching up to claw at his friend, his betrayer.

Oh the nightmare lingered after waking. Bill Tibbs knew it by heart. And there was only one antidote for the horrible dream. The gunrunner crossed the room to his liquor cabinet, fumbled with the latch, and swung the door open. He reached for the Irish whiskey, uncorked the bottle, and poured a river of fire down his gullet.

"Take that, old friend," Tibbs gasped.

He returned to his bed and sat on the covers, his hand closed around the hilt of the scimitar, the Eye of Alexander, the last of the treasure that had cost him his honor. The rest of the baubles he'd squandered in ill-ventured speculations and lost on the gaming tables in Mobile's cantinas. But he owned the *Alejandro*, free and clear.

When British agents approached him about running guns to the Creeks, Tibbs had sensed the opportunity to recoup his losses. The British paid him well for each trip upriver.

Tibbs took another pull on the bottle. A knock sounded softly at his door. He strode over to a heavy oaken table on which was strewn a map, an oil lamp, pistols and shot, a few coins, and a plate of congealed stew beside a cup of cold coffee. He sat in a leather-covered wing chair.

"Yes?" Tibbs said.

The door opened and Arturo Gomez, the riverboat's first mate and Tibbs's right-hand man, entered the cabin. "Well, what is it now? More bad news?"

"No, my captain."

Gomez doffed his cap to reveal a shaved head. He was slight of build. A thin mustache outlined his upper lip below a hooked nose and narrow-set eyes. He wore a gold ring in his right ear. Pistols jutted from the leather belt encircling his narrow waist.

"Miguel has repaired the ship's engine, a valve in the boiler or something." Gomez shrugged and smiled his bucktoothed grin. "And the patch is complete; we no longer take in water. Tomorrow morning we finish digging out and with the engines in reverse, we will be free!" Gomez liked having good things to report.

His gaze moved toward the scimitar. *My, such a sword of wondrous beauty.* His heart seemed to skip a beat just to behold the jeweled weapon. Maybe one day Captain Tibbs would have an accident and the wonderful sword would pass to Arturo Gomez. He caught himself staring and returned his attention to the man behind the desk.

"You bring me excellent tidings, *mi amigo*."

Tibbs tossed the dregs of his coffee into the nearest corner and then poured a measure of the Irish whiskey into the cup and slid it toward Gomez, who grabbed it up, offered a silent toast to his captain, swilled the spirits, and slapped the cup down on the tabletop. He sucked in a lungful of air and smacked his lips. His eyes began to water.

"Tell the men well done, and break out the rum. See that each man has a tankard, but I want no one staggering blind and too sotted to work come morning."

Tibbs glared at the leftover stew. He took the plate and set it on the floor. A calico cat trotted out from beneath the bed and hurried over to make a meal on the leftover pork and potatoes.

"When you've seen to that, assign the guards and

then come back here and help me kill this bottle,"
Tibbs added.

"It will be my pleasure, *el jefe*," Gomez replied,
and hurried from the captain's quarters.

Tibbs was under no illusion as to the sincerity
of Gomez's loyalty or affections. Both ran as deep
as the linings of Tibbs's pocket. The gunrunner
lifted the scimitar and stared into the gleaming ruby
on its hilt.

Even with his back to the wall and desperate for
money, Tibbs had not been able to part with the sword.
There was magic in it. This he believed. As long as the
blade was his, Tibbs felt invulnerable, the conqueror
of worlds. He pressed the cold jewel to his forehead
and imagined he could hear the Macedonian armies
tramping across Persia, sense the carnage of battle and
experience the rush of victory that Alexander the
Great must have known.

Part with this treasured blade, give it up? No.

"You are mine," he whispered to the curved steel
and the pulsing, blood-red jewel reflecting Tibbs's own
image. "You will always be."

Miguel Medrano was not a violent man by nature.
Nor could he rattle off the names of many enemies. At
the age of fifty he considered himself above the vices
of drunkenness and debauchery that permeated the
character of the rest of the crew. They were a mixed
lot, Spaniards and Frenchmen and Yankees from the
north, and a couple of mixed-bloods that Miguel
suspected of being cannibals.

Yes, they were an unsettling blend, thirteen rivermen
and any one of them capable of violence. But only
Miguel could keep the small steam engine running. He
took pride in the fact that he was aboard for a skill

other than with musket or cutlass. He kept clear of quarrels and avoided confrontations with other members of the crew. He did his job well and expected an ample reward and perhaps even another bonus when Captain Tibbs returned to Mobile after a successful river run. The bonus Miguel received this night came as quite a shock.

The round-shouldered, weary engineer rubbed his eyes and then stretched out on his bedroll near the woodpile by the furnace when he heard the scrape of wood against the paddle wheel. He started to ignore the sound, then thought the better of it. Some stretches of the Alabama River were an obstacle course of half-submerged logs and floating brush that could damage the paddle wheel by catching in the steam-driven blades.

Miguel crawled out of his bedding and stepped around the engine house. He sucked in his belly and then inched along a narrow walkway that led back to the paddle wheel. He yawned and wondered if it was midnight yet. Miguel squinted in the darkness and wished the moon hadn't ducked behind clouds. Still, he managed to locate the source of the peculiar noise. Something indeed had drifted into the blades. He peered through the gloom, a slow frown wrinkling his bushy eyebrows. He eased down into the shallows, his bare feet sinking into the sandbar as he worked around to the *Alejandro's* stern.

"What is this?" he grumbled. *Madre de Dios*, it was a raft piled with— A hand clamped over his mouth, shutting off his cry as a knife blade sank into his back.

Young Otter lowered the dead man into the shallows and pulled his knife free. Kit McQueen made his way past the raft and up onto the sand. He caught a glimmer of movement on the hurricane deck side of the riverboat. The guard above sauntered off toward the bow. Behind Kit, a third figure huddled by the raft. Stalking Fox waited to light the kindling.

On the riverbank, Raven O'Keefe watched in the darkness of the forest, her rifled musket loaded and ready. A screech owl swooped down from a nearby sweetgum and startled her so badly she came to within an inch of firing her gun. Sweat beaded her forehead. She took a deep breath and slowly exhaled. Then she prayed silently:

> *"God of my mother's people,*
> *All-Father, Spirit Healer,*
> *Guide my steps*
> *And help me to walk in courage."*

Her companions were hidden from view now, on the opposite side of the *Alejandro*. She felt helpless, with nothing to do but wait. She thought of Kit and the change that had come over him. Who had he seen aboard the riverboat? She had found the courage to ask him as the two worked side by side, lashing the poles together for the raft.

"An old friend," the lieutenant had replied.

It was the tone of his voice that unsettled her. The matter of the *Alejandro* had become more than some military duty, a plan to destroy the Creek rifles and capture a British agent. Now it was personal: Kit McQueen was out for blood.

Raven stared at the riverboat. Lamplight filtered through the shuttered windows along the main deck. Music from a concertina carried across the water to be swallowed up by the forest, dark and still. There was laughter aboard the *Alejandro* and the cheerful din of a spontaneous celebration. Tapping a keg of rum had put everyone in a festive mood.

It wouldn't last long.

Young Otter crouched in the shadow of the wood-pile. He looked nervously from the hurricane deck rail to the open doorway on the main deck that led down to the riverboat's storage hold. The Choctaw repositioned himself beneath the wrought-iron stairway that led to the deck above. He heard footsteps and tightened his grip on his rifle, holding his breath.

River water lapped against the hull. A moth fluttered past and alighted on the warrior's gun barrel, resting a moment before flying off toward the lights amidships. The sentry on the deck above turned on his heels, grumbled a complaint as to how he deserved to be in the crew's quarters enjoying the comradeship of his friends and a hearty draught of grog.

Kit appeared in the entrance to the cargo hold. He held an oil lamp minus its glass chimney and had removed the wick. He arrived at the top of the stairs, having left a trail of whale oil in his wake. He poured the last of the lamp's contents at the top of the stairs and knelt by the puddle. Young Otter hurried to join him. The warrior was anxious to be off this boat and into the relative safety of the forest.

"There are rifles and powder below. Enough for the Red Sticks to start a war," Kit said. He handed his tinderbox to the Choctaw. "Light it and run like hell, my friend."

Kit stood and started toward the black iron stairs. Young Otter caught him by the arm. "Where are you going? See, Stalking Fox has already lit the fire raft. We must hurry."

Kit glanced over his shoulder and saw for himself

the stream of smoke coming from the kindling and the faint pinpricks of orange firelight as Stalking Fox blew upon the embers and coaxed them to life. Once the raft was ablaze, the flames would consume the paddle wheel, crippling the boat. Finding the powder kegs below deck inspired Kit to plot a more explosive ending to the craft.

Young Otter knelt by the puddle of oil and prepared to strike the flint and send a shower of sparks onto the flammable liquid. He hesitated only because he was unwilling to jeopardize Kit's safety, since Kit obviously intended to remain aboard.

"Go ahead," Kit whispered harshly.

"What of you?" Young Otter retorted beneath his breath.

"I'll be along."

Kit started up the iron steps and vanished before the Choctaw could offer further protest. Kit had a rendezvous to keep and a debt to settle once and for all.

Chapter Twenty-eight

Kit moved soundlessly along the hurricane deck until he reached the captain's quarters. Around the corner and toward the bow, the two men assigned to keep watch stood together in muted conversation as they stared out across the black river and regaled one another with stories of the women they had known from the bordellos of Mobile and New Orleans. Below, on the main deck, the rest of the crew merrily attempted to drain the recently tapped barrel of rum despite the one-tankard limit ordered by their captain.

Kit placed his ear to the door and to what he took to be a heated interchange between two men.

"But, señor, I tell them, only a tankard to a man. They do not listen."

"You get them in line or I'll find another first mate!"

Suddenly the door latch turned beneath Kit's hand and the door swung open. Kit drew his pistol from his belt. Arturo Gomez stopped short. Seething with anger, he wasn't in any mood to be confronted by what he took to be a member of the crew. Then it dawned on him that the redheaded stranger was no one he knew. Kit's hard left fist caught Gomez flush on the jaw and sent the ship's mate flying back into the cabin, where he sprawled unconscious at the foot of the brass frame bed.

Bill Tibbs bolted out of his chair. His own flintlock lay in the center of the map on the table, alongside a whiskey bottle and two cups. But the gunrunner froze in midreach toward his weapon. He was rooted in place by this materialization of his nightmares.

With jaw slack and mouth agape, Tibbs watched as Kit slipped into the room and shut the door. He walked across the room and stood opposite the man behind the heavy oaken table. He looked around the room, noting the scimitar dangling in its scabbard at Tibbs's side.

Except for the bed, table, and a couple of chairs, the room had little else in the way of furniture. Only the liquor cabinet, now unlocked and with its door ajar. Two leather-and-wood-paneled chests lay against the wall. These were padlocked and no doubt would hold any wealth or contraband that Tibbs could not trust to the hold below to which his crew had easy access. Brass lanterns hung from two of the walls. A gun rack holding a shotgun and several pistols dominated the third, directly across from the door. Yet there was something bleak about the room, as if it reflected its occupant's frequent disposition.

Tibbs seemed to have aged ten years since Kit had last seen him. The gunrunner's hair was flecked with silver and his normally cleanshaven face was covered by a salt-and-pepper stubble. There were dark shadows like crescent moons beneath his eyes.

The room smelled of spilled whiskey and cigar

smoke. The faint residue of a meal lingered in the air. And now there was the faint sick odor of fear as Tibbs fought to control himself, his mind reeling from images born of his nightmares, now embodied in the man who stood before him.

"I imagine you're surprised to see me, old friend," Kit said. "If you wanted me dead, you should have done it yourself and not left the job for Morales and his dragoons."

His voice dispelled one notion. Tibbs realized he wasn't seeing a mad vision, that Kit was flesh and blood. Somehow he had survived Florida and after all this time had tracked Tibbs to this river.

No, the gunrunner reasoned, *McQueen could not possibly have tracked me. Blind fate must have caused our paths to cross. Or maybe it was the sword, working its magic, bringing us together, so I can kill him once and for all and put an end to my nightmares.*

"You are a lucky man, Kit. Smart and shrewd."

"Not so smart," Kit retorted. "I picked you for a friend."

He searched for something more to say. After all this time, finally to come face to face with the man who had left him to die, at last to confront him... Kit shook his head, feeling the hatred leak out of him like juice from an overripe fruit, leaving a part of him empty and even a little sad. He thought this would mean more. Kit gestured with his pistol toward the jeweled sword at the gunrunner's side.

"Is that the last of it?" he asked.

Tibbs glanced down at the hilt. The Eye of Alexander glimmered, and Tibbs took courage. Even under Kit's gun, Tibbs knew the sword would protect him and turn the situation to his favor.

"Yes. There wasn't all that much, really. And I'm

ashamed to say, my poor head for business squandered it. Yet the sword continues to bring me luck." Tibbs pulled a silk kerchief from the sleeve of his frock coat and dabbed at his upper lip and forehead. "I have this boat, which I named after the one treasure I will not part with. And I have made new friends, profitable friends."

"Like British agents who pay you to play traitor to your own country," Kit said. "Sword of luck? Sword of evil! Up until this moment I thought I hated you— hated you enough to shoot you on sight." Kit stepped back, and his eyes seemed filled with sorrow. "But now, all I have is pity for the man you used to be: I didn't die in Florida, Bill. You did."

The clatter of boots on the walkway outside the door cut short the moment as the men on guard hurried toward the ship's stern. Cries of "Fire! Fire!" drifted through the walls.

Tibbs looked toward the door.

"What have you done, you bastard?" he exclaimed.

The burst of activity brought Kit out of the past and back to the uncomfortable present. He was aboard a riverboat that at any moment might blow sky high.

"You're coming with me," Kit said, and waved his pistol in the direction of the cabin door.

"I don't think so," Tibbs snapped, a look of malevolent triumph glittering in his dark eyes. He inadvertently glanced past Kit.

Kit sensed the danger and heard the click of a gun being cocked. He lunged to his left, dropped and spun, and hit the floor shoulder first.

He fired at the same time as Arturo Gomez. The Spaniard was propped against the bed, a small-bore pistol in his hand.

The simultaneous gunshots boomed with deafening effect in the confines of the cabin. Kit felt a searing tug at his left sleeve and a flash of pain from a flesh wound. His own shot struck Gomez high in the chest a few inches below the throat and flung the smaller man against the bedding, then dropped him forward in a twisted contortion, where he lay still and bleeding to death.

Tibbs roared and overturned the table. Kit rolled and freed his other pistol as the captain's table came crashing down upon him. The whiskey bottle shattered near his face. He grunted, worked his legs beneath the heavy piece of furniture, and squirmed free. He sat upright, pistol leveled, in time to catch a glimpse of Bill Tibbs disappearing through the open doorway.

Kit scrambled to his feet and, leaping the rubble, gave chase. He lunged out into the night air, which wasn't so dark as it had been before. The stern of the *Alejandro* was engulfed in flames, the paddle wheel, the entire aft section of the riverboat, completely ablaze.

Several men had already abandoned ship, and more followed, leaping over the side. A few of the crewmen in the shallows opened fire, shooting toward the shore, only to be answered by rifle fire that dropped two of their number and silenced the guns of the other crew members.

Kit turned and headed toward the bow. "Tibbs!" he shouted.

The hurricane deck was empty. Kit ran to the stairway leading to the main deck and took the steps two at a time. He paused at the bottom of the landing and looked back toward the flames. A heavyset man clad only in a pair of canvas trousers emerged from the crew's quarters. He carried a rucksack of food over one shoulder and brandished a cutlass in his right hand.

"Save yourselves, mates," he yelled, wiping a forearm across his soot-smeared features before he clambered over the rail and dropped to the sandbar. The boatman began wading across the shallows to the riverbank.

Kit tied a kerchief around his nose and mouth to filter out some of the smoke, then started to work his way toward the bow of the ship. Where the hell was Tibbs? Had he jumped over the side? The stench of smoke and burned flesh filled his nostrils. The breeze shifted, blowing thick, black clouds across the bow, cloaking the walkway in a lung-searing fog. Kit staggered past the sternwheeler's cabins, rounded the corner, and headed for the bow. The deck tilted where the boat had hung up on the sandbar. The incline was just enough to keep a man off balance. Kit managed to stumble to the bow.

His eyes streamed tears and his lungs felt like he'd choked down live coals. He could see no one on the river and turned to face the flames and shout.

"Tibbs! It isn't finished!"

A tall, grim figure materialized out of the smoke like a demon summoned by the sound of Kit's voice. This spectral figure, nigh mad with rage, roared out in a cry more beastlike than human, and with scimitar raised, Tibbs charged his foe.

Kit raised his second pistol, sighted on his attacker, and squeezed the trigger. Nothing? Kit, dumbfounded, stared at the pistol in his hand while an old adage replayed in his mind. *Keep your powder dry.* The damned river...

"Oh, shit!"

Tibbs swung the scimitar. The blade sliced down in a mighty arc. Kit braced himself, vainly attempting to parry the sword with the pistol in his hand. There came a blinding flash, and Kit thought for a minute he was dead. He tumbled weightless, hurling through the air with all manner of debris.

The thunderous clap came almost as an afterthought as the gunpowder in the hold ignited and the *Alejandro* exploded in a mushrooming column of fire and smoke that rained debris over the entire channel. The force of the blast that blew Kit off the bow tossed him like a smoldering rag doll into the cooling waters of the river.

He gulped water and fought his way to the surface, feeling the tug of the current as he struggled to stand. His feet sank into the muddy river bottom. The battered lieutenant gasped and took his weight off his left leg. He stared at his arms as if they were appendages belonging to some stranger.

He saw that his right hand, if indeed it was his hand, still clutched the pistol that had misfired. He frowned, another concern coming to mind, and searched for the medal beneath his shirt. Kit's hand closed around the British crown dangling against his chest, and he experienced a rush of intense relief.

Except for the fact that he was deaf, near blind, bleeding from the nostrils and the arm, had a broken leg, and had patches of his hide singed off, he was none the worse for wear.

Kit smiled, satisfied, and toppled face forward into the river.

Chapter Twenty-nine

In a clearing along both sides of Willow Creek, the Choctaw gathered. From the hills to the north they came, the survivors of the Creek raid, and from the west where the tribes had settled in the delta country of the Yazoo. They came from the rich, black prairie land where their crops had flourished. They came from dense pine forests where game was plentiful and the berries sweet. The war belt had traveled across the territory and to all the Choctaw villages.

The camp by Willow Creek was arranged like any other Choctaw settlement, ordered on a cleared square of ground. Houses, framed with stout poles, with sides of cane woven tightly into a solid wall, then covered with clay and grass, served as dwellings for the warriors and their families. A public square in the center of the village was dominated by a low-roofed ceremonial house whose floor, three feet below ground level, had been dug out of the rich earth. Here the chiefs sat in council, to listen to the young braves talk of war and the elders' wish for peace.

It was the middle of November, the time of the Leaf-Falling Moon. Some mornings the air was crisp, but beneath the sun's steady glare the temperature lost its edge and became quite pleasant, although on overcast days men and women donned leggings and buckskin shirts for comfort. Food was brought into the village, edible roots were harvested from the forest, and the supplies of corn, beans, and squash brought from the delta were pooled together and stored in common grain houses. There were common smokehouses for the storage and preserving of meat to ensure that no family would go hungry, even if the men of that family fell in battle.

These were the days of a war in which hardly a battle had been fought. Under the leadership of the chiefs—Iron Hand, Little Elk, and Crow Path—the Choctaw waited and watched, uncertain of General Jackson's intentions, wondering whether or not the Tennessee Volunteers were at war with them. As for Wolf Jacket and his Red Sticks, a few Choctaw hunting parties had skirmished with Creek raiders, but nothing worthwhile had been achieved for the lives lost.

Alabama Territory had become a theater of war, the principle players primed to take their places upon the stage.

These were the worries plaguing Iron Hand O'Keefe in the final days of Indian summer as he stood outside his lodge and watched the children at play in the village square. He thought of Star Basket, the woman he had loved, mother of Raven and mother too of the son he'd held in his arms, stillborn, during the long night that had cost the woman her life. Raven was his joy, but he had also longed for a son.

Iron Hand puffed on his pipe and watched a young boy toss a deerhide ball from one player to the next. Each player held a yard-long cane pole with a reed cup at one end in which they could carry the ball. Two oaken posts had been set ninety feet apart at each end of the playing field, a trampled patch of earth. The two teams engaged in a free-for-all, working the ball up the field and down, accompanied by a pack of yipping dogs that now and then entered the fray to nip at the heels of the players. The object of the game was to strike the opposing team's post with the ball.

Iron Hand smiled, observing how much like their fathers these brown-skinned children were, for just as many fights were breaking out during their game as when the adults took the field. But for a tragic twist of fortune, one of those lads might have been his.

He shifted his stance, inhaling the strong tobacco. *A cup of hot chicory root coffee would go down mighty good right now*, he thought. O'Keefe lowered his pipe and sniffed the air. He breathed in the aroma of the cornmeal porridge Raven had laced with dark honey and cooked over an open fire. And when she emerged from around the corner of the lodge, holding a wooden bowl with steam curling over the top and a cup of strong, bitter tea, O'Keefe's stomach started to growl. He sat on the tree stump outside the door, and his big, ugly face split in a grin.

"Now, there's a proper daughter, bringing her father his morning meal." He tapped the ashes out of his pipe and returned it to his pocket.

Raven skirted his outstretched hands. "I left plenty for you, Father, and you can help yourself."

"I might have guessed. Bound for the young lieutenant, eh?" he said, jabbing a thumb toward the lodge next to theirs. "It is mighty personal care he's received, nursed back to health by the daughter of a chief. I hope McQueen appreciates you."

"Oh, he does." Raven beamed.

"Hmmm. Well, then, maybe he better not appreciate you quite so much." Iron Hand glowered. He sensed something in her reply. By heaven, did the two of them think he was blind? He'd been their age and felt the same stirring below his belt. O'Keefe saw the look of amusement on Raven's face, and try as he might, the Irishman couldn't work enough bluster to intimidate the headstrong girl. He leaned back and appraised her ripe figure. *Aye, she is like a dark, sweet plum bursting with the juices of life and ready to fall. I might just have a son, after all—leastways, a grandson.*

O'Keefe propped his elbows on his broad thighs and leaned forward, his massive girth straining his buckskin shirt.

"Well, daughter, you're too late for him; best you leave that bowl with me."

"Where has he gone?" Raven asked, her eyebrows arched as she spoke.

O'Keefe shrugged. "He was gone when I looked in on him. You healed him up so well, I'm surprised he hasn't joined the game yonder, crutch and all." The Irishman shrugged. "His trail oughtn't be too difficult to follow. I must admit McQueen moves pretty quick for a fella I figured for dead when you brought him in."

Iron Hand O'Keefe still remembered the pale, gaunt-looking man Raven had returned with from their venture downriver.

Young Otter and Stalking Fox had hauled the man on a litter all the way from the headwaters of the Alabama across the hills to the village at Willow Creek. The Irishman had hardly recognized Kit. Raven had managed to splint Kit's badly broken left leg, but infection had set in, and though she had treated the wounds along the arduous trek upriver, the lieutenant was still sick with fever when they arrived at the village. Most men would have succumbed. But O'Keefe had to admit, Kit was different.

Exhibiting the same bullheaded toughness as when he charged the Spanish dragoons armed only with an empty flintlock, Kit McQueen fought for his life. And Raven was constantly at his side, helping to bring him back from death, one step at a time.

Raven stood in front of her father and handed him the food she had prepared for Kit. "I will find him."

"The women will laugh behind your back. They will say, 'See how the mixed-blood daughter of Chief Iron Hand chases after the white lieutenant.'" O'Keefe knew well the propensity for gossip among the women. He and Star Basket had once endured the same talk until he proved himself in battle against the Creeks and gained acceptance into the tribe.

"Let them talk. It keeps them from worrying about the Red Sticks. They are even afraid to walk the woods, seeing Wolf Jacket behind every shadow."

"A little caution seems prudent in time of war," Iron Hand said, balancing the bowl on his knees and spooning a mouthful of porridge into his mouth. He wiped his forearm across his grizzled features and smacked his lips. "You honor this old man, offering me the food you'd intended for your lieutenant."

Raven refused to be baited. She turned and walked off among the lodges. O'Keefe watched her leave. She was the best thing in his life. It would be hard to let her go. He returned his attention to the game of chunkey, as the Choctaws called it, and noticed Little Elk, one of the chiefs of the tribe attempting to cross the gaming field.

The gray-haired, dignified-looking war chief narrowly missed being pummeled to death as the game swept over him. The elderly chief was a revered figure who enjoyed O'Keefe's company. But today, Little Elk found himself surrounded by two dozen young men and boys, each trying to scoop up the hardened ball while battering their opponents senseless.

O'Keefe scratched at his jaw with his hook as the muscles twitched along one side of his neck.

"Weather's fixing to change," O'Keefe muttered. "Or trouble is on the way."

Once his armpit had toughened up, the crutch wasn't all that much of a bother, Kit decided. But he was anxious to be rid of it. Knowing Raven would protest his attempts, he had left the village and followed Willow Creek into a stand of timber, a mixture of oak and hickory and sweet gum trees. Here and there a few plum trees grew wild in the moist bottomland.

It might have been Eden, Kit thought, save for the fact that a man must go armed.

He glanced around and decided he was alone. The sounds of the village were muffled by the densely intertwined branches. A breeze stirred the tree limbs and a flurry of leaves showered about him thick as snowflakes. Kit was determined to be walking, unaided, before winter.

The lieutenant paused by the creek to study his reflection in the placid surface. He saw a changed man. His face was leaner now. And though he'd regained his normal ruddy color, there were wrinkles, like crow's feet at the corners of his piercing eyes. He was dressed in buckskins like a Choctaw warrior. His pistols, the "Quakers" Raven had saved for him, were tucked in a belt adorned with shells and glass trade beads, another gift from Raven. But the most important gift of all had been his life. Deep in his memory, often at morning just before rising, he could dimly recall fragments of his rescue. He could almost taste the black water. If he concentrated, he could produce a mental image of himself floating, drowning, and feel hands beneath him, lifting his head out of the water, dragging him to the safety of the riverbank.

There were other images, too brief at times to fully comprehend, sometimes just the sound of a voice, the rocking of the dugout in which he lay, the smell of the wood and the stink of infection, and the moments of pain as if his leg were afire. Another memory lingered as well, of a tender touch, warm eyes in a woman's face, sweet face, coppery skin and lips like wine and a voice to cling to when the fire returned and the darkness of death came to claim him. But he had refused. He had clung to a voice and black hair and green eyes, and the longing that became the desire to live and deny death.

He leaned his crutch against a plum tree. Kit's left leg was free of the wood splints he'd worn for the past eight weeks. It was tightly bound with deer hide straps that had been soaked and then tightly wrapped about his calf and thigh. They allowed for a little movement yet provided adequate support for his healing limb.

Kit chanced a step, followed it with another. His leg began to ache by the time he'd traversed thirty feet, slow and steady. He started back toward the plum tree and had covered two thirds of the distance when his feet slipped in the muddy bank and he toppled into the creek with a yelp.

He spat water and sat upright, the creek flowing over and around him. But the cold bath was far easier to take than the laughter drifting toward him from the forest. He recognized Raven's voice and scowled. He tried to stand, but his stiffly bound leg kept slipping in the mud.

Raven walked down to the creek, and wearing a look of resignation, she retrieved his cane and held it out for him to reach. He caught hold, she pulled him upright, and he hobbled out of the creek.

"It appears you're called to keep me from drowning."

"Then I had better stay near you," Raven replied as he joined her on the creek bank. "But if you break your leg again, I shall let Blue Swallow set it. He can be as gentle as a wounded panther."

"No, thanks. I'll be careful."

Kit was familiar with the Choctaw medicine man. Blue Swallow had straggly silver hair and a filmy gaze, and the fingernails on his hands were long and clawlike. He had come from a village on the Yazoo in Mississippi, to work his magic against the Creeks. Kit doubted the aged shaman would affect the outcome of a war one way or the other. Still, the lieutenant intended to stay in good standing with the healer, just to be on the safe side. There had to be something to his powers, for it was Blue Swallow's medicine that broke the infection in Kit's leg.

Kit leaned against the tree. Its branches had been picked clean of fruit by the denizens of the forest, both feathered and furred, not to mention the women and children from the Choctaw camp.

"Raven," the lieutenant began, searching for the right words. So much had happened over the past months. He had expected to find trouble in the territory and had been prepared for whatever shape or form it took. But Iron Hand's daughter was something else again. Nothing had prepared him for Raven. "I grow stronger every day, thanks to you and all you have done," he continued.

The young woman stood before him, willowy as a wood nymph, with eyes so warm and inviting a man could lose himself in her gaze and never care.

"My heart is filled with gratitude."

She nodded, waiting, perhaps even expecting more. He was struggling to speak what was really within, what had become a part of him since meeting her.

"No, my heart holds more than gratitude," he managed to say.

He looked up at the sunlight filtering through the branches, turning them into a latticework of gold. Scissor tails darted and dipped into the creek, spattering the amber surface that flowed peacefully on. The morning was drenched in this lazy, quiet beauty. What better place to speak his heart than paradise?

"I love you," he said. The words hung on the stillness like the petals of the last wildflower, clinging to these final days of autumn, this healing time.

In reply, Raven stepped forward and put her head against his shoulder and her arms around his waist.

Her mother had taught her the Choctaw way. The man calls you to his blanket, the two becoming one ceremony, the warrior who is broken by what is in his heart so that the woman may make him whole.

But Kit McQueen was not a Choctaw and the words of her mother's people were not his. He had followed his own path, and it had led him to her side.

"When all this trouble with the Red Sticks is over, I will not leave without you," he warned. He nuzzled her black hair and kissed her on the forehead when she looked up at him.

"I will go with you," Raven said, a hint of a smile upon her wine-red lips. "If only to keep you from drowning."

"Aaahh..." Kit growled, and pulled her to the

ground, where they lay together, laughing. They made love, on this last sweet morning, lulled by the sighing wind and the singing creek.

The sun burned high overhead when Kit awoke with Raven nestled at his side, one arm stretched across his stomach.

Raven stirred, yawned, and, sensing he was awake, rose up on her elbow, one coppery brown breast brushing his arm. She smiled and began to trace circles in the rust-red ringlets matting his chest. He covered her hand with his.

"Now, none of that," he cautioned, and then chuckled. "I've yet to recover my full strength, remember."

Raven pouted, then resigned herself to the reality of the moment, rolled away from his side, and slipped into her buckskin dress. "I can wait till you are healed," she replied.

Kit kept his comments to himself. One thing for certain, he was going to be in for a pretty wild time of it. He'd need all his stamina. The lieutenant dressed hurriedly. He imagined bringing Raven home to the Hound and Hare Inn on the Trenton Road. His mother would be . . .

He glanced at Raven, seeing in the Choctaw woman many of Kate McQueen's own qualities. Both women were strong and determined and fiercely courageous. Yes, Kate would approve. And as for Esther Rose—she would be delighted. *One day I will bring her there*, Kit resolved silently. *But we will not stay.*

Raven was a woman of the frontier. The wilderness was her home, not some drawing room or parlor in Pennsylvania.

Kit looked around at the shuddering branches, the climbing bittersweet: he breathed in the fragrances of the forest and reveled in the serenity. He knew, in that moment, the wilderness was his life as well, for the freedom it offered and the love he had known.

He reached down and cupped the medal lying against his chest. The coin felt warm in his hand, and the longer he stared at it, the more he began to understand how love and freedom had a price, that the peace he had experienced must sometimes be defended, bought with sacrifice. Such was the duty his father had accepted and the legacy he had passed along to his son.

"Where are your thoughts now?" Raven asked, her hand upon his arm.

"Our time together slips through my fingers like grains of sand. Soon I must make the journey to find General Jackson. And somehow convince him not to make war on your people."

"Your words are true. Jackson will see your heart and know it is good."

"I don't think the general works that way, looking into people's hearts and all."

Raven was about to offer further encouragement when she noticed her father following the creek toward them. Man and woman exchanged looks of relief. If O'Keefe had chosen to find them any earlier, there might have been a lot of explaining to do.

O'Keefe's ruddy features held none of his usual good humor; indeed, his square-jawed countenance was almost grim as he hurried toward them. He seemed oblivious to the surroundings and the sheepish expressions on the faces of his daughter and Kit. Kit rubbed the back of his neck as a chill crawled up his spine.

"So there you be," O'Keefe said as he lumbered up from the creek bank by an old hollow log. "Your 'friend,' Stalking Fox, just brought the news. Jackson's finally on the move. He's crossed into the territory, set up a fort on this side of the Tennessee, and is coming on south. They burned a Hillabee village. I don't understand. The Hillabees have always been on good terms with the white settlers." Iron Hand fixed the lieutenant in a smoldering stare. "I been with these people many a year. I think more like a Choctaw than I do white. If those Tennesseeans march against us, by my oath, I'll see them dance in rivers of blood before they bring me down."

"Jackson won't march against you," Kit said. He leaned on his crutch and looked from Raven to her resolute father.

"What's to stop him?" O'Keefe replied somberly.

"I will," the lieutenant answered.

Kit noticed the look of disbelief in O'Keefe's eyes. Even Raven looked a trifle incredulous.

"Trust me."

As the setting sun streaked the sky with cinnamon wisps of clouds etched in golden light, the throbbing cadence of war drums reverberated throughout the Creek village at the Horseshoe Bend on the Tallapoosa River.

As leader of the Medicine Belt Clan, Wolf Jacket sat in a place of honor. He was silent and outwardly impassive as the other war chiefs began to assemble in the council house of the Red Stick village. All the leaders of the Upper Creeks, "the people of war," had been summoned to council.

The Fox Clan under Red Eagle, newly arrived only a day ago, fresh from raids that had terrorized settlers from Alabama to deep into Georgia, had stationed themselves in front of the council house while Red

Eagle entered the long-walled, low-beamed cabin and joined the other clan leaders who were gathered about the ceremonial fire.

Runs Above, the new leader of the Bear Clan, was present. His shrewd eyes were constantly shifting, as if he were expecting an attack instead of being among friends.

Other chiefs arrived as the night wore on: Clubs the Runner and Tall Willow, famed warriors in their own right. The Hawk Clan answered the call of the drums, and many of them demanded to sit at council. The Hawk Clan was always a problem, Wolf Jacket thought with a sigh. So many of the warriors were young and hotheaded, too eager to rush headlong into battle. Still, Wolf Jacket approved of their courage; he knew how to make the best use of them.

The red-coated chief knew wars were not won by reckless conduct. Each of his own forays had been carefully planned. And now he had another scheme, to draw Andrew Jackson into waging war against the Choctaws. And when the army of Tennesseans was depleted and the volunteers counting their dead, the Creeks would strike hard and fast and in overwhelming numbers.

Wolf Jacket knew the others were waiting for his counsel, to hear what he had to say. Finally Blue Kettle, a swarthy, quarrelsome warrior, glanced at Runs Above, who nodded. As if acting on an unspoken command, Blue Kettle stepped forward and, indicating Red Eagle, began to speak.

"Our brothers of the Fox bring us word of their many victories against the white settlers who steal our land. Songs will be sung of their bravery and great deeds. But what will be sung of we who hide behind the walls of our village? Let us march against this

General Jackson and destroy him once and for all. Then the white men in their great village to the north will see that the Creeks will keep their land and not be driven out."

Blue Kettle looked about and saw that many of the young men, especially among his own clan, supported him.

Red Eagle, a mixed-blood whose clean-cut features were hidden behind his war paint, stood up and waited for the others to cease their comments and be quiet.

"I have fought the white soldiers. They have no stomach for fighting. We have nothing to fear from them." Red Eagle folded his arms across his muscular chest. His close-cropped hair was adorned with a pair of eagle feathers, which added to his stature. He turned to Wolf Jacket and added, "Still, I will hear the words of he who wears the medicine belt."

Again there was murmuring among the braves as Wolf Jacket stood and walked to the center of the circle of warriors.

"We are not women who hide from the soldiers who have crossed the Tennessee. Nor are we children who shake our weapons and run to the first sound of rifle fire." His eyes swept over the faces of the men seated in the council house. He fixed his gaze on Blue Kettle, who lowered his eyes and sat down among the other young men of the Hawk clan. "This is no game for children," Wolf Jacket continued. "The Red Sticks are strong because our numbers are many. We are many because we do not waste our young men in battle." Embers in the fire crackled and split apart. "Let the soldiers make war against our enemy, the Choctaw. Let them weaken one another. Then we will destroy them both."

"Jackson may march against us. How do you know he will choose to attack Iron Hand?" Runs Above said, rising to confront Wolf Jacket. As an elder and leader of the Bear Clan, he had a right to challenge the war chief.

"Can you see what has yet to happen?" Red Eagle asked. He too had begun to doubt the wisdom in delaying a strike against Jackson's army.

"It will happen as I say," Wolf Jacket stated flatly.

"And will you lead this Jackson and his army against the Choctaws at Willow Creek?" Runs Above said. He thought he had Wolf Jacket caught by his own words. Runs Above was wrong.

"Not I," said Wolf Jacket. "Him!" He turned and pointed toward a figure in the shadows, who upon command started forward. The recent arrivals to the Creek village began to marvel aloud as the firelight played off the ruby and gold hilt of the shadow man's long knife. Here was a weapon of great power and magic.

Bill Tibbs had survived the explosion, survived the river. Battered and bleeding, he had blindly followed where the sword led him. He had lived. And with his every step the Eye of Alexander had fueled the black hatred in his heart for Kit McQueen, this shadow man, Bill Tibbs.

Chapter Thirty

"I'll shoot the first man who starts for home," the gaunt general bellowed. He had planted himself smack-dab in the middle of the open gate, a few yards out from the stockade walls of Fort Strother. The men who were huddled in the gateway knew they could overpower any guard, but not one of the sixty men wanted to be sacrificed for the good of all the rest.

The volunteers were tired and hungry, and they had lost their enthusiasm for this war. Supplies were low, and reinforcements had yet to arrive. But these farmers had dutifully followed Jackson and did as they were ordered and built Fort Strother on the banks of the Coosa. It had taken the last week in November and the first fifteen days of December to erect the stockade walls and finish a cabin for the general, and cabins, no matter how incomplete, for the remainder of his command. Then the army began to vanish.

Men who had signed up for ten, twenty, or thirty days simply packed their meager belongings and left in droves. Most of the time, Jackson was the last to hear of these departures, as they usually occurred in the dead of night. Some volunteers simply went out on patrol and never came back. Jackson had crossed the Tennessee River with nearly a thousand volunteers; now his force had dwindled in size until it numbered barely a hundred and twenty men. And that wasn't the end of his problems.

On this morning of the sixteenth of December another sixty men were preparing to depart, anxious to return to their farms and loved ones. Their leader, a hulking, buckskin-clad frontiersman by the name of Axel Griffin, had refused to sneak away. He was a solid, plainspoken man whose reputation for hard work, honesty, and courage had never been questioned. He had brought his Blue Ridge boys down from their hardscrabble farms to serve with Jackson. But their thirty days of service was ended. And as of yet, not a man among them had fired a gun in anger.

"Gen'l, you ain't about to shoot me," Griffin said. "Stand aside. If we leave now, chances are we'll be home before the first snow."

Jackson remained rooted in place. A wintry December breeze tugged at the hem of his black frock coat. The wind brushed his silvery hair forward, and he looked like some half-starved Medusa, threatening to turn these mutineers to stone.

Jackson leveled the pistol he had grabbed from Marcus Bellamy's belt when the captain had brought word of Griffin's intentions. The general had quite literally sprung from his sickbed, stolen his subordinate's gun, and rushed across the campground to the gate, where he waited in the cold, gray light of morning for Griffin and his Blue Ridge boys to appear.

"What day is it?" Jackson called out to the husky farmer.

Griffin scratched his head beneath his coonskin cap. "Don't rightly know, Gen'l."

"It is the sixteenth of December," Jackson replied in a hard, clipped tone. He aimed right between the woodsman's eyes. "A man ought to know the day he dies. Even a mutineer like yourself."

The Blue Ridge farmers ·behind Griffin began to grumble and move out of the line of fire, an action not lost on the amiable leader. Big Axel Griffin stared down the barrel of Jackson's pistol. At a distance of fifteen feet the farmer was under no illusion that Jackson might miss.

"See here, Gen'l. There ain't hardly enough food for the men you got. If'n we go, there'll be fewer mouths to feed. We ain't taken nothing but a handful of cornmeal and some jerked beef. Me and the boys can forage the rest and live off the land till we reach home." Griffin held his work-roughened hands palm out in a gesture of peace. A pistol and a tomahawk remained tucked in his belt. He licked his lips, then scratched at his bushy brown beard.

Behind the men from the Blue Ridge Mountains, the remaining volunteers under Jackson's command watched from their longhouses or straggled out into the compound for a better view of the confrontation. One man in particular, a tall, brooding figure with long, black hair, watched from the makeshift stable where he'd been saddling Bellamy's horse and preparing to make a wide circle of the forest in search of any Choctaw scouts that might have ventured north.

Bill Tibbs had appeared at Fort Strother three weeks ago and presented himself as a survivor of the Hope Station massacre. Tibbs remembered with smug appreciation of his own cleverness how he had affixed the blame for the slaughter on Iron Hand and his warriors.

Wolf Jacket's plan was working like a charm. Jackson not only accepted Tibbs's story, but appointed him scout since he knew the countryside, and allowed him the use of the horses. Tibbs grinned as he watched the general try to stop another mutiny.

"If only you knew what the Red Sticks have in store for you, General, you'd join those Blue Ridge boys and skedaddle on back across the Tennessee River." Tibbs adjusted the shoulder strap of the buckskin bag in which he kept the scimitar hidden from the soldiers in the fort.

"Yes, sir," Tibbs muttered. A horse stamped and pawed the packed earth. Flies cut hectic spirals above the droppings. "Your troubles are just starting."

Back at the gate Andrew Jackson quickly estimated the strength of his command at a hundred and thirty men. The loss of Griffin's volunteers would be disastrous, depleting his force by half and leaving him with only a handful of soldiers to defend Fort Strother while awaiting Colonel William Carroll with reinforcements and the supply train. Jackson knew he had to stop this latest threat here and now.

"General, you got no right to call us mutineers," Griffin exclaimed, stalling for time. He'd begun to believe Jackson meant business and intended to shoot him down. He wiped a hand across his mouth and stared up at the gunmetal-gray sky.

It was a cold, damp day with the smell of rain in the air. Griffin considered making a run for the woods; after all, the general only had one shot. But a man Griffin's size made a good target, and the land on three sides of the fort had been clearcut, leaving forty yards of open ground. The Coosa River bordered the fourth side, and a man would be a fool to wade it under fire.

For a single fleeting moment the farmer considered a try for his own weapons. But that course only led to the gallows, certainly not home.

"We signed on in Nashville for thirty days. Captain Bellamy was there. Thirty days is up. And that's what we agreed to. Ain't that right, Captain?" Griffin turned toward the thickset, nervous officer standing off to one side. Bellamy, while not the most capable of officers, had exhibited an earnest desire to learn and showed compassion for the common soldier, qualities that had won him the respect of the volunteers.

Griffin glanced in Bellamy's direction, but the captain was no longer paying attention to the confrontation at the gate. He was staring past both parties, toward the direction of the forest opposite the south wall of the fort, where two white men, the smaller one walking with a slight limp and the other nearly as large as a bear, approached the fort. Griffin looked in that direction, stepping aside to stare past Jackson. The general, muttering to himself, turned to look down the well-trampled path.

The trail disappeared once it reached the thicket of red bur oaks and sweet gum trees and shagbark hickory, the dense beginnings of a forest that peppered the hills and offered concealment to a thousand imagined enemies on blustery moonless nights.

But two strangers hardly posed a threat, so Jackson held his ground. He wasn't about to scurry into the stockade like a frightened pup. He could see now that these newcomers were at least white men. They were no doubt stragglers from some other massacre perpetrated by the likes of that renegade O'Keefe. *Poor souls*, he thought. *Well, I'll greet them myself.* The general from Tennessee wasn't motivated by politeness. Whatever news he could glean from these new arrivals, Jackson wanted to be the first to hear.

The closer he came to Fort Strother, the more Iron Hand O'Keefe began to lag behind his companion.

Kit McQueen glanced aside at the big man. "Take courage, my friend."

"Easy for you to say," O'Keefe grumbled. "It ain't you, McQueen, putting your head in the bear trap."

"You've been in worse spots," Kit replied. If Kit could keep the Irishman talking, the man wouldn't bolt and make a dash for the tall timber. Kit studied the stockade.

That had to be Jackson standing before the gate, gun in hand. Kit had heard enough descriptions of the man to identify him on sight.

"What the devil is going on?" O'Keefe muttered. He eyed the stockade and counted half a dozen riflemen behind the parapets. More men were massed at the gate, and they looked armed to the teeth.

"Just like your runners said," Kit replied. "Jackson's been losing men. Looks like he's about to lose some more."

"Blast my soul, we should have waited," O'Keefe lamented, scratching at his jaw with his iron hook.

"Rest easy, there," Kit said. "Five can shoot us just as dead as fifty."

"A discouraging notion—"

"And tuck away that hook, or you'll have them opening up on us before I say my piece."

Kit quickened his pace. He was dressed in his linsey-woolsey shirt and leather boots, but the remainder of his attire was Choctaw, from his buckskin overshirt to his fringed breeches that Raven herself had made for him, stitching the leggings with fine sinew.

O'Keefe wore the garb of his adopted people. His shaggy mane was adorned with a raven feather and fell in a silvery cascade across his massive shoulders. Both men could see the growing suspicion in Jackson's eyes and in the faces of those behind him. Kit reached inside his shirt and removed a leather packet as he crossed the last few feet.

"General Jackson?" he asked, just to be on the safe side.

"Yes," Jackson replied, studying the new arrivals. "Are you scouts for Colonel Carroll?"

Captain Bellamy left his position by the gate and moved up alongside his commanding officer. Axel Griffin and his Blue Ridge boys hung back inside the safety of the fort. The men on the walls anxiously scanned the line of trees, sensing movement in the underbrush.

"I am Lieutenant Kit McQueen of the United States Army. These papers will introduce me and explain why I am here." He held out the leather pouch.

"So you are the young Hotspur," Jackson said gruffly. His gut had begun to spasm, and his side ached. "Harrelson already alerted me as to your arrival. However, he made no mention as to your disregard for promptness, much less for military attire." Jackson took the pouch and passed it to Bellamy, then briefly appraised Kit. "Save for your hair, I would have took you for a Creek or Choctaw. Hardly an officer." Jackson stroked his lean jaw as he studied the young lieutenant. "Hmmm. So Dan McQueen was your father. I expected you to be larger."

"As for my attire, I have been among the Choctaw,"

Kit replied. "And I owe them my life. And as to my stature...I can hold my own."

"The Choctaw let you live?" Bellamy blurted out. "We have heard they take prisoners only to torture them to death. Did you escape?" Realizing he had interrupted his commanding officer, Bellamy lapsed into an awkward silence.

"So you've visited the Choctaws," Jackson continued, his disbelief obvious. "And I suppose you've brought Chief Iron Hand here as your prisoner," he added jokingly. The general had yet to comprehend the identity of the rough-looking man standing behind Kit.

But O'Keefe wasn't about to keep Jackson waiting. He brought his left arm out from behind his back and held the hook up in plain view.

"I ain't nobody's prisoner, General, sir. And never will be. I come along of my own free will."

"By heaven, it is the renegade himself!" Bellamy exclaimed, and reached for his pistol.

Jackson snapped up the flintlock in his hand. The name spread among the ranks of the Blue Ridge boys and carried to the stockade walls. Iron Hand O'Keefe— war chief of the Choctaws!

One of Griffin's men bolted across the compound, eager to spread the news that the Choctaw chief was outside the stockade. In the shadowy interior of the stable, behind the stout log walls that shielded the horses from the elements, Bill Tibbs cleared away a layer of chinking with his knife and watched through the peephole he had made for himself.

At the gate, Kit moved quickly to place himself in General Jackson's line of fire. "Iron Hand comes as an ally," he said.

"The butcher of Fort Mims and Hope Station and

Lord only knows how many farms has the affrontery," Jackson sputtered, "to come before me and expect me to welcome him instead of clap him in irons?"

"I suggest you lower your gun, General Jackson," Kit said.

"Not until this villain is in chains!" Jackson answered.

"I wondered how best to convince you of O'Keefe's intentions," Kit began. He noticed the soldiers on the walls were increasing in numbers, and many of the men had their rifles trained on the Irishman. "Then it dawned on me, if I couldn't do it alone, I'd bring help." Kit slowly drew one of the pistols from his belt. Bellamy visibly tensed as Kit raised the weapon and fired into the air. The gunshot reverberated among the green hills, repeating itself as it faded into the somber gray sky. On his signal, the help he spoke of showed themselves. Three hundred Choctaw warriors materialized out of the forest and moved silently toward the fort. The effect on the men inside the stockade was instantaneous. Even Griffin's volunteers forgot all about their Blue Ridge homes. They grabbed their rifles and headed for the walls.

Captain Bellamy looked thunderstruck. He stared in horror at the Choctaw host advancing on Fort Strother. His eyes fairly bulged in his head, and his mouth went dry.

"My God," the captain croaked. "What have you done?" He began edging toward the gate.

Jackson glanced over his shoulder at his subordinate. "Hold your ground, dammit!" Then, to Bellamy's surprise, the general lowered his pistol and returned it to the captain.

"Tuck this back in your belt, Marcus. If this was an attack, we'd be dead by now."

"But General—" Bellamy began to protest.

Jackson silenced him with a castigating glance. He faced Kit and the lumbering giant of an Irishman. "Well, Lieutenant McQueen, perhaps you'll kindly inform me as to just what the hell is going on."

"I'd be glad to, General," Kit replied. He nodded to O'Keefe, who waved to the advancing Choctaw. Acting on his gesture, the warriors halted and waited in the meadow about thirty yards from the fort.

"First of all, Wolf Jacket and his Creeks are responsible for Hope Station. They raided the Choctaw camp as well."

"Killed a bunch of old men and boys and carried off many of our women and children," O'Keefe said. Truth seemed to radiate from the Irishman's ugly, honest war map of a face. "We aim to fight 'em to the death," O'Keefe finished. "The Red Sticks have us outnumbered. But the way I see it, General Jackson, together we could give them Creeks a licking that they'd never forget."

"And to show good faith," Kit added, "Chief Iron Hand and his people have brought supplies for your command. There's corn and meat, dried berries and squash. Enough to tide your men over until your pack train arrives."

He searched Jackson's stern countenance and hawk's eyes, hoping to find some manner of acceptance. The general's resolve began to falter. Such an unexpected development had caught him completely off guard. Kit pressed his point while Jackson seemed to be wavering, struggling to comprehend all Kit was telling him.

"I'm sorry to make such a show of this, General Jackson. You see, it's the Creeks who are working with the British. Agents—renegades, actually—are issuing guns to the Red Sticks. I caught one of the turncoats, a

man named Bill Tibbs, and would have brought him to
you, but he was either killed or escaped me when..."
His voice trailed off as the general's jaw went slack and
his eyebrows arched in astonishment.

"Who did you say?" Jackson leaned forward.

Kit glanced at O'Keefe. The Irishman shrugged.
"Bill Tibbs," Kit repeated. "He was in the pay of the
British. I lost him, though, on the Alabama River."

Andrew Jackson's sallow complexion grew livid.
His emaciated frame trembled, and there was murder
in his burning gaze. "Tibbs lost? I think I can help you
find him."

Kit reached the door to the stable a few paces
ahead of O'Keefe and the soldiers. Brandishing the
"Quakers," those heavy-bore pistols that had served
his father so well during the Revolution, Kit ducked
through the doorway and flattened himself against a
dark patch of wall. He crouched in the shadows until
he could see past the horses in their stalls to the rear
of the stable, where a crudely fashioned back door
swung ajar. Several soldiers immediately filled the
entrance and crowded through the doorway, their rifles
cocked and primed. One sandy-haired young man in
woolen breeches and a waistcoat over his naked, hair-
less chest yelped as Kit dislodged himself from the
darkness. The soldier whirled and fired. Kit's reactions were lightning quick. He slapped the rifle barrel
up away from his face, causing the startled soldier to
blast a hole in the roof.

"Christ!" Kit said, staggering back, his ears ringing.

"Sorry," the Tennessean replied sheepishly, and
lowered his rifle. Powder smoke trailed from the barrel.
He began to reload. Kit snatched the powder horn
from the soldier's grasp and tossed it aside and, after

one final glower, trotted off down the middle of the stable and out the rear door. He had just stepped into pallid sunlight when a second round of gunfire shattered the autumn stillness.

"McQueen!" It was Iron Hand, bellowing Kit's name from the compound. Kit groaned and came on at a dead run, wondering what other trigger-happy fools were up to mischief.

Kit could see the burly Irishman lumbering back toward the front gate and with sinking heart feared what he'd find, that Bill Tibbs had eluded him again.

He dashed past the stable and caught up to O'Keefe as the man turned toward him.

"Your friend Tibbs came galloping out from behind the longhouse yonder." O'Keefe hammered out his words. "Rode right past the lads at the gate. Shot one, on my oath."

Another volley sounded from the men on the walls, the crack of gunfire rolling back toward the soldiers in the compound. Andrew Jackson was just ahead, walking with a long-legged gait that brought him up to the wounded Tennessean sprawled in the shadow of the log walls.

It was Axel Griffin. One of his kinsmen had propped him up against a water barrel. He watched as Andrew Jackson and then Kit McQueen and half a dozen soldiers reached him.

Kit limped outside the walls. The Choctaw warriors waited with their weapons ready and fearing treachery. Tibbs had skirted O'Keefe's people and followed the winding riverbank. Kit shaded his eyes and glimpsed the fleeing horseman as he left the Coosa and vanished at a gallop into the forest.

"He took my horse," a voice beside him spoke. It was Captain Marcus Bellamy. "She's a born runner.

Fastest horse in the command. Even faster than General Jackson's, but he doesn't like to admit it." Bellamy sighed and wiped a hand across his mouth and double chin.

Kit started back into the fort and waved O'Keefe forward.

"You better settle your warriors down. Those rifle shots made them kind of nervous."

"Weren't any tonic for me, neither," the Irishman muttered. "That Tibbs lives a charmed life." The war chief started down the trail toward the Choctaw warriors, who seemed to visibly relax at his reappearance.

Kit thought on what O'Keefe had said. *A charmed life.* Maybe there was something to that damn evil sword. Maybe it had not only corrupted Bill Tibbs but protected him as well. It was hard to disregard such a notion as he stood off to the side and watched Griffin die. At last the Tennessean's chin tilted down toward his blood-soaked chest.

When it was ended, another of Griffin's Blue Ridge boys stepped forward, his coonskin cap in hand. He looked around at those companions who had elected him spokesman.

"General Jackson," the volunteer began. "I be Otis Potts. And I speak for us mountain folk." He glanced down at Griffin, then back to the general. "If it's all the same to you, we changed our minds and figger to stay on with ye for a while, till we settle things, eye for eye, blood for blood." Potts turned on his heel and returned to the ranks of the volunteers.

There would be no desertions today.

PART FOUR

Horseshoe Bend

Chapter Thirty-one

There were drums in the afternoon. They beat a solemn, reverent cadence, accompanying the soft, trilling melody played upon wooden flutes. The ceremonial music, though muffled by the settling snow, managed to rise from the Choctaw encampment outside the walls of Fort Strother and settle on the log cabins where an army of Tennesseans endured the bitter cold. For this troop of recent arrivals, a warm fire and boring inactivity was reward enough, for they had just returned from a skirmish with the Creeks and there had been casualties.

In the cabin that served as his headquarters, Andrew Jackson loomed like a brooding gargoyle over his map of the territory. His shadow covered all of Alabama and stretched as far as New Orleans, his silhouette shifting in subtle ways with the flickering of the lamplight and the flames leaping up from the logs in the fireplace.

To his left stood Colonel William Carroll, a man in his middle years, short and stout and solid, a man who loved a good fight. Across from Jackson, Carroll's own adjutant, Captain Owen Kelly, a darkly handsome young man, showed fatigue in his spattered blue waistcoat and trousers; the dull brass buttons on his wide lapel no longer gleamed in the lamplight.

Kelly came from a good family of Tennesseans who owned several hundred acres of rich bottomland a few miles south of Nashville. Up until a few months ago Kelly had been studying medicine at Yale, but the lure of the frontier had caused him to abandon his schooling in Connecticut. Returning home, he had gained his father's grudging consent and joined Carroll's infantry. Kelly's parents had permitted him to embark on this campaign if the young officer promised to take up his studies once the Red Sticks were defeated. Kelly had happily struck a bargain, though it was one he had no intention of keeping. He'd found soldiering to his liking.

The former student touched the point of his dagger to a scrawled line that indicated the upper reaches of the Tallapoosa River. Despite his weary state, he eagerly described the excursion that had taken him into battle. He had run into a Creek war party quite by accident. After a liberal exchange of gunfire both sides had retreated to opposite banks of the river. At last Kelly finished his vainglorious account of his first battle. He smiled smugly at Captain Bellamy, standing to his left. The two adjutants had become rivals since Carroll's infantry had joined with Jackson's command. Kelly came from a better family and considered himself Bellamy's superior.

Captain Marcus Bellamy figured quite the opposite. He was older and more experienced and was Jackson's trusted aide, and that ought to settle any claim to rank, he felt.

"Well, Marcus, did you and your Choctaw allies

have any luck?" Kelly asked. "I understand you beat me back to the fort by three days."

Bellamy nodded and indicated another location on the map that Jackson had already marked with an X. He had taken the men from Blue Ridge along with a contingent of Choctaws led by Kit McQueen and a warrior named Young Otter.

"We met a force of Cherokee some twenty miles from the fort," Bellamy said. "They brought word of a Red Stick war party ranging along Emuckfaw Creek. We caught up with them a couple of days later."

Kelly tried to remain unimpressed. "And your Choctaws, did they actually fight?"

"Like a pack of red wolves. And Potts's lads held their own as well. And when we had left the field, there was no doubt as to who had carried the day, on my oath," Bellamy replied pointedly, to put this up-start Kelly in his place.

The former medical student sipped his brandy and struggled to remain impassive, but his companion's tone got the better of him.

"See here, sir, if you are implying any cowardly defeat on my part, I heartily take offense." Kelly's cheeks reddened, and he was already reaching for the glove in his belt.

"Enough," Jackson interjected. "Both of you have deported yourselves with honor." He glared at Kelly. "I will not permit either of my officers to engage themselves in a duel. I need all of you in good health." The general winced. The cold seemed to aggravate the pain in his side. Carroll had brought a physician, but Jackson would not allow the man to probe for the pistol ball.

"All your officers?" Colonel Carroll grumbled, taking a seat in the nearest chair. "One seems conspicuously absent."

"Ah, the young Hotspur." Jackson chuckled. He'd begun to take a liking to Kit despite himself. The lieutenant had proved true to his word and brought the Choctaws under General Jackson's command. Next, the Cherokees had followed O'Keefe's example and come into Fort Strother. Carroll's reinforcements had entered the fort on Christmas day. Jackson had never received such a welcome gift. He could now place almost a thousand men in the field against the Creeks. But how best to use his men and when to use them, that was the question. The door to the general's cabin swung ajar, and a frigid gust of wintry air followed Kit McQueen into the room.

"Hmmm. Speak of the devil," Kelly replied haughtily. He could not help but hold in contempt this man who so preferred the company of another race to his own. Kelly was appalled at the rumors he had heard concerning Kit and a mixed-blood Choctaw woman. The two were often seen together.

Kit ignored the captain's tone of voice and dusted the snow from the greatcoat he wore over his shirt of brushed buckskin, military breeches, and boots. His red hair was as shaggy as a Choctaw's. A reddish blond beard covered his jaw now. His sharp eyes revealed caution and wariness befitting that of a hunter. His experience with the "long-haired people," as the Choctaws called themselves, had seasoned him in ways a man like Owen Kelly could never guess. Kit walked to the fire and held out his hands to the blaze in grateful supplication to its warmth.

"You are late, sir," Kelly added. Kit walked to a table set against the wall and laden with round loaves of bread, a quarter wheel of cheese, and an enameled bowl of beans and chunks of pork.

The table, like all the other furniture in the general's quarters, was hand-hewn and fastened together with wooden pegs. Patches of bark on the side of one of the legs revealed the carpenter's haste. It was a roughly appointed room, with only a few touches of home to make the winter seem not so interminable to the man the Tennesseans had taken to calling "Old Hickory." A silhouette of Jackson's wife, in a gilded gold frame, rested on a small table near the general's bed. A matched pair of engraved dueling pistols in a black walnut case had been left upon the table with the map.

Jackson filled a blue enameled tin cup with a measure of hot buttered rum. He slid the cup across the table for Kit.

"Captain Kelly is tired and therefore a trifle brusque," Jackson said.

"I understand him, General," Kit replied. He tried the rum and found it to his liking. Warmth spread from his belly to his limbs. "The Choctaws are burying their dead, the two warriors who scouted for Captain Kelly. And I was obliged to be there."

Colonel Carroll was quick to rush to the defense of his well-to-do subordinate. "Well, now...a tragic loss...but it could not be helped. In war, men die."

"I had no way of knowing the damnable Red Sticks were on the opposite bank when I sent your Choctaws across the shallows," Kelly spoke up, his mouth full of cheese. "They were killed in the first volley. Were they...uh...friends of yours?" He swallowed and ran his tongue over his teeth, searching for any remnants of cheese.

Kit looked at the young officer. "I hardly knew Big Turtle. As for Stalking Fox, he hated my guts. But he had courage, and I respected him for that even while I disliked him. Just like I respect you, Captain Kelly."

Kit's meaning was obvious. Kelly turned livid. His lips tightened into a thin line. "Respect, Mr. McQueen? Perhaps one day I might have the opportunity to teach you the meaning of the word."

"Perhaps," Kit replied. "If the Red Sticks let you live that long." He turned and winked at Marcus Bellamy, who had to stifle his own laughter so as not to further aggravate the situation.

"I asked you all here for a reason," Andrew Jackson began. "And it wasn't so that you might stuff your bellies on the last of my good cheese and make bold threats over tankards of rum like common roisters!"

He paused and sucked in his breath as the bickering around him ceased. Then he leaned over the map and placed the tip of his knife blade on the Tallapoosa River at Horseshoe Bend.

"There they are. Wolf Jacket, Red Eagle, and the whole Red Stick confederacy. That's the stronghold we must take, or the territory will never know peace." Jackson traced a line with the dagger from the location of Fort Strother to the fortified Creek village. "Our next line of march must bring us straight to the Tallapoosa. Once we break winter camp there will be no turning back. The longer we take to achieve victory, the longer we leave New Orleans and the underbelly of our country open to British invasion."

Jackson set aside his dagger and rolled up the map of the territory, revealing Iron Hand O'Keefe's own rendering of the fortifications at Horseshoe Bend. The Creeks had chosen their encampment well. They had placed their village in the center of a peninsula surrounded on three sides by the Tallapoosa River. Across the landward base of the peninsula the Creeks had erected a palisade from which they could direct a murderous fire. The Tallapoosa itself was an equally challenging barricade, wide enough to slow an advancing force and leave them sitting targets for Red Stick marksmen on the riverbank.

Carroll and Bellamy studied the map of the stronghold. Kelly quickly joined the men at the table. He was curious as to this new dilemma and eager to offer his suggestions.

"Give me a couple of hundred fighting men, and we'll storm their palisade and drive the Creeks back to the village," he bragged.

Jackson did not reply. Instead, he shifted his gaze to Kit and waited for the lieutenant to comment on the map.

"Without a doubt the palisade must be stormed," the general agreed when Kit made no remark.

"Such an assault, over open ground," Captain Bellamy observed, his tone thoughtful, "would no doubt result in a frightful loss of life."

"Determination will prevail," Kelly retorted.

"A frontal assault is a fool's gambit," Bellamy said.

"I take offense, Mr. Bellamy."

"Blast your pride! We are talking about human lives!"

"Both of you are right," Jackson flatly interrupted, putting an end to the heated exchange. "We must take the palisade. But such an attack cannot hope to succeed without a diversion." He looked once more at Kit, waiting. . . .

Kit sighed and traced a line along the river until he stopped at the tip of the peninsula. "O'Keefe and I could lead a force of Choctaws and Cherokees across the river under cover of night. By morning we could be in position to strike the Red Sticks from the rear while you rush their fortifications."

Captain Bellamy paled. "Think what you're saying,

man. If they've posted sentries and an alarm is given, you'll be caught in the river and cut to pieces."

"No alarm will sound."

"You place great trust in your luck, Lieutenant McQueen," Colonel Carroll remarked.

"Indeed," Kelly added.

Kit drew his broad-bladed knife from its sheath. It was duel-edged and razor sharp, capable of slitting a man's throat from ear to ear. He stabbed the knife into the tabletop, skewering the Creek stronghold. "I trust in this!"

No one had anything else to add. General Jackson nodded in appreciation. He couldn't have said it better himself.

Kit could have shared quarters with Bellamy and Kelly, but he had no apology for his preferences, and with the snow settling on his shoulders and coat he made his way out of the fort and to the lodge some of the Choctaw people had built for him. As he had fought at their side, so the long-haired people accepted him.

He picked his way unerringly through the cluster of pole-and-woven-reed huts until he came to his own, a small, adequate shelter erected close to O'Keefe's. Kit paused at his entrance and looked longingly at O'Keefe's. His innermost thoughts reached out to Raven across the transformed setting, for the snow had begun to work its magic, drifting and swirling in a tempest underscored by the ceremonial drums.

A hand closed over his. He jumped, startled. Raven drew him into his lodge. She wore a woolen blanket and a teasing smile and nothing more, and she led him to his bedding of rushes covered with soft pelts.

"What are you doing?"

"I have wept for the dead," she said, pulling him down beside her. "Now I will sing, my body to yours, my heart to yours." She looked up into his eyes and grew troubled by what she saw there. He sat beside her, but his gaze was filled with worry, not passion. A small fire burned in the center of the lodge. But all the warmth seemed to emanate from Raven O'Keefe.

"What has happened?" she said, moving closer to him. She abandoned, for the moment, her attempted seduction.

"I may have killed your father myself, and many of your people tonight," Kit told her, and quickly recounted his plan for a diversionary attack upon the Creek stronghold. He looked at her. "You ought to run to your father and tell him to take his people and go from here."

"This is our land. Have you learned nothing?" Iron Hand's daughter said. "The Choctaws will be the first to draw blood. My people will think you honor them." She sat on her haunches and faced Kit. "The Red Sticks slaughtered our old ones, carried off the young. It is our right to strike them first."

"You think and talk like all the others," Kit grumbled. Fording the Tallapoosa could get a lot of them killed."

"I *am* one of the others," she said. "Do you think being a mixed-blood makes me any the less a Choctaw? Is that what you hope?" she added coldly.

Raven opened the blanket, revealing her lithe form, her coppery skin, and the soft, sweet curves of her breasts and thighs.

"What *do* you see?"

Kit reached around the young woman and pulled the blanket up about her shoulders. "Life," he told her.

And taking her hands he kissed each palm, lifting first the left, then the right to his lips.

An ember cracked and popped like a pistol shot. Firelight leaped and fell; shadows crouched and danced like gypsy angels.

"When will you leave?" she asked.

"Two weeks, three, maybe longer, maybe when the weather clears or worsens and the Red Sticks do not expect us."

"Then we have time," Raven said, and pulled him down beside her.

"Listen," Kit said.

The drums had ceased their mourning toll. The reed flutes finished their trilling whispers. And all that remained beneath the silent, settling snow was what had always been there and always would be—death and life.

Chapter Thirty-two

It was in the time of the First Budding Moon, on the twenty-sixth day of March, and the Creek stronghold at Horseshoe Bend waited out the death throes of a savage thunderstorm. Rain pummeled the new-growth branches of white oaks and sweetgums. Winds as cruel as a cat-o'-nine-tails lashed the log barricade and sent the Creek defenders Wolf Jacket had posted scurrying to the safety and comfort of their lodges.

One solitary figure seemed immune to the bruising downpour. Wrapped in a heavy blanket that he clutched about his head and shoulders, Bill Tibbs continued his rounds of the hundred-acre encampment. His keen eyes probed the storm-lashed line of trees across the river.

When will they come? From which direction? Tibbs noticed the lack of Creek guards by the dugouts. If Jackson was foolish enough to try a crossing, the sentries would need to sound the alert. Tibbs, his back to the Tallapoosa, peered one last time through the curtain of rain at the stockade walls. The Red Stick defenders could hold that barricade against twice the number Jackson had under his command.

Old Hickory was on the move, bringing his Tennesseans and his Choctaw allies with him.

And bringing McQueen, Tibbs thought. *My friend, my enemy.*

He tightened his grip on his blanket and, skirting a puddle, made his way through the village, his long-legged gait carrying him across the newly tilled fields where Creek women had planted corn and beans. His boots sank in the soft earth, and for a few minutes, Tibbs had to fight for each step. By the time he reached the lodges at the east end of the peninsula, a trickle of water had begun to work its way beneath his makeshift cowl and send a rivulet down his back.

Eventually he reached firmer footing, but his woolen trousers were mud-soaked up above his ankles. Tibbs made better time as he headed straight for Wolf Jacket's lodge. The gunrunner was about ten feet from the entrance when Wolf Jacket, half naked, bolted through the doorway. His features were mottled with anger.

Behind him, a naked young girl of fifteen winters flailed away at the war chief of the Red Sticks. His right hand, entangled in her hair, held her at arm's length. He dragged her out into the rain and with a mighty backhand sent her sprawling facedown in the mud. Wolf Jacket wiped a forearm across his bloody lip.

"Long-haired she-welp!" he cursed. When the hapless girl tried to crawl out of harm's way, Wolf Jacket moved in and delivered a kick to her midsection that tumbled the girl over in the mud, where she lay clutching at her belly and gasping for breath. Another well-aimed kick snapped her head back, and she lay still.

Wolf Jacket noticed Tibbs standing off to one side and motioned for the white man to join him, then ducked back through the entrance, leaving his poor captive motionless in the rain. Pity for the Choctaw was a luxury Tibbs could not afford. He ducked through the entrance and followed Wolf Jacket into his lodge.

The interior of the lodge smelled of smoked venison, boiled beans, and cornmeal cakes. Wolf Jacket squatted by the cook fire, warming himself while carving a portion of venison from a roasted haunch brought to him by one of his wives. Tibbs glanced around at the willow backrests and folded blankets. The lodge, about twenty feet across from wall to wall, seemed empty without them. "Your wives, Calling Shadow and Little Willow?" Tibbs asked.

Wolf Jacket shrugged. "The long-hair poisoned them against me. Their eyes were like knives; I could not be with the long-hair woman while my wives watched from their blankets. I sent them both to the lodges of their mothers." Wolf Jacket wrapped a blanket around his shoulders, his torso rippling with coppery muscles thick as cordwood. The Red Stick grinned.

"Ah, but the long-hair was too much trouble." He gingerly touched his swollen lip where she'd cracked him in the mouth with a bowl. "Now I have no woman to keep me warm." He crawled back to his bedding and began to eat.

Tibbs removed his blanket and dried himself by the cook fire. He removed the pistols from his belt and laid them aside. The scimitar with its baleful eye he placed close at hand upon the ground.

"We don't need women to keep us warm," Tibbs said. "You and I have our hate."

Wolf Jacket studied Tibbs. Here was one white man the war chief could tolerate. Tibbs brought guns, traded for plunder, and then left. He made no claim to the Creek lands. But there was something more to Bill Tibbs than guns and gold. Wolf Jacket had offered the renegade an escort to see him safely to Mobile once General Jackson had found him out. But Tibbs refused, insisting that he remain at Horseshoe Bend.

Now Wolf Jacket had an inkling why. He too was waiting for an enemy.

"I understand you," the war chief said. "Our hearts are one in our hate." Wolf Jacket stretched out upon the tanned skins and soft pelts that served for his bed. Leaning against his backrest, he watched the smoke from the fire curl up through the hole in the woven reed roof. The smoke hole was shielded from the elements by a reed flap.

The Red Stick surveyed the familiar surroundings. His weapons were stacked nearby, a fine British rifled musket, a short-barreled pistol, its stock ornately engraved with swirls and floral designs. Wolf Jacket had personally bludgeoned to death the pistol's former owner at Hope Station. Next to the firearms lay his favorite weapon, an iron-bladed tomahawk whose shaft the war chief had decorated with brass studs. The walls of his lodge were hung with tanned hides and British blankets to catch any wayward draft that might slip between the logs where the chinking had cracked.

Wolf Jacket searched beneath his blanket and produced a brown clay jug, just another bit of plunder that he'd kept for such a night.

"This is Creek land, from the Tensey,"—he waved the bottle in a northerly direction—"to the great waters." He gestured toward the south, then sloshed the contents of the jug and passed it to Tibbs, who chanced a sip.

"By heaven, that's whiskey," Tibbs gasped, savoring the warmth that spread from his nose to his toes. "You cunning devil, you've been hiding this."

He lifted the jug to his lips and, while he drank, caught the war chief studying the scimitar. He knew Wolf Jacket coveted the weapon. The Eye of Alexander had woven its spell and captured the Red Stick's imagination. He recognized the weapon's spirit power.

"My runners tell me the white chief Jackson will soon be here. He is camped two day's walk from our village. The Choctaws and Cherokees follow him like camp dogs, hoping to feast on our bones."

"You should not have attacked their village," Tibbs remarked. "They might have joined you."

Wolf Jacket's brows momentarily knotted, and for a moment, like sparks from flint or lightning against the night sky, fire danced in his dark eyes. But when he spoke, his tone was cordial. "Maybe when the storm ends and the sky clears, I will lead my people out and we will surprise the white chief and his red dogs." Wolf Jacket raised up and reached toward the jeweled hilt gleaming close to the cook fire. "I will carry this into battle."

"The hell you will," Tibbs snapped. He set the jug down between the scimitar and the warrior's outstretched hand.

Wolf Jacket froze at the sound of a pistol being cocked. Tibbs had dropped his left hand to the smooth-bore weapon lying beside him. The weapon was cocked and primed, and though he did not bring it to bear, the flintlock's presence was warning enough. Wolf Jacket wanted the long knife with its fire eye. All he had to do was kill Tibbs to get it. But the white man was his only link with the British and their guns and powder and shot. He hesitated on the brink of violence. The Eye of Alexander held him transfixed in its blood-red stare.

The long knife was power. Once its spirit magic was in his possession, there would be none to stand against him or challenge his leadership. Men like Runs Above and Blue Kettle had been too outspoken of late. They also had questioned his attack on the Choctaws, and other Creeks had begun to listen to them. *Somehow, I will have the long knife, when I no longer need this white man. Then I will rid myself of Runs Above and Blue Kettle.*

The Creek war chief relaxed, curled his fingers around the neck of the clay jug, and poured the contents onto the ground by the coals. He settled back and began to eat. His shell necklace rattled with each movement, and a trickle of juices glistened at the corner of his mouth. Thunder rumbled like cannon fire beyond the walls of his lodge.

Tibbs stared ruefully at the puddle slowly soaking into the ashes and earth.

"A waste of good whiskey," he muttered.

"White man's poison, another gift that kills my people," the Red Stick replied.

"You don't seem to mind the gift of our guns," Tibbs reminded the Creek war chief.

"That's because we can kill *you* with them," Wolf Jacket said, setting his bowl of roasted meat aside. "Kill and kill with the guns you give us until the white man no longer travels our rivers or hunts in our forests. Until you are driven back to your great villages to the north." Wolf Jacket grinned, and veins stood out in stark relief along the shaved sides of his skull. In battle, he would smear the shaved areas with a paste of yellow warpaint made from bear fat and sulfur. "Do not worry, Bill Tibbs. You have nothing to fear. You are my brother, eh?"

"Sure I am," Tibbs answered. He found a wooden bowl and served himself some beans with a gourd dipper. He squatted down alongside his guns and the Eye of Alexander. "Sure I am."

Outside the lodge, the slanting downpour at last resolved to a trickle and then ended. A half hour later the sun appeared, but only as a bone-white orb peeping through a somber veil of clouds. Beneath its baleful glare, a chorus of dogs began to yip and growl and paw at the mud-covered body of a Choctaw girl, quite naked, quite lifeless.

Chapter Thirty-three

By midnight the wind had scoured the thunderheads from the sky, and all that remained of the previous day's storm were a few spectral clouds abandoned like gossamer ghosts and doomed to haunt the moonglow, to drift silently across the face of time. Stars reflected upon the rain-swollen surface of the Tallapoosa shimmered and danced as Kit McQueen lowered himself into the river. He paddled with his left hand, keeping a firm right-handed grip on the cane basket that carried not only his own firearms but those of several warriors who had preceded him into the river here at the easternmost tip of the Red Stick village at Horseshoe Bend.

The cold water cut right through his weary state and revived him from the effects of the forced march that had brought them to the river. He wasn't the only one to suffer the shock of emersion. A few yards upriver he heard Iron Hand O'Keefe mutter a curse as the Irishman lowered his bulk into the river. Kit briefly smiled. It was all the humor he could manage. After all, the Choctaws might be walking right into a trap.

It all depended on how many guards had been stationed by the dugouts and how watchful they were.

Kit glared at the sky as the moon lost its cover of clouds and turned the river's black surface a molten orange, making the host of Choctaws little more than bobbing targets. Kit braced himself for the inevitable burst of rifle fire and the shouted alarms that would arouse the village and bring a thousand Creek warriors down to the riverbank. He groaned inwardly, ruing the day he had ever volunteered O'Keefe's people for this rear assault. And yet, the Choctaws, true to Raven's word, had jumped at the chance to attack their enemy.

Kit shifted his gaze and saw Young Otter gain the opposite bank. Kit leaned into the water as the mud underfoot dropped off where the river deepened. He kicked and pulled a sidestroke, dragging the basket in his wake. Another half dozen braves joined Young Otter on the peninsula. This was the moment of truth. Heart throbbing in his chest, Kit struggled against the current; he fought the river and won.

Suddenly his feet plunged into the muddy river bottom, and he slogged the remaining few yards up onto dry land. He dragged the basket onto the shore and left it alongside one of the Creek dugouts. He crouched low and took a moment to catch his breath, unable to believe the Red Sticks hadn't found them out. The outlying earthen lodges began a mere stone's throw from the tip of the peninsula.

He grabbed the "Quakers" out of the basket and made sure each of the heavy-bore flintlocks was loaded and primed. Then he helped himself to an extra pair of pistols. The Choctaws around him hurried to retrieve their own guns.

Kit chanced revealing his position to a Creek sniper. He stood and studied the shoreline both upriver and down. He estimated there must be at least fifty dugouts that had been dragged up onto the riverbank just in this area alone. But he did not spy one single guard.

"The Red Sticks do not fear us. They think we have no heart for fighting," Young Otter whispered.

Iron Hand O'Keefe came slogging toward them. Water dripped from his greasy buckskins, and his silver hair was matted to his head and shoulders. He carried a Kentucky rifle in the crook of his arm. Pistols and ax were tucked in the belt that circled his waist.

"By heaven, I can't figure it," he said, keeping his voice low. The big man stabbed a thumb in the direction of the Creek village. Smoke curled from their cane roofs. Obviously the village wasn't deserted. He had already covered one circle of ashes that might have earlier warmed a lookout. The violent storm might have driven the Red Sticks to shelter.

"Maybe it is the work of the Above Ones who have blinded the Red Sticks to us," Young Otter offered.

"They think we're still two days' march from here," Kit said. "Come morning they'll know different."

"This damn silence worries me more than if they'd posted guards," O'Keefe complained. He wiped a thick hand across his mouth. His breeches were soggy and uncomfortable. "Soaked on the outside and dry as grandpa's bones on the inside."

"Best we spread your people out along the point," Kit suggested. "We can use the dugouts for cover."

Young Otter nodded and with a couple of his companions trotted off to pass the word to the Choctaws and the Cherokees as they emerged from the Tallapoosa. The warriors of both tribes wasted little time in arming themselves, and then they set to work, building a makeshift barricade by stacking the dugouts. It was all the elder warriors could do to keep the young warriors from charging the Red Stick encampment right then and there. But cooler heads at last prevailed. Once the dugouts were rearranged, even the hotheaded warriors settled down to await O'Keefe's signal.

Kit sat beside the Irishman and, leaning against a dugout, stretched out his legs. He guessed sunrise was about three hours away. He was grateful for the opportunity to rest. But there was something he had to bring out in the open.

Ever since leaving Fort Strother, he had wanted to speak to O'Keefe about his daughter. But there had been too many excuses along the way, and each time he found himself alone with the Irishman Kit faltered, courage failed him. *This is hardly an appropriate time*, he thought, *on the verge of battle.*

Time was running out. And so these wee hours of the morning would have to suffice. He took a breath, tightened his resolve, and spoke.

"O'Keefe?" Kit glanced at the man at his side. "We need to talk. Well, I do, at any rate."

"Do you, now?"

"Yes. It concerns Raven and me."

"Oh. . . ." the big man replied, and stroked his chin with his fiercesome hook. "And it's about time, I'll warrant you. Never seen two carry on so, as if they think a man can't see them, sneaking off to be alone."

"Then you know?"

"See here, Lieutenant McQueen, I lost my hand, not my eyes," the Irishman answered sternly. "If a lesser man had tried to take my daughter, I would have slit him open and flung his innards to the treetops." O'Keefe shrugged, then folded his arms across his massive chest. "Trouble is, I like you. So I reckon once the two of you cool down enough for you both to think with clear heads, you'll do right by one another." O'Keefe leaned over, and his voice became deadly serious. "Don't you be going and getting your skull split today. Raven would shoot me on sight if I let that happen."

"I'll try my best," Kit replied.

Images of the girl flashed through his mind from the first moment he saw her, defying Wolf Jacket along a flood-swollen creek, to the last, when he said good-bye and she watched him ride from Fort Strother on one of Jackson's own horses. Kit felt as if he had crammed a lifetime into the space of a few short months. What were her final words spoken, the poignant, private moment before he joined the column of volunteers? Her eyes were moist as she entered his embrace in the fragrant stillness of her father's lodge.

"I half expected you to grab a rifle and follow us, despite your father's objections," Kit had said.

"Once I might have," Raven had answered in all honesty. "But not now, when our hearts and our flesh have been one. You would be worrying about me and not looking after yourself when some Red Stick knife might find you. And take your life. And mine."

Outside the walls of the lodge an army of Tennesseans, Choctaws, and Cherokees had begun its march toward destiny. And Kit's place was among them. It had taken a selfless act of courage for Raven to hold him close then send him on his way.

Kit rested now, finding comfort in memories of Raven's brave smile, the pride shining in her eyes, and the warmth that would never leave him.

Kit McQueen and Iron Hand O'Keefe sat together in silence. Minutes lengthened into an hour. One hour become two. And gradually the stars faded and the sky shed its night shade. A blush appeared above the forest east of the Tallapoosa. A scarlet tanager perched atop a ceremonial pole in the center of the village heralded the onset of morning with its piping song.

"I love her," Kit told the Irishman as if they had just ended their conversation minutes, not hours, ago.

"Yes, lad," O'Keefe replied. His eyes were closed, but he hadn't slept a wink. "I know."

Both men stood together, and three hundred Choctaw warriors, who had waited so long for this moment, rose from the ground and started forward.

Their day of vengeance had arrived.

Like some Roland upon his horn, O'Keefe sounded a blast loud enough to wake the dead. At their war chief's signal the Choctaw rushed the village. Several of the warriors held torches and paused to set afire the first lodges they came to. Kit could smell the aroma of burning cane and hear the crackle of the reeds as the flames devoured them, spreading up and over the lodges. He dashed headlong toward the center of the village.

Creek warriors, alerted by O'Keefe's horn and the rippling gunfire, swarmed from their lodges, angry as wasps. The Choctaw advance slowed as more and more Creeks hurried to defend their village. Soon the Creeks would outnumber the attacking Choctaws three to one. If Jackson's volunteers delayed their assault on the palisade, O'Keefe's warriors would be overwhelmed and annihilated.

Rifle fire rattled throughout the village; powder smoke blotted out the rising sun. Kit raced past one lodge and headlong into a tomahawk-wielding Creek warrior looking for someone to kill. The two men shoved clear of one another. Kit fired his rifle and blew the warrior back against the lodge wall.

The warrior slid to the ground, his legs outstretched and blood pumping from a hole in his chest. A chunky young woman with bruised features crawled out of the lodge. She straightened and stared at Kit for a brief moment; then, noticing the warrior Kit had shot, the woman rushed forward and grabbed up the fallen man's tomahawk and began to strike him with it about the head and shoulders. Kit hurried off to rejoin the attack, leaving the Choctaw captive to her own grisly revenge.

Wolf Jacket rubbed the sleep from his eyes, snatched up his red coat, rifle, and tomahawk, and bolted out into the encampment, with Bill Tibbs close behind him. Powder smoke stung their eyes but didn't blind them to what was going on. The village was a flurry of activity as the lodges emptied themselves of red warriors scrambling en masse to block the attacking Choctaws and drive them back to the river.

From out of a mob of Red Sticks, Runs Above veered toward Wolf Jacket and the white man at his side. The gray-haired warrior trembled with anger as he confronted the war chief. No longer would he be cowed by Wolf Jacket. No longer would he couch his defiance, but speak it plainly and openly.

"The Choctaws and Cherokees have come against us. See what your pride and your foolishness have done!" he shouted.

The old warrior pointed his rifle toward the sound of the gunfire and the flames rising up from the burning lodges. At least a third of the encampment was already engulfed by the blaze.

"Blue Kettle and his brothers of the Hawk are dead.

They were killed by those who should have been our allies. You will answer for it! We follow you no more!" Runs Above was finished. He had enemies to slay. The gray-haired warrior turned away and with rifle in hand rushed off toward the east end of the encampment and the spreading flames.

Wolf Jacket impassively watched the warrior depart. In all the confusion and gunsmoke and screaming, one more death wouldn't be noticed. He snapped up his rifled musket and squeezed off a shot.

Bill Tibbs jumped in surprise, then stared through the acrid discharge and saw Runs Above stumble, clutch his back, and pitch face forward in the trampled earth.

Wolf Jacket loosed a savage war cry and charged into battle. He leaped the crumpled form of the man he had murdered and without so much as a sideglance raced toward the sound of battle.

Tibbs hesitated, uncertain of his role. There should have been guards posted by the dugouts and outlying sentries stationed in the forest. Red Stick braves brushed past him, drawn to the din of shrieking men and thundering guns. Somewhere in all that furious bloodletting, Kit McQueen waited. As sure as morning followed night, Kit waited for him. Tibbs smiled and drew the scimitar from its gold-inlaid scabbard. He stared at his elongated reflection in the length of razor-sharp steel.

"Take me to him," he said aloud, and joined the Creeks as they prepared to retake the eastern end of the village.

On the ceremonial pole in the heart of the encampment, the scarlet tanager whose sunrise song had awakened the dawn left its perch and rode the morning breeze up and over the lodges and the newly tilled and planted fields. It swooped and soared above the stockade walls left virtually undefended in the wake of the Choctaw attack. The tanager flew on toward the woods and glided down toward the branches of a white oak, then altered its glide and rose once more into the sky, frightened off by the column of soldiers emerging from concealment.

General Andrew Jackson had arrived.

The horn of Iron Hand O'Keefe blared once again. It pierced the tumult and summoned the Choctaws and Cherokees to fall back, which they did in good order, swiftly and almost in unison. They broke off the fighting and retreated through the smoldering ruins of the Creek encampment. Dead men, mostly Creek but some Choctaw, littered the ground.

As O'Keefe's people headed for the dugouts, many a former captive followed them. Choctaw women and children gathered rifles, powder, and shot from the slain and joined in the retreat to the tip of the peninsula and the riverbank of the Tallapoosa, whose muddy waters effectively prevented any escape. They were cornered.

Kit had trouble keeping up with the wild-eyed Choctaws as they fled through thickening clouds of ashen smoke. His leg, though healed, was not as limber as it used to be. Kit's buckskin shirt was ripped and blood oozed from his slashed shoulder. A red welt streaked his powder-burned cheek. Lead slugs whirred past, searching for him. Gray smoke from the burning village drifted over the peninsula, obscuring the combatants who had blindly stumbled into the stinging mist.

A Cherokee warrior staggered. Kit caught him by

the arm, then saw the man was already dead, the back of his skull blown away. The riverbank at last materialized up ahead. The Choctaws scrambled into positions behind the dugouts and prepared to make their final stand. Kit redoubled his efforts and, with his lungs burning, managed to vault the makeshift barricade.

As he reached the tenuous safety of the dugouts, half a dozen rifle balls flattened against the side of the nearest boat and showered him with splinters.

The first wave of Creeks followed close on the heels of the Choctaws. The Red Sticks, in their fury, never slowed but descended on the dugouts in a wild assault through the billowing smoke. The Choctaws loosed a ragged volley that broke the attack as quickly as it had begun and further obscured the riverbank.

Kit fired into the acrid mist, then dropped below the dugout and reloaded. By the time he swung his rifle over the edge of the barricade for another shot, the Creeks had already retreated into the smoke to regroup and lick their wounds. At least fifty of their number were sprawled upon the ground, dead or dying.

Kit crawled the fifteen feet to the river's edge and dunked his head beneath the cooling waters. He was not alone. The rest of the Choctaws hurried to slake their thirst before the next onslaught. Kit raised up. Water matted his red hair and beard and dripped from his face. O'Keefe loaded his pistols a few yards farther up the bank and Kit scrambled across to the Irishman. O'Keefe gripped a pistol between his knees and poured a charge of powder down the barrel, then rammed home a patch and shot. Kit noticed the Irishman's iron hook was caked with blood. Someone had died a nasty death.

"They'll come at us full force this time," the Irishman grumbled.

"I imagine so," Kit replied.

He looked east to where the morning sun struggled to be seen through the billowing wood and powder smoke shrouding Horseshoe Bend. Kit then glanced down at his torn shirt where the medal of Daniel McQueen dangled against his chest. He placed his hand over the British coin that George Washington had initialed and presented to his father thirty-six years ago. In those early days of the Revolution, things must have looked pretty hopeless . . . same as now.

"Well there's one good thing," O'Keefe said.

"What?" Kit asked.

"We won't have time to get scared," the Irishman said, and squatted behind the barricade. The dugout was hard-pressed to provide cover for a man his size.

Kit shouldered his Kentucky rifle and knelt alongside O'Keefe. All along the riverbank Choctaw warriors began to taunt the Creeks, who no doubt were massing to attack. Kit's chest swelled with pride. He had never been among more gallant men.

The Red Sticks advanced through the haze, a dim, ghostly army on the move. Kit, O'Keefe, and the rest of the Choctaws prepared to meet them with another volley.

Suddenly, on the verge of the attack, a thunderous exchange of rifle fire sounded at the opposite end of the village. The Creeks halted, uncertain whether or not to continue their advance. Behind them, the rifle fire increased in intensity, and now could be heard the cries of the dying and the war whoops of the Blue Ridge boys and enraged Tennessee mountain men wild as any savage to be found on the peninsula.

"By God, it's him!" O'Keefe was jubilant. He stood and raised his horn to his lips and sounded a blast. "C'mon, you bloodthirsty bastards. You've a choice now. Old Hickory or Choctaw steel!'' O'Keefe danced a jig and laughed aloud. The Choctaw warriors grinned at his display.

Kit reached up, caught O'Keefe by the arm, and pulled him back behind the barricade.

"The white chief Jackson has taken the village. The Red Sticks are trapped," Young Otter exclaimed. The stocky warrior had worked his way along the riverbank until he had reached them with this news.

"Yes, trapped," Kit said. "With only one way out," Kit replied. "Through us."

At the first report that Jackson's troops had stormed the stockade and were loosed in the village, Wolf Jacket knew he was finished. Now his sole concern was to live to fight another day. Standing before his assembled warriors, he sent most of them back into the drifting smoke, back into the encampment in a vain attempt to rout the soldiers.

The war chief held in reserve the warriors of the Bear Clan and those of the Turtle Clan. With these men he would storm the dugouts, cut his way through the Choctaw, and make good his escape. He spied Bill Tibbs standing close at hand. From the expression on Tibbs's face it was plain that the gunrunner had guessed the purpose of the war chief's strategy.

Tibbs rubbed his watering eyes. He'd lost his stomach for the fight. He peered at the dugouts through the haze. Kit might be there, yes, but Tibbs had a bad feeling about charging into those Choctaw rifles.

"Give me the long knife," Wolf Jacket said, his dark eyes fixed on the scimitar.

"Go to the devil," Tibbs replied.

Wolf Jacket nodded to the Red Sticks standing to either side of Tibbs. They jabbed their rifles into his sides and cocked their weapons.

"I will not ask again," Wolf Jacket said.

Bill Tibbs's long, lean frame tensed. His left hand closed into a fist. The paleness of his flesh was positively cadaverous and stretched taut over his bony brow and prominent cheekbones.

A pitched battle was raging in the village, coming closer, ever closer. He was wasting time. Tibbs, his expression as if etched in stone, tossed the Eye of Alexander on the ground before Wolf Jacket. The Creek retrieved the weapon. As he grasped the hilt, energy surged through his limbs. The warrior's lips curled back in a feral snarl. He spun, lunged with the scimitar, and buried the blade in Bill Tibbs's vitals.

Tibbs gasped and clawed his belly, astonished, feeling the violation of the blade. "No. . . ." he moaned, and sank to his knees as the blade slid out, drenched with his blood. He collapsed upon the smoke-shrouded ground.

"Now I have the power!" Wolf Jacket raised the crimson blade, gleaming hilt, and ruby eye for the Red Sticks to see. Then, with an ear-splitting shriek, he charged the barricade, the Bear Clan and Turtle Clan at his side, following Wolf Jacket and the spirit weapon he held.

Kit McQueen heard the inhuman-sounding cry and sighted his rifle on the shifting clouds of smoke. The oncoming Creeks again materialized out of the ashen fog within a few yards of the dugouts. Creek and Choctaw rifles belched flame. Men dropped on both sides, fell clutching their shattered limbs and spurting wounds. Men stumbled and cried and begged for water and died. And that was only the beginning. Creek warriors leaped the barricade and closed with the defenders, who rose to meet them. Choctaw tomahawk and Cherokee knife and Creek rifled musket continued the butchery. The fighting was hand to hand: stab, club, kick, or gouge. Pistols fired at close range also took their toll.

Kit, his rifle empty, tossed the weapon and drew his pistols, the "Quakers." A Creek warrior climbed atop the dugout and leveled a pistol of his own. Kit shot him dead and fired with the second pistol. The heavy-caliber slug knocked a second warrior to the ground. A pistol roared to his right and Kit saw O'Keefe drop one warrior with his flintlock. The Irishman disemboweled another victim with his hook.

"McQueen!" O'Keefe bellowed a warning. Too late. A blurred figure in a red coat leaped over the dugouts and barreled into Kit. The two men rolled down the riverbank. Kit caught a glimpse of curved steel; then the thin razor-sharp blade cracked, slicing into Kit's side. He groaned, staggered, kicked free, and finally faced his assailant through a haze of gunsmoke.

He recognized Wolf Jacket. And the Red Stick remembered this white man who had stolen away Iron Hand's daughter and humiliated the war chief of the Creek nation.

Wolf Jacket feinted with the scimitar, whose shattered blade still posed a threat, a foot of jagged steel sprouting from its jeweled hilt. Had it been an actual thrust, Kit would have died then and there, for he was dumbstruck and rooted in place at the shock of seeing the weapon Wolf Jacket held, the Eye of Alexander.

The war chief howled in triumph, darted forward, and slashed at Kit's throat, assuming the sword's magic would continue to hold his intended victim spellbound. Wolf Jacket was wrong.

Kit ducked beneath the thrust, caught the war

chief's wrist, and wrenched the man off balance, flinging him into the shallows. Kit dove after the Red Stick and, using his weight and leverage, turned the sword against Wolf Jacket. Kit shoved down through the muddy water and plunged the shattered length of steel hilt-deep in the warrior's heart.

Wolf Jacket screamed and choked as water poured into his mouth and muffled his agonized cry. Bubbles rippled the surface. The warrior's legs thrashed the water but he could free himself neither from the weight of the man atop him nor from the cruel bite of the blade that took his life.

The legs settled in the water. The bubbles stopped. The struggle ended. Kit straightened, stood, and pulled the broken-bladed weapon free, leaving a bloody trail on the river's silt-churned surface. Kit gradually became aware of the silence, broken only by a scattering of gunshots. He looked up and saw that the battle at the dugouts had ended. The surviving Creeks had lost their stomach for the fight and had surrendered to O'Keefe's people.

Gripping the Eye of Alexander, Kit stumbled as if in a dream walk out of the river and through the Choctaws, who stood aside to let him pass. O'Keefe spoke to him, but the Irishman's voice seemed far away. He said something about the scimitar being worth a fortune.

Up ahead, a war-weary line of soldiers straggled from the village. Kit recognized Captain Bellamy, alive and clutching a broken left arm. And there was General Jackson astride a fine chestnut stallion. Gritty black powder smoke lapped at the stallion's belly. Old Hickory waited, the general no doubt expecting Lieutenant McQueen to make his report.

But the general could wait.

Kit picked his way among the dead warriors. The half-glimpsed corpses of three tribes lay twisted and still beneath the hellish mist, the residue of war.

Then Kit McQueen heard the voice, and he knew what had drawn him from the river. He saw the arm reach up from among the dead and extend a hand above the shifting charcoal-colored shroud.

"Mine," said a voice that might have belonged to Bill Tibbs but sounded as if it called from the land of the dead. "Miiiinnnnnne..." The man who had been his friend beckoned.

The Eye of Alexander gleamed and glittered, and Kit saw his own reflection in the jewel. It was worth a fortune, that sword—no, more than a fortune. The Eye of Alexander was power. And all Kit had to do was keep the sword. Keep it. Keep it for his very own.

Keep it.

Kit shuddered and gingerly reversed the shortened blade and fitted the jeweled hilt into the outstretched fingers of what had once been Bill Tibbs. And Kit thought he heard a kind of sigh. A death rattle? Or the horrid, sibilant sound of a man's soul being sucked out and imprisoned in a blood-red stone? The hand sank out of sight. Kit McQueen turned, and parting the black mist, he kept walking until he reached the sunlight.

A Note from the Author

The Medal is a series of novels that chronicles the exploits of the McQueens, a family whose devotion to the dream of what America can be involves them in our nation's most turbulent decades. Passing along their own unique "medal of honor" from one generation to the next, the McQueens embody the proud spirit of the country they serve.

Guns of Liberty began their story, and Sword of Vengeance continues it. And I recently completed the third volume of the Medal series, Only the Gallant.

I write about frontier America and who we are as Americans. I write about the opening of the West and the tragedies and triumphs of those who have gone before. With every landmark paved over to make a new industrial park or shopping mall, we lose a little more of our precious identity. What's the point of rushing to the future if we lose the richness of where we've been? So I'll continue to tell my tales and spin my yarns and do my part to keep the legends alive, and if you find pleasure in them, well, my friend, I am satisfied.

★ ★ ★

Kerry Newcomb lives in Fort Worth, Texas, with his wife and two children.

Turn the page for an exciting preview of the third volume in best-selling author Kerry Newcomb's saga of an American military dynasty.

★ Only the Gallant ★

This Bantam original will be on sale September, 1991.

Jesse Redbow McQueen bit the hand that tried to hang him. The man with the lynch rope, a Creole by the name of Maurice Charbonneau, was a stocky, thick-necked ruffian with a belly full of whiskey's false courage. No, Charbonneau wasn't afraid of any man whose wrists were securely bound behind his back. Then Jesse clamped down, showing his teeth, and Charbonneau howled in pain, wrenched free, and stumbled back to safety. Jesse McQueen had bought himself a little time, but if he wanted to live through the hour he'd have to come up with a better plan. He couldn't believe his bad luck. One moment he had been hurrying through the storm back to his warm, dry room at the Orleans House on Toulouse Street. The next moment he'd found himself cornered by a gathering of the Crescent City's angry citizenry.

It was the twenty-fourth of April in the year 1862, and New Orleans was aflame despite a drenching downpour that obscured whole blocks from view. The nation was at war, split North and South by men with too many ideals and not enough patience. Cemeteries already teemed with the unfortunate blue- and gray-clad victims of this tragic conflict. New Orleans had considered itself impregnable, secure behind two mighty bastions, Fort St. Philip and Fort Jackson. But Commodore Farragut had proven just how wrong such a popular theory could be. After days of bombardment, the Union fleet had swept past the forts and up the mighty Mississippi and brought their guns to bear upon the city itself, at which point the city fathers surrendered. Word had spread like wildfire and ignited in the populace a sense of betrayal and outrage. As a result of this hysteria, strangers immediately became suspect, labeled as spies to be summarily shot or, in this case, hung. And Jesse Redbow McQueen was just such a stranger, toting a pack of lawbooks and professing a desire to practice in New Orleans.

Jesse focused his dark brown eyes on the two men who had been apprehended with him. One already dangled like a puppet on a string from the hotel's wrought-iron railing like a poor, broken toy discarded by a violent child. The man was E. M. Todd, a fellow boarder at the Orleans House. Jesse knew him as a seller of wine and imported spirits, an Englishman and hardly a spy. The second of the mob's intended victims was a portly, middle-aged man whose shrill appeals for mercy went unheeded by the bloodthirsty crowd. They were wounded and bitter and ablaze with righteous anger. Union spies had caused the city's downfall. And there must be a reckoning. No matter if a dozen innocent folks were slain in the process, the guilty must not escape retribution.

"I'm from Atlanta and loyal to the cause!" the portly man exclaimed. "My name is Robert Wilmont, portrait artist, nothing more!"

"And perhaps I am General Robert E. Lee," said a silver-haired Creole gentleman in the gray-and-red-trimmed uniform of the New Orleans Home Guard. He was a dapper, small-boned Creole with narrow features and blazing eyes. He sat ramrod straight in the saddle, oblivious to the downpour. His hair curled over his hard leather collar. Silvery white hair all but hid his ears. "But you see, in truth, I am Colonel Henri Baptiste, defender of this fair city—and you, sir, are a spy."

"But I'm not!" the frightened artist cried, and lifted his quivering features to the rain. Rivulets streaked his face like tears.

"Oh, hell! I'm the spy. Hang me and let him go," Jesse spoke up. His horse shifted its stance, and he had to grip tight with his knees to keep himself upright. Rain pummeled his head and shoulders and matted his shirt to his wiry frame.

"In good time," Baptiste remarked, glancing up at Jesse. It was obvious the colonel neither knew nor cared if either of the men was a spy. They were strangers to him, and that was guilt aplenty. "Private Charbonneau, put the noose on that man," the colonel called out, noticing Jesse's bare neck. Jesse was clad in nankeen breeches and a loose cotton shirt. The mob had stolen his hat and coat. His unruly black hair was plastered to his neck, and a black beard concealed the clean, aquiline cut of his jaw.

Charbonneau reluctantly walked his horse forward. Jesse took satisfaction in the crimson-stained bandage that the Creole had hastily applied to his mangled left thumb.

"Hang 'em both!" shouted a voice from the crowd. And the throng, about fifteen men, most of them dockworkers and riverboat men with a few merchants, heartily concurred. Time was wasting, and there were other rain-washed streets to check and other traitors to be apprehended.

"C'mon Charbonneau," Jesse snarled, his dark stare full of malice. "Put your hand out, and I'll bite it off at the wrist."

The Creole private hesitated. Then another Creole, a tight-lipped, imperious young man whose boyish expression could not conceal the bloodlust in his eyes, brushed Charbonneau aside and grabbed the lynch rope from the cowed private. Someone in the crowd shouted, "There's a lad, Gerard. Show the scoundrel."

Gerard, who was handsome and much sought after by the young ladies of the city, blushed and acknowledged his accolades with false modesty. He walked his horse close alongside Jesse. Up ahead, Henri Baptiste had already thrown the length of rope up to another of the home guard, who waited on the balcony. The militiaman quickly tied off the end and stared down at the portrait artist, who continued to protest his innocence.

Gerard held the noose up to Jesse while a couple of the men in the crowd steadied his horse and held him about the waist. With a quick flick of his wrist, the handsome young Creole flipped the noose over Jesse's head, and the mob cheered his dexterity. But his face was close and he forgot the lesson Charbonneau had learned; that a bound and cornered panther is still dangerous, still a panther.

Jesse lowered his head and butted the Creole square in the middle of his face. Gerard groaned and clasped a hand to his broken nose, and when he felt the blood flow and saw the droplets work their way through his clenched fingers to be spattered by the rain and splotch his greatcoat, he could stand no more. Gerard grabbed the noose and wrenched it tight about Jesse's throat.

"Damn you!" Gerard cursed. He nearly dragged Jesse from the saddle, the rough hemp tearing the flesh on either side of Jesse's throat. Colonel Baptiste at last intervened, walking his mount between Jesse and Gerard and forcing the young Creole with the broken nose to release his hold.

"Each man in his turn," Baptiste said. Rain poured from the brim of his gray hat whenever he tilted his head, and splashed his horse's neck. "This must be a proper execution, with as much dignity as time permits." Baptiste stared at his two subordinates, one with a cloth-wrapped thumb, the other cupping a hand over his disfigured features. The colonel glared at Jesse. "You, sir, are most troublesome."

"I've never been lynched before," Jesse rasped. "I am ignorant of the proper behavior. Why not take my place, and I'll study you?"

His reply elicited grudging laughter from the less rowdy of the mob, who were patiently enduring the downpour in order to see another enemy of the Confederacy receive his proper dispatch.

"Study me?" Baptiste replied in a silken tone. "Study him!" He slapped the end length of the hangman's rope down across the rump of the mare directly ahead of Jesse. The animal bolted forward; the mob cheered as Robert Wilmont, lately of Atlanta, danced death's jig.

Jesse closed his eyes, his heart full of pity for the poor little man. The stench of smoke and death clung to the rain-drenched air. Throughout the city, warehouses of dry goods and cotton had been torched to keep these supplies out of Union hands. The city had turned on itself like a mad animal, destroying itself and its own people. Jesse looked into the faces of the men surrounding him. There was no reason here.

Hatred and fear had reaped a bitter harvest among men of conscience. One death begot another; there was no stopping them. Two men twisted in the rain. It was time for a third.

Jesse Redbow McQueen struggled to free his wrists. The rope that bound him was soaked, and in another few minutes he'd be free. But Colonel Henri Baptiste wasn't going to allow him a few minutes. The mob was eager for blood, and so was the Creole colonel. Jesse would have to stall them somehow. He closed his eyes and focused his thoughts, and in his mind's eye he drifted out over the bedlam of the city and soared above the burning warehouses and the pall of smoldering bales of cotton to the barren branches of a magnolia in a garden apart from the destruction. And there among the twisted limbs he imagined a raven waited, fluttering and preening itself. The bird's bold, keen stare revealed an intelligence bordering on the supernatural. The trickster spirit of all ravens that had invaded his thought? "Raven, Grandmother spirit, help me," he shouted in Choctaw, the language of his grandmother's people. Jesse glanced around him and saw that his strange outburst had momentarily held the belligerent crowd at bay. Even Colonel Baptiste seemed taken aback. Baptiste and the other two Creoles, Gerard and Charbonneau, blessed themselves to protect one another against whatever demons they figured this stranger had attempted to summon.

But it was no demon or hell-spawned sprite that came to Jesse's rescue; it was a runaway pair of frightened mares hitched to a wagon whose load of hay was a pyre on wheels. Flames leaped from the bales of dry grass and singed the rumps of the frenzied mares, who raced down Toulouse at a reckless gait, desperate to escape the burning load they were hitched to.

Jesse alone saw the wagon as it careened along the narrow street, trailing orange streamers of fire through the pouring rain. The attention of the mob was riveted on this next man to dance at the end of the colonel's rope. "I'll silence your hoodoo talk," Baptiste declared, and tossed the lynch rope up to the man on the balcony. The line slipped from the guardsman's grasp and dropped to the street. A pair of rough-looking riverboat men broke from the crowd. Each man fought to claim the rope, as if it were some sort of prize.

"Tie off the end," came a shout.

"Raise him up with the others!"

Jesse ignored them. He tensed as the burning wagon bore down on the assemblage. It was close now, only a matter of seconds. At last the rattle of the traces, the pounding hooves, and a clatter of the wheels on the puddled surface of the street attracted the attention of the men on the fringe of the crowd. Their outcries alerted the rest. And the rabble that had called for another hanging suddenly lost its taste for death.

The runaway mares, blinded by pain, plunged head-on into the mob, trampling one man underfoot and scattering the rest.

Jesse drove his heels into the flanks of the horse beneath him. The bay mare, already made skittish by the crowd, needed no prodding to escape the burning wagon and the terrified team. The bay plunged forward, away from the Orleans House and out into Toulouse Street. Riding bareback, Jesse gripped the mare with his knees and bent forward, lowering his head to the rain. Behind him the team of mares swerved to avoid the hotel porch and the bodies dangling from the balcony. The wagon careened to one side as the mares lunged in the opposite direction. The wagon toppled over, its axle cracking under the strain. The singletree snapped as the burning bales spilled onto the porch of the hotel, crashing chairs and setting the columns ablaze.

"The rope!" shouted Baptiste, dodging a fiery death and fighting to control his steed. Gerard leaped from horseback as the frazzled end of the hangman's rope slipped past. It flopped and bounded along the street just out of reach. If the rope snagged even for an instant, the man at the other end would have his neck snapped. Jesse McQueen had escaped the frying pan only to jump into the fire.

Back at the Orleans House, the Creole guardsmen dismounted and led their horses away from the hotel, whose residents had already begun to rush from the burning building. One woman saw the hanged men and fainted. Baptiste and Charbonneau chanced a couple of shots. Jesse winced as hot lead whined past his ear. Charbonneau was a good shot and Henri Baptiste was fully his equal, but the downpour and the decreased visibility ruined their aim. Both men holstered their weapons as Gerard brought up their horses and walked the high-strung animals away from the spreading flames. The two mares dragging the broken remains of the singletree fled down the street after Jesse, further ruining the Creoles' aim.

"After him!" Baptiste roared. "He'll not escape us, by heaven. I swear it!" Jesse had already disappeared behind a wall of water. But the colonel was determined to avenge the honor of the Baptistes and that of the Creole guardsmen. He was confident of recapturing Jesse. After all, just how far could a man get riding bareback through a downpour with his hands bound behind him and a hangman's rope trailing from his neck?

The frightened bay veered to the right and rounded the corner from Toulouse onto Bourbon Street. Somehow Jesse managed to stay astride the animal. Jesse had grown up riding bareback across the plains and foothills of Indian Territory. He was a horseman, first and foremost. But the downpour, while concealing him from his pursuers, also worked against him. It took all his skill to cling to the mare's rain-slick back. His legs were growing numb from the effort.

The mare splashed through a puddle and galloped past a half dozen raggedly dressed looters who had broken into a bootmaker's shop and were helping themselves to his wares. The thieves were too absorbed in their own pilferage to take notice of the mare and its hapless rider. As Jesse flashed by the shop, the lynch rope worked its way to a corner step and ground a furrow in the splintery wood. Jesse felt the noose tighten around his neck. He considered sliding from horseback and taking his chances, which were none too good without a pair of hands to break his fall upon the hard street. Then the last of the rope cleared the steps, sparing Jesse yet again. But he knew he was living on borrowed time. Sooner or later the rope would wrap around a hitching post or catch beneath a wagon wheel, and that would end it. Buildings skimmed past, blurred by the rain and the dense smoke that drifted up from the waterfront and hung like a pall over the city, choking entire blocks in its black embrace. The bay showed no signs of slowing its pace. Smoke and flames, distant explosives, the bedlam of a rioting populace drove the animal onward in its headlong flight. Jesse McQueen needed a miracle if he was to see another sunrise. And he got one, a block from Canal Street. Fifty pounds of Mississippi blue heeler darted from an alley alongside Le Bon Nuit Café. The short-haired hunting dog darted out into the middle of Bourbon Street in front of the bay mare. Horse and hound caught each other off guard. The heeler's gray-speckled coat rendered the dog almost invisible in the rain until the hound bared its fangs, snarling and barking, its hackles raised along its powerful shoulders.

The bay mare skidded on the slick street, rearing and whinnying in terror, its hooves pawing the air. Jesse relaxed his hold, slipped from horseback, and landed on his back in a puddle. He sat up, sputtering, just in time to see the bay mare reverse its course. Jesse rolled to his left as the mare charged through the puddle. The bay missed trampling him by an arm's length. Jesse staggered to his feet and looked about at the empty, rainswept street. Well, almost empty. A silhouette of a narrow-shouldered man in a greatcoat and beaver hat materialized out of the shadows. Jesse retreated toward the nearest oil lamp streetlight, which cast a fitful radius of amber light that the storm threatened to obscure.

"Help me," Jesse rasped. "My hands are tied."

The man in the greatcoat reached up and shoved his wire-rimmed spectacles back off the bridge of his nose. He continued to stare at the torn, mud-spattered figure confronting him.

"Untie my hands," Jesse said. Still the man in the coat made no move. "At least take this noose off me. I'd do it myself, but you see I'm sort of at the end of my rope."

"Don't know you. Ain't none of my business," the stranger muttered at last. "But I could use your horse." And with that he brushed past Jesse and ran off after the bay.

"Son of a bitch," Jesse muttered. He was alone

again, save for the blue heeler, who continued to growl and bark. Every time the dog came within range to snap Jesse, the bound man aimed a kick at its head. At last the dog retreated, finding something new to inspect.

The blackened, shattered window of the café looked promising. Jesse staggered up onto the porch. The foyer of the café reeked of smoke damage. Its soot-blackened windows stared vacantly back as Jesse peered inside. The place stood empty, its clientele frightened back to their homes and apartments once word had reached them of the impending arrival of the Union fleet. Jesse took a moment to catch his breath, grateful for the porch and the shelter it offered from the elements. He wrinkled his nose as the damp, charred smell of the fire-gutted front of the café wafted out through the ruined windows. Jagged shards of glass still jutted from the whitewashed wooden frame like dragon's teeth. *Just the thing*, Jesse thought, and he backed over to the remains of the window. He chose the largest shard and began to saw at the ropes binding his wrists. Suddenly the lynch rope went taut and pulled him off balance even as it constricted his windpipe. The blue heeler had found the hangman's rope to be of keen interest. Tail wagging, the dog clamped its powerful jaws around the rope and began to play tug-of-war.

"Not now," Jesse gasped. "Christ Almighty!"

The dog continued to pull and tighten the noose around Jesse's throat. The blue heeler was enjoying this new game. Jesse held his ground, though barely able to draw breath. CHOKED TO DEATH BY A DAMN DOG was a hell of an epitaph, Jesse thought. He continued to saw at his bound wrists. *Come on. Come on.* He was beginning to lose consciousness. The already murky street was beginning to darken even more at the edges and slowly... ever so slowly... tilt. Pain jolted him. He straightened and yelped as the glass shard sliced across his flesh. The wrist bonds fell away, and his arms swung free. *Yes!* He clawed at his throat, worked the slipknot loose, then pulled the hemp necktie up past his ears and tossed the lynch rope into the street. Then he sagged against the nearest post, where the café posted its menu for the day. Tonight's main course would have been smoked oysters, pork loins in a mushroom sauce, sliced wild onions and tomatoes in a vinaigrette, and scalloped potatoes drizzled with butter. *And dog, if I had a knife or gun,* Jesse reckoned. But his anger faded because he could not imagine anything sweeter than being able to breathe, even with the stench of burned cotton permeating the air. He was bruised and cut and his clothes were torn, but he was alive. He had made good his escape from Colonel Baptiste and his rabble.

Almost.

A bullet blew away a fist-sized chunk of the wooden menu board and thudded into the windowsill. Jesse dove for the street as a voice shouted "Here! I've found him, Colonel. He's here!"

It was Charbonneau, and he was coming on at a gallop, eager to atone for his past mistakes. He had a score to settle with Jesse McQueen.

The author of **In the Season of the Sun** and **Scalpdancers** begins a multigenerational saga that will span the history of America, as seen through the lives of one family.

THE MEDAL

From a nation born of strife and christened with patriots' blood, there arose a dynasty of soldiers. They were the McQueens of America -- a clan hungry for adventure; a family whose fiery spirit would kindle the flame of a country's freedom. Keeping that flame from blazing into tyranny through the generations would take more than merely courage and determination. It would take a sacred secret: the proud legacy they called THE MEDAL.

Look for the first two books in this series,

THE MEDAL BOOK ONE: GUNS OF LIBERTY
THE MEDAL BOOK TWO: SWORD OF VENGEANCE

on sale wherever Bantam Domain Books are sold.

TERRY C. JOHNSTON

Winner of the prestigious Western Writer's award, Terry C. Johnston brings you his award-winning saga of mountain men Josiah Paddock and Titus Bass who strive together to meet the challenges of the western wilderness in the 1830's.

☐ 25572 **CARRY THE WIND–Vol. I** $4.95

☐ 26224 **BORDERLORDS–Vol. II** $4.95

☐ 28139 **ONE-EYED DREAM–Vol. III** $4.95

The final volume in the trilogy begun with *Carry the Wind* and *Borderlords*, ONE-EYED DREAM is a rich, textured tale of an 1830's trapper and his protegé, told at the height of the American fur trade.

Following a harrowing pursuit by vengeful Arapaho warriors, mountain man Titus "Scratch" Bass and his apprentice Josiah Paddock must travel south to old Taos. But their journey is cut short when they learn they must return to St. Louis…and old enemies.

Look for these books wherever Bantam books are sold, or use this handy coupon for ordering: